A R
MOU
CHR

A ROCKY MOUNTAIN CHRISTMAS

WILLIAM W. JOHNSTONE

with J. A. Johnstone

PINNACLE BOOKS
Kensington Publishing Corp.
www.kensingtonbooks.com

PINNACLE BOOKS are published by

Kensington Publishing Corp.
119 West 40th Street
New York, NY 10018

PUBLISHER'S NOTE
Following the death of William W. Johnstone, the Johnstone family is working with a carefully selected writer to organize and complete Mr. Johnstone's outlines and many unfinished manuscripts to create additional novels in all of his series like The Last Gunfighter, Mountain Man, and Eagles, among others. This novel was inspired by Mr. Johnstone's superb storytelling.

ISBN-13: 978-0-7860-3138-2
ISBN-10: 0-7860-3138-7

First printing: November 2012

10 9 8 7 6 5 4

Printed in the United States of America

PROLOGUE

Lambert Field, St. Louis, Missouri—
December 20, 1961

Rebecca Daniels Robison awaited her flight in the comfort of the Admiral's Lounge. A huge Christmas tree sparkled with blinking lights and shining ornaments and Christmas music played softly over the lounge speakers. Rebecca was reading the newspaper when she was approached by a very attractive young woman.

"Ambassador Robison? My name is Margaret Chambers, and I'm a reporter for the *St. Louis Globe-Democrat.* I wonder if you would consent to an interview?"

"Why would you want to interview me, dear? I'm no longer an ambassador."

"No, but you are still active on the international scene, and a recent poll put you as the country's most admired woman."

"Nonsense, my dear. Eleanor Roosevelt is the most admired woman."

Margaret laughed. "You came in second, and Mrs. Roosevelt doesn't count. She's been the most admired woman for the last thirteen years."

"And rightly so," Rebecca said. "She has certainly been most gracious to me, over the years."

A voice came over the intercom. "Attention passengers, all flights are on temporary hold until the runways can be cleared of snow."

"I was about to say there wouldn't be time for an interview," Rebecca said. "But it appears that my flight has been delayed, so I would be happy to talk to you. I suppose you want to hear about my time as ambassador to Greece."

"No, ma'am," Margaret said. "I'm doing a story for our special Christmas edition. I understand you once had a most harrowing Christmas experience when you were a child."

"Harrowing? Yes, I suppose it was, though that's not exactly the word I would use. But it was also the most uplifting experience of my life."

"Could you share that story with our readers?"

"How much do you know about that incident?"

"Hardly anything. Just that you've been very reluctant to discuss it in all these years and that you've turned down every request for it. Your father was a U.S. Senator then . . ."

"A state senator in Colorado," Rebecca corrected.

"Yes, thank you. According to what little information exists, you and your family were on a train going from Pueblo to Red Cliff, Colorado, during a blizzard."

"That's correct. But that is only part of the story. If I told you everything, I'm afraid you would have a very difficult time believing it. Which is why I have never told the story before."

Margaret held her little narrow reporter's pad on her knee and raised her pencil, poised to take notes. "Why don't you try me? I would love to hear the entire story."

"Margaret, is it?"

"Yes ma'am."

"Well, since my plane is delayed, Margaret, I will tell you the whole story of that Christmas so long ago. I'm almost eighty years old and don't much care if people think I'm a crazy old lady or not. I guess now is as good a time as any to finally tell it. "

"Thank you, Ambassador Robison."

"Let's sit down, Margaret. And please, no questions until I am done."

Chapter One

New Orleans, Louisiana—July 9, 1889

The *Delta Mist* was moored to the bank, running parallel with Tchoupitoulas Street. Matt Jensen showed his ticket to the purser, then boarded the vessel, a packet boat that made the run between St. Louis and New Orleans and back again. Instead of going directly to his stateroom, he stopped at the rail of the texas deck, looking back toward the city of New Orleans, at the flower-bedecked iron-work trellises and balconies, and the belles of New Orleans strolling the streets in butterfly-bright dresses under colorful parasols.

Of all the cities he had visited, New Orleans was one of the most unique. Although it was an American city, it retained much of its French heritage, and although it was a Southern city, it had its own unique culture, making it stand apart from other cities of the South. Aromas of food, flowers, and a "perfume" distinctive only to New Orleans wafted toward the boat. Music, interspersed with laughter—loud guffaws of men and high trills of women—came from a riverfront bar on Tchoupitoulas Street.

The captain of the boat stood on the lower deck, frequently pulling out his pocket watch to check the time. It was obvious he was waiting for someone, and whoever it was, was late, contributing to an increasing agitation.

Matt watched a cab approach the river, the horse in a rapid trot, then pull to a stop at the river's edge. A woman got out, handed a bill to the driver, and hurried across the gangplank and on to the boat.

"Uncle, I'm so sorry. I was shopping and lost track of the time," the woman apologized.

"Jenny, I can't hold up the entire boat because my niece can't keep track of the time," the captain said.

From his spot on the texas deck, Matt was able to examine the woman rather closely. She was an exceptionally pretty woman with red hair, a peaches-and-cream complexion, blue eyes, and prominent cheekbones. If one had asked her about her lips, she might suggest they were a bit too full.

"Mr. Peabody!" the captain called.

"Aye, sir," answered one of the other officers.

"Away all lines. Pull in the gangplank."

Matt maintained his position at the rail on the texas deck, watching as the boat crew performed the ordered tasks. Captain Lee had reached the wheelhouse, and once the boat was free of its restraints, a signal was sent to the engine room. Smoke belched from the twin, fluted chimneys and the stern wheel began to turn, pushing the boat away from the bank and into the middle of the Mississippi River. The boat turned upstream, and the great red and yellow paddle wheel began spinning rapidly, leaving behind it a long, frothing wake.

Jenny Lee worked for her uncle as a hostess in the Grand Salon of the *Delta Mist.* It was her duty to see to the comfort and needs of the passengers who came into the Grand Salon. She also arranged friendly games of whist, checkers, and even poker for the passengers who wanted to participate.

Over the past two days, the boat had been averaging twelve miles per hour and was approaching Memphis, 704 miles by river from New Orleans. She was passing pleasantries with some of the passengers when a loud, angry voice got the attention of everyone in the salon.

"No man is that lucky! You have to be cheating!"

The speaker was standing at one of the tables, and the object of his anger and the subject of his charge was Matt Jensen.

Unlike the angry man, Matt was composed as he sat across the table.

Not so the other two players who, at the outburst, had stood up and backed away from the table so quickly they knocked over their chairs.

For a long moment there was absolute silence in the Grand Salon, with nothing to be heard but the sound of the engine, the slap of the stern paddle, and the whisper of water rushing by the keel.

"Mister, nobody cheats me and gets away with it," the man addressed his hostility toward Matt.

"You're out of line, Holman." Dr. Gunter was one of the other players at the table. "Nobody has been cheating at this table."

"The hell there ain't nobody been cheatin'! I ain't won a hand in the last hour. And he's won the most of 'em." Holman reached for the money piled up in the middle of the table. "I'm just goin' to take this pot to make up for it."

"That's not your pot." Jay Miller, a lawyer from St. Louis, was the fourth player at the table.

"Yeah? Well, we'll just see whose pot it is," Holman said contemptuously as he started to put the money in his hat.

"Leave the money on the table, Holman." Those were the first words Matt had spoken since being challenged.

"The hell I will. This money is mine, and I'm takin' it with me."

Jenny hurried over to the table. "Mr. Holman, please. You are creating a disturbance, and your behavior is making the passengers uneasy."

"Yeah? Well, to hell with the passengers. What kind of boat is this, anyway, that you allow cheaters in the games?"

"I wasn't cheating," Matt pointed out dryly.

"Mr. Jensen is tellin' the truth, Miss Lee." Dr. Gunter pointed toward Matt. "He wasn't cheatin'."

"What do you say, Mr. Miller?" Jenny asked the third man.

"I've played a lot of cards in my day, and I think I can tell when someone is cheating. I don't believe he was."

Jenny looked back at the angry gambler. "These gentlemen don't agree with you."

"Of course they don't. They are probably in on it. I wouldn't be surprised if they all get together later on and divide up the money. *My* money." Once again, he leaned over the pile of money on the table. "Like I said, I'll be taking this pot."

"Miss Lee, I've played cards with Mr. Jensen," declared a passenger who wasn't currently in the game. "I've never known him to be anything but honest."

"Same here," another put in. "I wasn't in this game, but I've played a few hands with him since we left New Orleans, and I found him to be an honest man. If these two gentlemen who were in the game say he wasn't cheating, then I would be inclined to believe them."

"Mr. Holman, that makes four people who say Mr. Jensen wasn't cheating. When you play cards for money, you are accepting the possibility of losing. The only thing protecting the game is the honesty, integrity, and honor of the players."

"You!" Holman pointed at Jenny. "You are in on it too, aren't you? You are all in it together."

"Look. We were in the same game as you. You think we would take up for him if he was cheating? Hell, we lost money, too," Miller said.

"Yeah, well, neither one of you lost as much money as I did."

"That's because neither of them is as bad at cards as you are," Matt gracelessly pointed out.

"What do you mean, I'm a bad player? Why, I'm as good at cards as any man."

"No, you aren't," Matt insisted. "You can't run a bluff and you raise bets in games of stud when the cards you have showing prove you are beaten. You should find some other game of chance and give up poker."

Jenny turned to Matt. "Mr. Jensen, I believe the pot is yours." She reached for the money to slide it across the table toward him, but Holman pushed her away from the table so hard that she fell.

He pointed down at her. "Keep your hands off my money. Like I said, I'm takin' this pot, and there's nobody here who can stop me."

Matt and another passenger helped her up. "Thank you for interceding, Miss Lee, but I think you had better let me handle this now."

"Ha!" the angry gambler cried. "You are going to handle this? What do you plan to do?"

"Oh, I'll do whatever it takes." Matt's calm, almost expressionless reply surprised the angry man.

The shock showed in his face, but was quickly replaced by an evil smile. He stepped away from the table and flipped his jacket back, showing an ivory-handled pistol in a tooled-leather holster.

"Mister, maybe it's time that I tell you who I am. My name ain't John Holman like I been sayin'. My actual name is Quince Justin Holmes, only some folks call me Quick Justice Holmes because I tend to make my own justice, if you know what I mean."

"Quick Justice Holmes," A passenger repeated in awe. "That's Quick Justice?"

"This is gettin' downright dangerous," another said.

"What do you say now?" Holmes asked.

"I say the same thing I've been saying. You aren't getting that pot," Matt said resolutely.

"It won't matter none to you whether I get the pot or not, 'cause you ain't goin' to be around to see it," Holmes said, his voice menacing.

"Does this mean you are inviting me to the dance?" Matt asked, still calm.

Holmes laughed. "Yeah, you might say that. I'll even let you make the first move."

Despite his offer, his hand was already dipping for his pistol, even as he was speaking. He smiled as he realized his draw had caught Matt by surprise. But the smile left his face when he saw Matt's draw.

To the witnesses, it appeared Matt and Holmes fired at the same time. But in actuality, Matt fired just a split second sooner and the impact of his bullet took Holmes off his aim. Holmes's bullet whizzed by Matt's ear and punched through the glass of one of the windows of the Grand Salon.

"I'll be damned! I've been kilt!" Holmes cried as he staggered back from the blow of the bullet.

"You could have prevented it at any time," Matt uttered.

Holmes dropped his gun and clamped his hand

over the wound in his chest. Blood spilled through his fingers, and he opened his hand to look at it before he collapsed.

Matt returned his pistol to his holster. Looking over toward Jenny, he saw a horrified expression on her face. "I'm sorry about this, Miss Lee."

"No," she replied in a small voice. "You . . . had no choice."

The boat put in at Memphis, and a coroner's inquest was held. The hearing lasted less than an hour. Enough witnesses testified that Quince Justin Holmes instigated the shooting and a decision was quickly reached.

Quince Justin Holmes died as a result of a .44 ball, which was energized to terrible effect by a pistol held by Matthew Jensen. This hearing concludes that Mr. Jensen was put in danger of his life when Holmes drew and fired at him. It is the finding of this hearing that this was a case of justifiable homicide and no charges are to be filed against Mr. Jensen.

Matt was welcomed back aboard the *Delta Mist* by those who had witnessed the shooting, as well as those who had only heard about it. He apologized to the boat captain for having been involved in the incident.

"Nonsense," Captain Lee replied. "Why, you've made the *Delta Mist* famous. People will want to take the boat where the infamous Quick Justice Holmes was killed. To say nothing of the fact that he was killed by Matt Jensen. You are truly one of America's best known shootists, as well known for your honesty and goodness of heart as you are for your prowess with a pistol."

"Hear, hear!" someone called, and the others cheered and applauded.

For the next 575 miles, the distance by river from Memphis to St. Louis, passengers vied for the opportunity to visit with Matt, or better, to play poker with him. His luck wasn't always as good as it had been during the trip from New Orleans to Memphis. By the time the boat docked up against the riverbank in the Gateway City, he had no more money with him than he had when he left New Orleans.

Jenny Lee stood by the gangplank, telling the passengers good-bye as they left the boat and thanking them for choosing the *Delta Mist.*

"Mr. Jensen, I do hope you travel with us again. You managed to make this trip"—she paused midsentence and smiled broadly—"most interesting."

"Perhaps a little too interesting," Matt suggested as he took the hand she had offered him.

Chapter Two

At sea—September 23, 1890

The ship was the *American Eagle*, a four-masted clipper in the Pacific trade. As much canvas as could be spread gleamed a brilliant white in the sunshine, and the ship was lifting, falling, and gently moving from side to side as it plowed over the long, rolling swells of the Pacific. The propelling wind, spilling from the sails, emitted a soft, whispering sigh as the boat heeled.

The helmsman stood at the wheel, his legs spread slightly as he held the ship on its course. Working sailors moved about the deck, tightening a line here, loosening one there, providing the exact tension on the rigging and angle on the sheets to maintain maximum speed. Some sailors were holystoning the deck, while others were manning the bilge pumps.

Twenty-four-year-old Luke Shardeen stood on the leeward side on the quarterdeck, his big hands resting lightly on the railing. From the age of seventeen he had been at sea, rising from an able-bodied seaman to first officer. His dark hair blew in the wind as his brown eyes examined the barometer for the third time in the last thirty minutes. There was no doubt it was falling, and that could only presage bad weather. Shrugging his broad shoulders, he left the quarterdeck and tapped on the door of the captain's cabin.

"Yes?" the captain called.

"Captain, permission to enter?"

"Come in, Mr. Shardeen."

Luke stepped into the cabin, which was as large as all the other officers' quarters combined. Captain Cutter was bent over the chart table with a compass and a protractor.

"Captain, the barometer has fallen rather significantly in the last half hour. I've no doubt but that a storm is coming."

"Do you have any idea how fast we are going, Mr. Shardeen?"

"It would only be a guess."

"We are doing nineteen knots, Mr. Shardeen. Nineteen knots," Captain Cutter said. "It's my belief that if we can maintain this pace, we'll outrun the storm."

"We won't be able to maintain this pace, Captain, if we rig the storm sails."

"I have no intention of rigging the storm sails. Certainly not until it is an absolute necessity."

"Very good, Captain." Luke withdrew from the captain's cabin and returned to the quarterdeck.

"Mr. Shardeen," the bosun called. "Will we be taking in the sail, sir?"

Luke shook his head. "Not yet."

He looked out over the water. The sea was no longer blue, but dirty gray and swirling with white-caps. It was the kind of sea referred to by sailors as "green water" and so rough the ship dropped into a trough and took green water over the entire deck as it started back up.

Shortly, the storm was on them, with wind and rain so heavy it was impossible to distinguish the rain from the spindrift.

"Captain, we have to strike sail!" Luke shouted above the noise of the gale.

"Aye, do so," Captain Cutter agreed.

Luke sent men aloft to strike sail, praying that no one would be tossed off by the bucking ship.

The masts were stripped of all canvas without losing anyone, but the storm continued to build. By mid-morning, it was a full-blown typhoon. Fifteen-foot waves crashed against the side of the 210-foot-long ship. The *American Eagle* was in imminent danger of foundering.

"Captain, we have to head her into the wind!" Luke Shardeen shouted.

"No. Even without sail we're still making head-way," Captain Cutter shouted back.

"If we don't do it, we'll likely lose the ship!"

"I'm the captain of this vessel, Mr. Shardeen.

And as long as I am captain, we'll sail the course I've set for her."

"Aye, aye, sir."

The huge waves continued to crash against the side of the ship and the rolling steepened, going over as far as forty-five degrees to starboard. It hung for so long the sailors had sure and certain fear it would continue to roll until it capsized.

Below deck in the mess, cabinet doors swung open and plates, cups, and bowls fell to the floor, crashing against the starboard.

"Everyone to port side!" Luke shouted through a megaphone and, though the sailors found it difficult to climb up the slanted deck, their combined weight helped bring the ship back from the brink of disaster.

When the ship rolled back, the dishes tumbled to port, breaking into smaller and smaller shards until there was nothing left but a jumbled collection of bits and pieces of what had once been the ship's crockery.

Above deck the yardarms were free of sail except for the spanker sail, which had been left rigged, and was now no more than tattered strips of canvas, flapping ineffectively in the ninety-mile-per-hour winds.

Captain Cutter was standing on the quarterdeck when a huge wave burst over the side of the ship. He and three sailors were swept off the deck, into the sea.

"Cap'n overboard!" someone shouted, and Luke

ordered the helmsman to turn into the wind. That kept the ship in place and stopped the terrible rolling, but it began to pitch up, then down, by forty-five degrees. Luke put the men to the rails to search for those who had been washed overboard. They found and recovered two of the sailors, but there was no sign of the third sailor or the captain.

By late afternoon the storm had abated, and Luke ordered the ship to remain in place to continue the search. For the next two days, in calm winds and a placid sea, they searched for the captain and the missing sailor, but found no sign of either of them. Finally, Luke ordered the ship to continue on its original course.

They raised San Francisco twenty-three days later.

A tugboat met them in the Bay, a seaman shot a line up to them, and, with all sail gone, they were towed to the docks, where they dropped anchor. As soon as the ship was made fast by large hawsers, a ladder was lowered for the officers and a gangplank was used by the men to offload their cargo of tea.

Luke sat in the outer office of the headquarters for the Pacific Shipping Company. The walls were decorated with lithographs of the company's ships, including one of the *American Eagle.* Beside each ship was a photograph of its captain. Emile Cutter's face, stern and dignified in his white beard, was alongside the picture of the ship Luke had just left.

"Captain Shardeen, Mr. Buckner will see you now," a clerk said.

Luke wasn't a captain, but he figured the clerk didn't know that or had called him "Captain" because he had assumed command of the ship to bring it home.

Although Richard Buckner's shipping empire had made him a millionaire, he had never been to sea. Nevertheless, his office was a nautical showplace, replete with model ships, polished bells engraved with the names of the ships from which they came, and the complete reconstruction of a helm, with wheel and compass.

Buckner was a man of average height, but in comparison to Luke's six-foot-four-inch frame, he seemed short. He greeted Luke with an extended hand. "Mr. Shardeen, you are to be congratulated, sir, for an excellent job of bringing the ship back safely. Please, tell me what happened."

Luke told about the storm, and how a huge wave hit them broadside, washing the captain and three other sailors overboard. Luke made no mention of the argument he'd had with Captain Cutter about bringing the ship into the wind.

"We rescued two of the sailors right away and stayed on station for two days, but we never found Captain Cutter or Seaman Bostic."

"Thank you. I'm sure that Mrs. Cutter will be comforted to know exactly what happened and will be grateful for the effort the entire ship showed in trying to rescue her husband."

"I wish we had been successful."

"Yes, well, such things are in the hands of God. Now, Mr. Shardeen, if you would, there are some reports you need to fill out. After you are finished, please come back into the office. I have something I want to discuss with you."

"Aye, sir." Luke normally didn't use *aye* except when he was at sea, but he knew Buckner enjoyed being addressed in such a manner.

As he was filling out the reports, Luke was given a stack of letters that had been held for him until the ship's return. One of them was from a lawyer's office in Pueblo, Colorado. He had never been to Pueblo, Colorado, and as far as he was aware, didn't know anyone there. Tapping the envelope on the edge of the table, he wondered why he would be the recipient of a letter from a Pueblo lawyer. His curiosity was such that he interrupted the paperwork in order to read the letter.

1 February 1890

Dear Mr. Shardeen:

It is with sadness that I report to you the death of your Uncle Frank Luke, who passed away on the 5th of August from an infirmity of the heart.

As you were his only living relative, you are the sole beneficiary of his will, in which he leaves you the following items:

18,000 acres of land
A four room house

All the furniture therein
A bunkhouse
A barn
1500 head of cattle
20 horses with saddles and tack
$1017.56 (remaining after all final expenses)

In order to claim your inheritance, you must present yourself at the Pueblo courthouse on or before November 1st, 1890.

Sincerely,
Tom Murchison
Attorney at Law

The letter came as a complete surprise. Luke had not seen his uncle Frank in over ten years, had no idea he'd lived in Colorado, or that he even had anything valuable to leave in a will. And he'd left everything to him!

Conflicting emotions quickly rose in Luke—elation over what appeared to be a rather substantial inheritance and guilt because not only had he not seen his uncle Frank, he had corresponded with him only three or four times in the last ten years.

Setting the letter aside, he finished the paperwork and returned to Mr. Buckner's office as requested.

"Mr. Shardeen," Buckner said. "With the unfortunate death of Captain Cutter, we have to find a new captain for the *American Eagle.* You know the ship and the men, and you brought her successfully through a terrible storm. I would like for you to be her new captain."

Had this offer been made to Luke one month earlier—or even one hour earlier—he would have accepted it immediately. But the letter from Tom Murchison had changed all that.

"I thank you for the offer, Mr. Buckner. I am extremely flattered by it." Luke took a deep breath before plunging on. "But I believe I will leave the sea for a while. I'll be submitting my resignation today."

"What?" Buckner replied in shocked surprise. "You can't be serious! Mr. Shardeen, this is the opportunity of a lifetime. How can you possibly pass it up?"

"Simple. Until today, I had no anchor. But now"—Luke held up his letter—"I am a man of property and can no longer afford to sail all over the world."

"Are you absolutely positive of that? If you are, we will have to promote someone else to captain."

"I am positive."

"Very well. The company will hate to lose you, Mr. Shardeen. You have been a good officer. If ever you wish to return to the sea, please, come see us first."

"I will do so," Luke promised.

Chapter Three

New Orleans—October 5

Nate McCoy boarded the *Delta Mist* and immediately entered the Grand Salon, interested in getting into a game of poker. He dressed well, had impeccable manners, and seemed able to get along with everyone. He was also the most handsome man Jenny had ever seen.

For the next two days, she watched him as he played, though she stood on the far side of the salon so nobody could see that she was watching him.

As evening fell, she took a quick break from her duties and she leaned on the railing of the texas deck, looking down at the great stern wheel, its paddles spilling water as they emerged from the river.

A man spoke to her. "You have been watching me."

Turning toward the speaker, Jenny saw Nate McCoy. "I'm supposed to watch people in the salon. That is my job."

"You're not watching me as part of your job. You're watching me for the same reason I'm watching you."

"Oh? And why is that?"

"I think you know why that is," McCoy quipped.

Jenny was lost from that moment, falling head over heels in love with him.

Three months later, On January 3, 1891, they were married.

Jenny learned quickly that marrying Nate McCoy was the biggest mistake she had ever made. Although he'd told her he was a broker who dealt with "other people's money," that was an extremely broad interpretation of his actual profession. McCoy was a professional gambler, and not an honest one.

Caught cheating on the *Delta Mist*, he was barred from taking passage on that or any of the passenger boats that plied the Mississippi. When he left the boats Jenny left with him, and for the next eighteen months, her life with McCoy became little more than running from town to town just ahead of a lynch mob.

"Why do you cheat?" Jenny asked her husband.

"Why do I cheat? Isn't it obvious? I cheat to make money. Where do you think we get the food we eat? The expensive clothes you wear? How do we pay for the fine hotel rooms? From my winnings, that's where. The odds of winning are not good enough for all that unless I give myself an edge. And that is exactly what I do, my dear. I give myself an edge."

"By cheating."

"You call it cheating, I call it increasing the odds."

"When you were caught cheating on the boats you were barred from taking any further passage on them. But if you are caught cheating in a saloon or a gambling house, the consequences could be much more severe. You could be killed."

"Ahh, it does my heart good to know my darling wife is frightened for me," Nate said sarcastically.

"Nate, why don't we make a living doing something else? I have an education. I could teach school." Jenny made that offer, even though she knew most schools had a provision in their contract that the teachers they hire be unwed.

"Assuming you could get around the obstacle of being married, what would you propose that I do, my dear? Become a store clerk perhaps?"

"Why not? It would be honest work. And we could settle down somewhere and have a real home like ordinary people."

"Like *ordinary* people," McCoy repeated, emphasizing the word.

"Yes."

"And this real home, no doubt, will have a white picket fence? Perhaps some flowers that you care for so tenderly? Maybe even a brat or two running around?"

"I-I wouldn't call them brats," Jenny mumbled, hurt by his sarcastic response.

"Yes. Well, my dear, as for your rather tedious dream, I am not *ordinary*, as you know."

"Yes," Jenny said, the dream now dead. "How well I know."

Colorado Springs, Colorado

Two days after that very conversation, Jenny and Nate had breakfast in the hotel dining room.

"I've never seen a town that had so many people who were ripe for the plucking. Why, I wouldn't be surprised if we didn't get out of here with between a thousand and fifteen hundred dollars."

"Nate, please be careful."

"Oh, don't you worry about that, my dear. I've been doing this for a long time. I know how to take care of myself." McCoy stood and left Jenny to return to their room alone.

Jenny tried to concentrate on the book in her hand, but her thoughts kept interrupting. Nate had been gone for over four hours, and it wasn't like him to be gone so long. He had told her they would have lunch together, but it was nearly one o'clock and he hadn't come back to the hotel room yet.

Feeling an overwhelming sense of foreboding, Jenny put the book aside and walked to the window, looking down onto the street below. When there was a knock at the door she gasped. She knew something was wrong. Nate wouldn't knock.

Turning away from the window, she took a sharp breath, and with trembling hands, crossed over to open the door. The man standing in the hallway was wearing the badge of a deputy city marshal.

"Mrs. McCoy?"

"Is he dead?" Jenny asked in a quiet and resigned voice.

If the deputy was shocked by her question, he didn't show it. "Yes, ma'am, I'm afraid he is."

"What happened?"

"I'm told he was caught with an ace up his sleeve. There was an altercation, your husband went for a gun, and he was shot."

"That isn't possible."

"Mrs. McCoy, are you saying your husband didn't cheat?"

"No, he cheated all right. But it isn't possible that he went for a gun. He never carried one."

"To be truthful with you, Mrs. McCoy, it doesn't matter whether he had a gun or not. There was a bitter argument precipitated by your husband, and the man who shot him believed McCoy was going for a gun. The belief that his life was threatened is all it takes to justify shooting your husband."

"Where is he now?"

"The undertaker has him. Will you be paying for his final expenses or will the city pay?"

"You mean the city would pay?"

"A plain pine box and a hole in the ground. I'm afraid there is nothing comforting about a city-financed burying."

"I'll go see the undertaker," Jenny said. "Perhaps we can come to an accommodation of sorts."

Learning that the undertaker's business was next door to the hardware store, Jenny left the hotel and walked down to see him. Surprised to see a rather substantial knot of people standing around in front of the undertaker's building, she wondered why they were there.

As soon as she arrived, she saw what was holding their attention. There, in an open casket, she saw her husband. His arms were folded across his chest, and he was holding a hand of cards. A hand-lettered sign read A CHEATING GAMBLER'S FATE.

"I'll bet all five of them cards is aces," a man in the crowd said, causing several others to laugh.

Jenny went into the establishment where she was met by a tall, gaunt man in a black suit, white shirt, and black string tie.

"Yes, ma'am. Is there something I can do for you?"

"There certainly is. You can remove my husband from that horrid display in the window," Jenny answered pointedly.

"Your husband? You mean the gambler?"

"Yes, Nate McCoy. He is—was—my husband. And what you are doing, displaying him like that, is disgraceful. I thought morticians were supposed to show respect for the dead and their families."

"I-I beg your pardon, madam. I wasn't aware the deceased was married, and I was especially unaware he had any family in Colorado Springs. Of course, I will remove the remains at once."

"Why would you do such a thing, anyway?"

"I thought the city would be responsible for burying him. They pay so little I don't even break even on the cost of the services I provide. Displaying his body in such a way draws people to satisfy their curiosity, morbid though it may be. And that is good publicity for my business."

"I will pay for his funeral," Jenny promised.

"Yes, ma'am. Will you want a church service and a minister in attendance during the committal?"

"I will."

"What is your denomination?" the undertaker asked.

"I am not particular."

"And how soon do you want the funeral?"

"As quickly as it can be arranged." Jenny opened her reticule and withdrew the roll of money Nate had won in the last city. It was to be his seed money for his next gambling operation. "How much will this cost?"

The undertaker looked at the wad of money and licked his lips. "I think, uh, one hundred and fifty dollars should cover everything."

"Yes, I should hope so," Jenny said, counting out the money.

"Yes, ma'am. Leave everything to me. I'll take care of all the details."

"How soon can we do this?"

"Oh, I'm quite sure we can arrange it for you as early as tomorrow."

"Today would be better, but if it is to be tomorrow, then that will have to do."

"Where are you staying, madam?"

"I am staying at the Dunn Hotel."

"I will get word to you when the arrangements have been made."

"Thank you."

The only people present for the church service the next morning were Jenny, the preacher, and the mortician. The preacher knew nothing about Nate McCoy, so instead of preaching a funeral service, he merely reread the sermon he had given the previous Sunday.

An additional person was present for the graveside committal. The gravedigger stood off at a respectful distance, leaning on his spade and smoking a pipe as he waited for the opportunity to close the grave so he could draw his fee, then go have a drink.

The committal service was short, consisting only of a single prayer, during which the preacher called him Ned, instead of Nate. The moment the preacher said amen, the gravedigger sauntered over and he and the mortician lowered the pine box into the ground.

As she walked away from the open grave, Jenny could hear the *thump, thump* as dirt landed on the pine box.

Leaving the cemetery, Jenny went directly to the railroad depot. "What time is the next train?" she asked the ticket agent.

"The next train to where, madam?" the ticket agent replied with a long-suffering sigh.

"I don't care where it is going as long as it is the next train."

"The southbound is due in about half an hour."

"I want a ticket on that train."

"Where to, madam?"

"Where is it going?"

"Pueblo, Salt Creek, Walsenburg . . ."

"Pueblo," Jenny said.

"Yes, ma'am." The ticket agent made out the ticket, stamped it with a rubber stamp, then handed it to her.

"That will be eight dollars."

"Thank you." Jenny handed him the money.

When the train rolled into the depot twenty-six minutes later, Jenny boarded it and found an empty seat, purposely choosing not to sit by the window. She had no wish for a last look at the town where all her fears had culminated. Though she would never admit it, even to herself, it was also where she'd gained freedom from a marriage that never should have been.

Chapter Four

Pueblo, Colorado—April 1893

The thirty-three children of Jenny's fifth grade class were gathered for a photo in front of the steps leading up to the school. Students in the first row sat on the ground with their hands folded across their laps. Those in the second row sat on a long, low bench, and the third and fourth rows were standing on ascending steps.

"Now, if the teacher would just sit beside her class." The photographer had a long mustache that curled up at each end. His camera, a big box affair, was sitting on a tripod in front of the class.

Jenny sat on a chair alongside the class, her hands folded across her lap just as she had instructed the children.

"Now, nobody move until I say so." The photographer put his hand on the shutter latch. "See the honey up in the tree, I wish you would bring some to me," he said in a monotone voice. "There. Now you can move."

"I can move," one of the boys on the front row exclaimed, and he pulled the hair of the girl beside him.

"Ouch!"

"Danny," Jenny scolded. "All right, children, school is dismissed. Don't forget your homework."

"Yea!" one of the boys shouted and the class, which had been so motionless a moment earlier, scattered like leaves before a wind.

Jenny picked up her chair and carried it back into her classroom. The principal and the superintendent of schools were waiting for her.

"Mr. Gray, Mr. Twitty?" she said, obviously surprised to see them.

"Miss McCoy, or should I say Mrs. McCoy?" The expression on Twitty's face was grim.

"I'm not married." Jenny paused for a moment. "I'm a widow."

"You were married to Nate McCoy, were you not?" Twitty asked.

"Yes, I was."

"It has come to our attention that Nate McCoy was a gambler of, let us say, questionable ethics. And, while you were married, you followed him from gambling den to gambling den. Is that correct?"

Jenny looked down. "Yes," she said quietly.

"I'm sorry to have to tell you this, Mrs. McCoy. The school board has asked for your dismissal."

"On what grounds?" Jenny asked.

"Moral turpitude."

"What? But I . . ."

"Please take your things and leave," Mr. Gray said.

"My class?"

"They are no longer your class. We have already hired a replacement teacher," Mr. Twitty informed her.

"Can't I at least finish the year? We've only one month to go. For the children's sake, don't you think it would be better for them to keep the same teacher until the end of the year?"

"Good-bye, Mrs. McCoy," Gray said coldly.

Jenny fought hard to keep the tears from welling up in her eyes. She stood and turned away from them, determined not to let them see her cry. She walked into the cloakroom, removed her coat, and left the schoolroom. There was nothing else she wanted to take from there.

Red Cliff, Colorado—July 8

The sign out front of the store read RAFFERTY'S GROCERY. One of three, it stood at the very edge of town. Michael Santelli stepped into the little store, and a bell attached to the top of the door announced his entry.

"Yes, sir, what can I do for you?" Mr. Rafferty asked. Mrs. Rafferty looked up from sweeping the floor and smiled.

Santelli took a quick glance around. Seeing nobody else in the store, he pulled his gun and pointed it at the shopkeeper. "You can give me all your money. That's what you can do for me."

"Yes, sir," Rafferty said nervously. "Just don't be

getting trigger happy there." He opened his cash drawer, took out thirty dollars, and handed it across the counter.

Santelli counted it quickly, then looked up at Rafferty, his face twisted in anger. "What is this?" he demanded.

"You said give you all my money. That's what I did. This is all the money I have."

"Thirty dollars? Do you expect me to believe that all you have is thirty dollars?"

"That *is* all I have," Rafferty said. "We deposited yesterday's receipts in the bank last night. I always start the morning with just enough money to make change."

"You're lyin'!" Santelli pointed his pistol at Mrs. Rafferty. "You better come up with more money fast, or I'll shoot the woman."

"Please, I don't have any more money!" Rafferty shouted desperately.

"I warned you." Santelli grabbed Mrs. Rafferty, pulled the hammer back on his pistol, and held it to her head.

With a shout of anger, Rafferty climbed over the counter toward him.

Santelli shot him, then turned his pistol back toward Mrs. Rafferty and shot her. Quickly, he went behind the counter and looked through the cash box, but found no more money. With a shout of rage, he picked up the cash box and threw it into a glass display case, smashing the case into pieces.

That done, and with no more money than the

thirty dollars Rafferty had given him in the first place, Santelli left the store, mounted his horse, and rode away.

Sixty-seven-year-old Burt Rowe witnessed the entire thing from the back of the store. Santelli hadn't seen him when he looked around. But Rowe recognized the gunman, Santelli, having seen him before.

As soon as he was certain Santelli was gone, Rowe stepped out in front of the store and began shouting at the top of his lungs. "Help! Help! Murder! The Raffertys have been robbed and murdered!"

Within moments the store was filled with townspeople, including the sheriff and deputy sheriff.

"You are sure it was Santelli?" the sheriff asked Rowe.

"I'm absolutely positive," Rowe said. "I've seen him before."

"When he left here, which way did he go?"

"I seen him heading south, but that don't mean he kept going that way. By the way, he only got thirty dollars."

"Thirty dollars?" the sheriff asked incredulously. "You mean he murdered Mr. and Mrs. Rafferty for no more than thirty dollars?"

"Yes, sir," Rowe said. "I know that's all he got, 'cause I heard 'em talkin' about it."

"What are you going to do about it, Sheriff?" one of the townspeople asked. "Mr. and Mrs. Rafferty were two of the finest people in the world. We can't let that animal get away with this."

"He won't get away," the sheriff promised. "I'll get the word out to other sheriffs and city marshals. We'll get him, and when we do, we'll bring him right back here to hang. I promise you that."

One week later Michael Santelli rode into the town of Kiowa, Colorado, sizing it up as he went along the main street. The little town was made up of whipsawed lumber shacks with unpainted, splitting wood turning gray in the sun. A sign over the door of one rather substantial-looking brick building identified it as the BANK OF KIOWA. Still angered by th slim pickings from Rafferty's Grocery, Santelli figured the bank might offer some promise for a bigger payoff.

So far, he had over five thousand dollars he'd stolen from a bank in Greeley and hidden in the bottom of an old abandoned well near Gunnison. His plan was to put together enough money to buy a saloon in Texas. The idea of owning a saloon appealed to him—unlimited access to whiskey and beer. And the whores working for him would be available to him anytime he wanted them. But he figured he would need at least ten thousand dollars . . . to set himself up for the rest of his life.

Santelli was a wanted man. There was so much money on his head every bounty hunter in the state was looking for him. The sooner he was able to put together enough money to get out of Colorado, the better it would be. Once he got to Texas, he would be a model citizen. He smiled. He might even run for mayor.

Santelli rode up to the hitching rail in front of the Silver Nugget Saloon, dismounted, and patted his tan duster a few times, sending up puffs of gray-white dust before he walked inside. The saloon was busy, but he found a quiet place by the end of the bar. When the bartender moved over to him, Santelli ordered a beer, then stood there nursing it as he began to formulate a plan for robbing the bank.

Matt Jensen stood at the opposite end of the bar with both hands wrapped around a mug of beer. Something seemed familiar about the man who had just come in, but he couldn't place him. Studying the man's reflection in the mirror behind the bar, he took in his average height and weight and unkempt black hair. He had dark, obsidian eyes and a purple scar starting just below his left eye and disappearing in a scraggly beard.

The scar helped Matt make the identification. He had seen drawings and read descriptions of the outlaw Michael Santelli and just that morning had heard that Santelli had killed a grocer and his wife for no more reason than that they didn't have as much money in their cash box as he thought they should have.

Matt was neither a lawman nor a bounty hunter, but he didn't plan to let Santelli walk away. Before he could make any move, Deputy Sheriff Ben Mason came into the saloon, and Matt decided to wait and see how things played out.

He had met the deputy earlier, when he first rode into town, learning about Santelli's latest atrocity at the same time. Matt and Deputy Mason were about the same age, and Matt respected the lawman's dedication to duty.

When Mason saw Santelli standing at the bar, he stopped and stared for a long moment until he was sure it was the wanted outlaw.

"Santelli," Mason called out. "Michael Santelli."

Matt saw the way Santelli reacted, stiffening at the bar, but not turning around. The reaction gave him away, and Matt knew his first impulse had been right. The man was Santelli.

"You are Santelli, aren't you? Michael Santelli?" Mason asked. The lawman's voice was loud and authoritative.

Everyone in the saloon recognized the challenge implied in its timbre. All conversations ceased, and drinkers at the bar backed away so there was nothing but clear space between the lawman and Santelli. Even the bartender left his position behind the bar.

Matt stood in place at the opposite end of the bar, watching Santelli with intense interest as the drama began to unfold.

Santelli looked up, studying the lawman's reflection in the mirror, but he didn't turn around. "Lawman, I'm afraid you've got me mixed up with somebody else."

"No, I don't think so," Mason said confidently. "I know who you are. You are a bank robber and a murderer, and you are under arrest."

Not until that moment did Santelli turn to face the lawman, and he did so with a slow and assured nonchalance. "It looks like I can't fool you, can I?" he said as a frightening smile curled across his lips. "What are you, anyway? A city marshal? A sheriff?"

"I'm a deputy sheriff. Mason is the name."

"Well, now, Deputy Mason, you think you've got yourself a big prize, don't you? You're right. I am Michael Santelli, but there's not a thing you are going to be able to do about it. Because the truth is, mister, you have just bitten off more than you can chew. If you make a move toward your gun, I'll kill you right where you stand."

"And then I'll kill you." Matt added his voice to the conversation for the first time.

Santelli was startled to hear a new challenge from his left, and he turned his head quickly to see Matt standing away from the bar, facing him. Like Mason and Santelli, Matt had not drawn his pistol.

"Who asked you to butt into this?" Santelli asked.

"Nobody asked me. But I met Deputy Mason earlier today, and I found him to be a fine, upstanding gentleman. I don't plan to stand here and watch you shoot him."

"Thank you, Mr. Jensen," Mason said. "I appreciate your help."

Santelli's face, which had been coldly impassive, suddenly grew animated. His skin whitened and a line of perspiration beaded on his upper lip. "Jensen?" he said nervously. "Is that your name?"

"Matt Jensen, yes."

"You fellas seem to have me at a disadvantage, two of you to my one."

"I would say that is a smart observation, Santelli," Matt said.

"Take your gun out of your holster, using only your thumb and finger," Mason ordered.

Santelli reached for his pistol, then suddenly wrapped his entire hand around the pistol butt.

Seeing that, Matt made a lightning draw of his pistol, pulling the hammer back as he brought his gun to bear. The sound of the sear engaging the cylinder made a loud clicking noise.

Hearing it, Santelli jerked his hand away from his gun and held it, empty, out in front of him, imploring Matt not to shoot. "No, no! I ain't goin' to draw! I ain't goin' to draw!' he shouted. Holding his left hand up in the air as a signal of surrender, Santelli's right hand removed his pistol from the holster, using his thumb and forefinger as the deputy had directed.

"Now, lay your pistol on the floor and kick it over here," Mason ordered.

Santelli did as he was directed.

"I'll help you march him down to jail," Matt said.

"Thanks."

"Did you see that draw?" someone asked, the quiet voice reflecting his awe. "I ain't never seen nothin' like that."

"Didn't you hear who that is?" another asked. "That's Matt Jensen.

Deputy Mason put Santelli in handcuffs, then he and Matt walked the prisoner down to the jailhouse. Three minutes later, the cell door clanked loudly as it closed on him.

"Jensen," Santelli called out as Matt started to leave.

Matt turned to him.

"I have a feeling me 'n you are going to meet again, someday."

Matt nodded, but said nothing.

CHAPTER FIVE

Pueblo—August 4

Jenny was getting desperate. She had not been able to find a job, and she was nearly out of money. She'd paid her rent for August, but if she didn't find employment soon, she would have to give up her room. Sitting at her desk, she was writing a letter to her uncle, begging his forgiveness and pleading to be allowed to come back to work for him.

She was agonizing over the letter she didn't want to write when there was a knock at the door. Answering it, she saw a very pretty, elegant woman in her early fifties.

Jenny recognized her. Adele Summers was the proprietor of the Colorado Social Club, a house of prostitution.

"Miss Summers," Jenny said, surprised to see her. "What can I do for you?"

"I hope it is something I can do for you," Adele replied. "I've heard of your problem, and how the school board, a bunch of ninnies, fired you. I would like for you to come work for me, and I will pay you three times more money than you were making teaching school."

"Oh, Miss Summers, uh, I thank you, I really do. But I don't think I could do something like—"

"Hear me out before you reply. It isn't what you think."

"Oh?"

"I'm not asking you to be a prostitute," Adele said. "Not for a minute. I don't know what you know about the Social Club, but it isn't your ordinary house of prostitution. We have a very high-classed clientele. I would want you to meet our clients when they arrive, and for those clients who would enjoy such a thing, spend a little time with them, talking to them, having a drink with them, and making them feel welcome. That's all."

Jenny thought back to her time working in the grand salon on the *Delta Mist* and smiled. That was exactly what she did then. "You mean you want me to be a hostess."

"Yes!" Adele replied with a wide smile. "Yes, that is exactly what you would be. You would be a hostess and nothing more."

Kiowa, Colorado—November 11

A rather short, beady-eyed man with a red, splotchy face and thin blond hair dismounted in front of the Kiowa Jail. Tying his horse at the hitching rail, he went inside. Three men were in the front, two of them in conversation. The third sat behind a desk in the far corner of the room. The sign on his desk read ADAM CARTER—SHERIFF—ELBERT COUNTY.

"Can I help you?" one of the two deputies asked.

"You've got my brother in jail. I want to visit him."

"What's your name?"

"Ward, Bob Ward."

The deputy shook his head. "We don't have anyone by that name in jail."

"You've got Michael Santelli here, don't you?"

"Yes."

"That's my brother."

"Your brother?"

"We have the same mother. We don't have the same father."

Sheriff Carter looked up. "Ward? Isn't there some paper out on you, Ward?"

"Not 'ny more, Sheriff. I was let out of prison two months ago. You can check."

"All right. Mason, let him see his brother."

"Take your pistol belt off and lay it on the desk," Deputy Mason said.

Ward did as directed, then he was thoroughly searched for any hidden weapon.

"He's clean," informed the deputy who searched him.

"I'll take him back," Mason said.

"Deputy, is there someplace we can talk in private?"

"What do you want to talk in private for?"

"My brother's goin' to be hung, ain't he?"

"Yes."

"Well, then, we may have some private, family things to talk about."

Mason looked at his boss. "What about it, Sheriff?"

"Has Durham sobered up?" Sheriff Carter asked.

"Yes, sir, I'm sure he has." Mason chuckled. "He probably has a pretty bad headache, though."

"He's the only other prisoner we have right now. Turn him loose. That'll give Ward and Santelli the whole place alone."

"Come with me," Mason said.

Mason took the keys into the back of the building, while Ward followed close behind. Eight cells made up the back of the jail, four on either side of a center aisle. Mason opened the door to one of the cells. "Let's go, Durham."

Durham was lying on the bunk. "It ain't time for me to be turned out yet."

"You're getting out early."

"Damn. Can't you let a man sleep it off?"

"Let's go," Mason repeated.

Grumbling, Durham got up and plodded out of the cell.

"I'll give you half an hour," Mason said to Ward as he pushed Durham to the front. He closed the door to the cell area, leaving Ward and Santelli alone.

"Well. My brother has come to see me. I'm touched."

"They tell me you're goin' to hang," Ward said.

"That's what the judge said at my trial."

"So, look, I was thinkin'. I mean if you're goin' to hang anyway, why don't you tell me where the money is that you took from the bank in Greeley?"

"What makes you think I've got any of that money left?"

"I know you do. I just don't know how much."

"It's a little over five thousand dollars. I was plannin' on gettin' enough money to go to Texas and buy a saloon." Santelli shrugged.

"Yeah, that's a good idea. It's too bad you can't do it. So, look, why don't you tell me where the money is, and I'll buy a saloon and I'll name it after you."

"What do you mean, you'll name it after me?"

"Well, I mean you'll be dead. So it's only right that if I buy a saloon with your money, that I name it after you."

"What makes you think you're going to have my money?"

"Well why not, Michael? Like I said, you'll be dead. What good is that money goin' to do you, when you're dead? You may as well tell me where it is. 'Cause when you think about it, me 'n you is the only kin either one of us has got."

"Get me out of here, and I'll tell you where the money is."

"How am I s'posed to do that? There's only one way out of this building, and it's through the front door. There's a sheriff and two deputies up there with guns, and maybe you didn't notice, but they took my gun away from me before they would let me come back here."

"They're takin' me to Red Cliff to hang," Santelli said. "That's a long way, by train. Figure out some way to get me off the train."

"I don't think I can do it by myself. It's goin' to take three or four people to do somethin' like that."

"Then hire them. Promise 'em five hundred dollars each. That'll leave three thousand for me 'n you to split, half and half."

"Fifteen hundred sure ain't like five thousand," Ward said.

"How much money do you have now?"

"I don't know. About forty dollars, I reckon."

"Fifteen hundred is a lot more than forty," Santelli pointed out.

"Yeah. Yeah, I guess you're right. All right, I'll find some people to help me."

Santelli smiled, then walked back over to his bunk and lay down, with his hands laced behind his head. "Thanks for the visit, Bob."

"All right. Uh, listen. Just in case somethin' goes wrong, don't you think you ought to tell me where the money is? I mean, just in case."

"It's up to you to make certain that nothing goes wrong."

Ward stood outside the cell for a moment longer, frustrated that it didn't go as he had planned. But at least he saw a way of getting fifteen hundred dollars, and it had been a long time since he had had that kind of money.

"I've got a friend I was in the pen with. I'll get him to help."

"You do that," Santelli said in a dismissive tone. It was obvious that, as far as he was concerned, the visit with his brother was over.

Ward walked back out front, then looked toward the desk where he had put his pistol. "Where's my gun?"

Mason walked over to a cabinet, opened it, then handed it to him.

"Thanks."

"You'll need these as well," Mason said, handing Ward six bullets. "I unloaded your pistol."

"What'd you do that for?" Ward asked as he started to reload his pistol.

"No. Don't reload it until you get outside."

Ward nodded as he strapped on his pistol belt.

Pueblo—November 15

Luke Shardeen sat in the chair at the Model Barbershop, stroking his chin and examining his face in the mirror. It had been three years since he left the sea.

"Would you like a nice-smelling aftershave tonic?" Earl Cook the barber asked as he removed the cape from around Luke's neck. "Oh, the women all love it," he added with a smile.

"I have enough trouble keeping women away from me now," Luke teased. "Why would I want more coming around?"

For a moment the barber was surprised, then he realized Luke was teasing. "Yes, indeed, sir. I suppose a handsome fellow like you would have to put up with a lot of women. It must be quite a burden."

"Now, who is pulling whose leg here?" Luke asked, laughing as he paid the barber for his shave and haircut.

Cook laughed as well, then he looked around to make certain he wasn't overheard before he spoke quietly. "Have you seen the new young lady over at the Social Club?"

Luke chuckled. "I'm not one who visits such places. I'm not judgmental of those who do, you understand, but I'm not interested in a woman who will go to bed with anyone who meets her price."

The barber shook his head. "You don't understand. This new girl isn't like that. She used to be a schoolteacher, and they say she is very smart. She is also very pretty."

"So she is smarter and prettier than all the others. I still don't plan to pay her to let me take her to bed."

"Oh, I don't think you could pay this girl enough to get her in bed," Cook admonished.

"What are you talking about? Does she work at the Social Club or not?"

"Yes, she works there, but the only thing you can do is have a nice conversation with her. Oh, and maybe have a cup of coffee and some cookies. She's what they call a hostess. All she does is talk and smile."

"Do the people who go to the club know that?"

"Oh yes, they know that. And she is still the most popular girl there."

"How can that be, if she doesn't allow them to do anything?"

"It's because like I said. She is one of the prettiest women you'll ever see . . . and also the smartest. She has a way of talking with you that makes you feel like you are just as smart as she is."

"You talk like you know this first hand."

"I do know it first hand." Cook chuckled. "I'll tell you true, I never thought I would ever go to a place like the Social Club and not do anything but talk. But that's exactly what I've done, and I've done it more 'n once."

Leaving the barbershop, Luke thought about the conversation with Cook. He had to admit it had him intrigued. He walked by the Colorado Social Club three times before he finally got up the nerve to go inside.

He was met by a smiling, middle-aged, attractive woman.

"Why, Mr. Shardeen, how nice of you to visit us."

Luke was surprised to hear her call him by name. "You know me?"

"Oh, yes. You own Two Crowns Ranch and have

the reputation of being a real gentleman. I make it a point to know all of the . . . let us say *quality* . . . gentlemen of Pueblo. My name is Adele. What can I do for you?"

"I, uh, well, the truth is, this is all rather new for me. So I'm not sure exactly what to do."

Adele chuckled. "It's simple enough. I'll take you into our lounge, where you will see some of our young ladies. All you have to do is pick out one who interests you, and—"

"No. Not that."

Adele got a confused look on her face. "Then, I don't understand, Mr. Shardeen. What do you want?"

"I—uh, nothing, I guess. I'm sorry I wasted your time. Please forgive me."

"Oh, you didn't waste my time at all, Mr. Shardeen. It was a pleasure talking to you. Please come visit us again, sometime."

"Yes, uh, thank you. I'll just go now." Luke hurried out the front door, just as Jenny came into the foyer.

"Who was that?" she asked.

"That was Luke Shardeen," Adele said.

"What did he want?"

"I don't have the slightest idea. And what's more, I don't think he does, either."

Before returning to his ranch, Luke stopped by the post office to pick up his mail. He had a letter from Heckemeyer and Sons, a cattle brokerage company in the nearby town of Greenhorn. Anxiously, he opened the letter, hoping it was the answer he was looking for.

Mr. Shardeen,

Our company would be pleased to buy 500 head of cattle from you at the prevailing market price. Payment will be made upon delivery of the cattle.

Sincerely,
Anthony Heckemeyer
Broker

Greenhorn, Colorado—November 22

Luke shipped 500 head of Hereford cattle by rail to Greenhorn, paying five dollars per head to get them there. The railroad had off-loaded the cattle into a holding pen where they would keep them without charge for one day. If he made the sale, Heckemeyer and Sons would move the cattle from the pen.

"I tried to get you forty-two fifty, but the best offer I've been able to come up with, is forty dollars a head," Heckemeyer said. "That would be twenty thousand dollars for all five hundred head."

"Great," Luke said. "I was prepared to sell for thirty-five dollars a head. The five-dollar increase paid for shipping them over here."

"Well, then," Heckemeyer said with a broad smile. "We will both be happy, and you will be sure to tell others of the wonderful service provided you by Heckemeyer and Sons."

"Yes sir. I'll be glad to do that, Mr. Heckemeyer."

Luke signed the bill of sale, then left the office. Twenty thousand dollars was the most money he'd ever had, and he went on a short shopping spree, buying a new shirt, a pair of boots, and a rain slicker. After that he stopped by the saloon to have a celebratory drink before heading back to Two Crowns.

"Did you get your cows sold?" the bartender asked as he poured a shot of whiskey into Luke's glass.

"I did indeed. And a good price I got for them too," Luke replied. "Set the bar up for one round. This has been a most productive and profitable trip for me."

"One free drink to everyone," the bartender called. "Compliments of this gentleman."

With shouts of thanks, the other patrons in the saloon rushed to the bar as Luke saluted them with a raised glass.

In another part of the same saloon two men exchanged glances, then left the saloon.

"You think he'll have the money with him?"

"He just bought drinks all around, didn't he? Where else would the money be, if not on him?"

"Yeah, you're right. Where else would it be?"

"So, what do we do, now?"

"Let's get our horses. We'll watch the front of the saloon, and when he leaves, we'll follow."

* * *

Half an hour later, after exchanging good-byes with the new friends he had made, Luke left the saloon, mounted his horse, and started home.

"Tell me, Harry," he said, patting his horse on the neck. "How does it feel to be ridden by a rich man?"

Harry whickered and nodded his head.

Luke laughed. "All right, Harry, all right. I'm not really what you would call rich. But I'll have you know I am carrying more money than I have ever held in my hands in my entire life."

Chapter Six

"Here he comes," muttered one of the two men waiting for Luke.

"Let's go," the other instructed.

"Shouldn't we wait until he passes, then follow?"

"No, we'll ride ahead of him. That way he won't suspect anything, and we can set up and wait for him."

Shortly after leaving town, Luke noticed the two horsemen on the road ahead of him. Acutely aware of his environment because of the money he was carrying, he decided not to overtake them, but to keep them in sight. That worked well for the first fifteen minutes, and when he reached the top of the next rise he expected to see them still on the road just ahead.

They weren't there, and despite a very careful perusal, they were nowhere to be seen. Where did they go? There were no buildings to have entered nor crossroads to have taken, so what happened to them? He found it rather troubling that he could no longer see them.

Pulling his pistol, Luke checked the loads in the cylinder chambers, and satisfying himself that he was ready for any contingency, returned the gun to the holster. Shifting his eyes back and forth from one side of the trail to the other he rode ahead. Suddenly, through a break in the trees, he caught a glimpse of two mounted men waiting just off the side of the road. Drawing his pistol again, he cocked it and held it straight down by his side. Thus armed and alert, he continued forward.

When the two riders thrust themselves in the road in front of him, Luke was ready for them. Both men were wearing hoods over their faces, only their eyes visible through the eyeholes.

"Throw down your money!" one shouted.

"The hell I will!" Luke called back, bringing up his arm and firing in the same motion.

A little puff of dust flew up from the man where the bullet hit. A red spot appeared there as well, and the man who had challenged him fell from his horse.

The other rider, suddenly realizing he no longer had a two-to-one advantage, jerked his horse around and dug in the spurs.

Luke holstered his pistol and snaked his rifle from the saddle sheath. Jacking a round into the chamber, he raised the rifle to his shoulder and took very careful aim, but couldn't bring himself to shoot a man in the back. Carefully, he eased the hammer back down and lowered the rifle as he watched the rider flee.

Dismounting, Luke walked over to the man he had shot and saw that he was dead. The man's fate neither surprised nor bothered him. It had been a head-to-head confrontation, and the robber knew the chances he took when he set out. Luke pulled the hood off and tossed it to one side as he studied the man's face without recognition.

The road agent's horse had not run off, so, with some effort, Luke put the dead man belly down over the saddle. He thought about going back to Greenhorn, but he was almost as close to Pueblo, so he decided to take him there.

Riding up to the sheriff's office in Pueblo half an hour later, he was greeted by Deputy Sheriff Proxmire, who met him out in front of the office. "Who have you got there, Luke?"

"To tell you the truth, Deputy, I don't know who this man is," Luke answered. "But this fella and another man tried to rob me."

"Tried to rob you, you say?"

"Yes, I saw them ahead of me, saw them hiding behind some trees, so I got a little suspicious. I pulled my gun out and when they ordered me to give them my money, I shot one of them. This one." Luke nodded toward the body draped over the horse he was leading.

"What about the other man?"

"When I shot this fella, the other one turned and rode off. I could have shot him, too, but I don't have the stomach to shoot someone in the back. Anyway, I thought I may as well bring this one to you."

Proxmire turned toward the office and called, "Sheriff Ferrell, you want to come out now?"

The door to the sheriff's office opened behind Proxmire and another man stepped out. Luke was surprised. He believed it was the man who had gotten away. He was also surprised to see the man was wearing a star on his vest. There had been no star during the ambush.

"Deputy, I'm not sure, but I think this may have been the other man." Luke pointed toward the man behind Deputy Sheriff Proxmire.

"By other man, you mean he was with the man you shot?" Proxmire asked.

"Yes. He had his face covered with a hood, so I can't be positive, but he was about this size and was wearing the same kind of clothes. Only he wasn't packing a star when I saw him last."

"You say they were both wearing hoods?"

"Yes."

"What about the hood that was on this fella?" Deputy Proxmire asked. "Have you got it with you?"

"No, I just tossed it aside."

"What about you, Sheriff? Is this the man you encountered on the road?"

"It is, indeed. And you heard him, Sheriff. He just confessed to murdering Deputy Gates."

"What?" Luke replied loudly. "What are you talking about? I didn't murder anyone!"

"Did you, or did you not, shoot down my deputy?"

"Who are you?" Luke asked.

"I'm Sheriff Dewey Ferrell."

"Did you shoot his deputy, Luke?" Proxmire asked.

Luke pointed to the body that was still draped across the horse behind him. "If that man is this man's deputy, then yes, I shot him. But it was in self-defense. Whether this man is a sheriff or not, he and the man I shot tried to hold me up."

"We did no such thing," Sheriff Ferrell argued. "We were merely trying to stop him, so we could ask him a few questions. That's when he surprised the two of us by shooting."

"Deputy, I don't know what's going on here, but what happened is nothing like this man is saying. Both men were wearing hoods over their faces, and they demanded that I give them my money. You don't mask yourself with a hood if all you want to do is ask a few questions, do you?"

"You say we were wearing hoods, but you can't show the hood my deputy was wearing," Sheriff Ferrell pointed out.

"If the man you say tried to rob you was masked, how do you know this is the same man?" Proxmire pointed to the sheriff.

"He just said that he was."

"I'm going to have to take your gun and hold you in jail until this is all worked out," Proxmire said.

"Deputy, I'm telling you these two men tried to rob me."

"Why would they try to rob you, Luke? Do you carry so much money around all the time that someone would want to rob you?"

"I am now. I'm carrying almost twenty thousand dollars from the sale of my cattle. You can check with Heckemeyer and Sons over in Greenhorn. They will verify that I'm telling the truth."

"Oh, I don't doubt but that you sold some cows," Proxmire said. "But that's not the question. The question is, did the sheriff and his deputy stop you to ask a few questions as he says or did he and his deputy actually try to rob you?"

"They tried to rob me."

"Look at it this way, Luke. Right now it's just your word against Sheriff Ferrell's word, and seeing as he is an officer of the law, his word carries a bit more weight. But perhaps you can convince a jury to believe you."

"A jury? Look here, are you actually telling me this is going to court?"

"It is," Proxmire said.

Luke looked at Ferrell. "Will he be in court?"

"I'll be there," Ferrell answered. "I intend to see justice done for the killing of my deputy."

"All right," Luke said. "I won't argue with you, Proxmire. If you'll let me put this money in the bank, I'll come quietly and I'll stand trial."

"Good idea," Proxmire said.

* * *

Judge Amon Briggs sat back in the chair in his chambers and put his hands together, fingertip to fingertip. He was listening to Sheriff Ferrell.

"Luke can make a lot of trouble for us if we don't take care of this situation."

"What do you mean trouble for us?" Judge Briggs growled. "I didn't attempt to hold him up."

"Did you, or did you not, give Gates and me the information about him going to sell his cows? And were you, or were you not, going to be in for a third of the take? And that isn't the only deal we've been in. You got your share from the coach holdup two months ago, too, as I am sure you well remember."

Briggs held his hand out to quiet Ferrell. "All right, all right. There's no need to say anything else. The walls have ears. Don't worry. I'll take care of it."

"You'd better take care of it," Ferrell pressed. "Otherwise we'll both be in trouble."

Pueblo—December 5

Luke's trial was going to be held in the local courthouse with Judge Amon Briggs presiding. He was in his chambers meeting with the prosecutor. "I want him tried for first-degree murder."

"Your honor, I don't think I can make the case for first-degree murder," Lloyd Gilmore said. "I mean, even if what the sheriff says is true, if all he and his deputy were doing was confronting him for questioning, it still wouldn't be premeditated murder."

"It doesn't have to be premeditated," Briggs said. "He was resisting arrest, and that is a felony. Any death that occurs during the commission of a felony is automatically first-degree murder."

"According to Sheriff Ferrell's own testimony, he wasn't making an arrest, he merely wanted to question him. That's not resisting arrest. A good lawyer could say that Luke thought he was being held up, and Tom Murchison is a good lawyer."

"You're the prosecutor. It's your job to make hard cases against good lawyers," Judge Briggs answered.

"All right, I'll try. But I don't think I'll be able to convince the jury."

As Prosecutor Gilmore and Judge Briggs were discussing the case, Tom Murchison arrived at the jail to meet with Luke Shardeen.

"You've got ten minutes," Deputy Proxmire said, escorting the attorney to Luke's cell.

"You are wrong, Deputy," Murchison declared as he entered the cell. "Mr. Shardeen is my client, and I will visit with him for as long as it takes."

"Yes, well, uh . . ." Proxmire knew he had no response to that, so he shrugged his shoulders and shut the cell door. "Just call out when your visit is finished." He turned and walked back to the front of the jail.

Tom Murchison was the lawyer who had handled the estate of Luke's uncle Frank. Since Luke's arrival in Pueblo, he and Murchison had become good friends. Compared to Luke, Murchison was relatively short, standing five feet nine inches tall. He wore a red bow tie, and held an unlit cigar at a jaunty angle in his mouth.

He sat down on the other bunk in Luke's cell. "Tell me what happened."

Luke told of selling the cows in Greenhorn, then seeing the two men waiting in ambush for him on the trail back to Pueblo. He told how they braced him with drawn guns and demanded that he give them his money.

"I'll do what I can for you, Luke," Murchison said. "The truth is, we are playing against a stacked deck. Judge Briggs seems to have an unusual connection to Sheriff Ferrell. But you have never been in trouble since you have been here, you have made a lot of friends, and I have an affidavit showing where you sold your cattle for twenty thousand dollars.

"So, while our case will be difficult because the deck is stacked against us, theirs will be equally difficult because they have no motive."

Chapter Seven

Luke's trial was held the very next day. The prosecuting attorney presented his opening remarks.

"Your Honor, and gentlemen of the jury, Mr. Murchison will, no doubt, claim that Mr. Shardeen had no motive for killing Deputy Gates. And he will attempt to use that claim as proof that what happened wasn't murder.

"But Sheriff Ferrell and Deputy Gates were conducting an investigation, and all they wanted to do was ask a few questions. Mr. Shardeen shot and killed Gates, and Sheriff Ferrell barely escaped with his life. If an officer of the law cannot question a citizen without getting shot, then where does that leave the rest of us?"

Murchison had been making notes, and when Gilmore sat down, the defense attorney stood and walked over to the rail separating the jury from the rest of the courtroom. He took his unlit cigar from his mouth and held it in his hand, sometimes waving it around as he talked.

"I am glad that my learned colleague has already conceded that Luke Shardeen had no motive for killing Deputy Gates. Who is Luke Shardeen?

"He owns Two Crown Ranch, and he is an employer who is well respected by the men who work for him. He has done business in this town for the last three years and, during that time, has earned the respect and admiration of his fellow citizens. Before that he was a seaman, and not an ordinary seaman, but a ship's officer—one who, when his captain was swept overboard during a typhoon, assumed command of the vessel and brought his ship safely into port, saving twenty-eight lives.

"Now, let us look more closely at the prosecutor's contention that all Sheriff Ferrell and Deputy Gates wanted to do was question Mr. Shardeen. If that is true, what were Ferrell and Gates doing asking such questions in Pueblo County in the first place? They are from Bent County. They have no business questioning anyone in Pueblo County. If they had a suspect they needed to question who happened to be out of their jurisdiction, the correct procedure would have been to contact Sheriff John McKenzie and ask that a deputy go with them.

"That's the way it's supposed to be done. But they didn't do that, and Sheriff McKenzie is prepared to testify that he was never contacted. That means Sheriff Ferrell has no corroboration for his story."

There was very little cross-examination during

the trial. Ferrell reiterated that all he and Gates wanted to do was question Luke, and Luke repeated his claim that the two men attempted to rob him.

After their testimonies, Murchison and Gilmore made their summation.

"Prosecution says Ferrell and Gates were two law officers who wanted only to question Mr. Shardeen." Murchison stood, facing the jury. "But neither of them were wearing a badge, and both were wearing hoods over their faces."

He walked back over to the defense table and reached down into a sack, withdrawing a piece of cloth. He spread the cloth out, then held it up before the jury, showing a hood with two eyeholes.

Several in the gallery gasped.

"Specifically, one of them was wearing *this* hood, which I found exactly where Mr. Shardeen said it would be. Wearing a hood like this is hardly the way a couple lawmen would stop a suspect for questioning. I'm going to ask that you do the right thing, and find my client not guilty."

Murchison stuck the unlit cigar back in his mouth, then returned to the defense table to sit beside his client.

"Mr. Prosecutor, your summation?" Judge Briggs asked.

Gilmore stood, hitched up his trousers, then approached the jury box.

"What it all boils down to is Luke Shardeen's word against the word of Sheriff Dewey Ferrell. On the surface, one man's word against another would balance the scales. But there are two things that tip the scales. One is the fact that Dewey Ferrell isn't just another citizen; he is a sworn officer of the law. And the other issue is the fact that we have a dead body. Deputy Brad Gates is dead, and we have the defendant's own admission that he shot and killed him. As to the hood, I've no doubt but that Mr. Murchison found it where Mr. Shardeen said it would be. But that proves only that he put the hood there. It is my contention that he did that just to build his defense. Under the circumstances, I feel you can bring no verdict but guilty of murder in the first degree."

In the judge's charge to the jury he suggested strongly that the evidence pointed to first-degree murder, and that it was his belief that they must find in accordance with the evidence.

"I don't care what the rest of you say, I don't intend to find Luke Shardeen guilty of murder in the first degree. Why would he do it?" one of the jurors said when they were sequestered.

"If Ferrell and Gates were questioning him about a crime he committed somewhere, he might have shot them," another juror said.

"What crime? All the prosecution said was that Shardeen was being questioned, and didn't even say what he was being questioned about. If you ask me, this thing is fishy."

"Yeah? Well, he did kill the deputy. That's a fact

that he doesn't deny. And I can't see lettin' him get off scot-free."

The jury continued to argue for the better part of an hour, before they came to an agreement and signaled the bailiff they were ready to return to the courtroom.

"Has the jury reached a verdict?" Judge Briggs asked when they were all seated.

"We have, Your Honor," Lynn Thomas, the jury foreman, replied. Thomas owned a leather goods shop.

"Would you publish your verdict, please?"

"We find the defendant guilty of manslaughter in the second degree."

There was an immediate reaction from the gallery, who, based upon the judge's public charge of the jury, expected a verdict of murder in the first degree.

The judge slapped his gavel several times to get order, then looked back at Thomas. "You were not given the option of finding for second degree manslaughter. The charge was for murder."

Thomas stared back defiantly. "Your Honor, you can accept the verdict of guilty of manslaughter in the second degree or not guilty of murder in the first degree."

Briggs glared at Thomas for a long moment before he pulled his eyes away and spoke. "Will the defendant approach the bench?"

Luke moved up to stand before the judge.

"You have been found guilty of manslaughter in

the second degree. The maximum penalty for that charge is to be incarcerated for forty-eight months and you are hereby sentenced to the maximum allowed by law. Sheriff, take charge of the prisoner. This court is adjourned."

December 16

Jenny McCoy stood at the window of the private reception room of the Colorado Social Club and looked outside. It was cold and a light dusting of snow was beginning to fall. She watched as a rider passed by, the collar of his coat turned up and his hat pulled down. Behind her a cheery fire snapped and popped in the fireplace.

Her beauty, bearing, and education had quickly made her a favorite of the more affluent "gentlemen" who visited the club.

One such visitor was The Honorable Lorenzo Crounse, Governor of Nebraska. He stepped up to the window beside Jenny and put his arm around her. "Doesn't it make you feel good to be all warm and cozy inside, when it is so cold outside?"

"It certainly does," Jenny answered with a smile as she casually turned out of his arm and walked over to the table where sat a carafe of coffee. "And a good hot cup of coffee makes it even better. May I pour you a cup?"

Governor Crounse chuckled. "Indeed you may, my dear." He watched her as she poured. "I must say, you are the most beautiful woman I have ever laid my eyes on."

Jenny brought the cup of coffee to the governor and handed it to him with a smile. "My goodness, Governor, if you flatter everyone that way, it's no wonder you got elected."

"Oh, but I mean it, my dear. I mean every word. You are—"

The door to the private reception room was suddenly thrown open, interrupting the governor's statement. Four men rushed inside, three had pistols in their hands, and the fourth was carrying a camera.

"Here, what is the meaning of this?" the governor asked angrily. "Do you know who I am?"

"Oh, yes, Governor, we know exactly who you are. Now suppose you just go over there, have a seat on the sofa, and don't make any trouble."

"Who are you? What is all this about?"

"If both of you do exactly what we say, no one will be hurt. We just want a picture, that's all."

"A picture?" the governor asked, confused by the odd request.

"A picture, yes. Miss," the armed spokesman said to Jenny. "I want you to take off all your clothes and go sit with the governor. We want a picture of you, naked, beside him."

"No! That will ruin me!" the governor said.

"I will do no such thing," Jenny replied indignantly.

"Oh, you will be photographed naked with the governor," the spokesman said. "Whether you are dead or alive when we take the picture makes no difference to us. The effect will be the same. You can take your clothes off yourself, or I'll shoot you and we'll strip your dead body."

"You had better do what they say, Jenny," the governor said. "I have a feeling these men have been sent by my political enemies, and I've no doubt but that they will do just as they say."

"Well now, Governor, you are smarter than I thought you were." The armed intruder grinned.

Frightened, Jenny removed her clothes, then sat on the sofa beside the governor. The photographer took a picture, and a moment later, two of the sheriff's deputies were brought into the room. Seeing Jenny nude, with the governor, was all they needed to bring a charge of prostitution against her.

Luke was lying on his bunk with his hands laced behind his head, looking up at the ceiling, when Proxmire and another deputy came into the cell area with a young woman.

Proxmire opened the door to the cell next to Luke. "All right, Miss, in there."

Luke sat up with a start. "Wait a minute! What are you doing? You can't put a lady in this cell."

"She ain't no lady, she's a whore," the deputy with Proxmire growled.

"She is a female. And you can't put women in jail with men. They have to have their own facilities. That is the law."

"Hah! Since when did you become a lawyer?" Proxmire asked.

"You don't have to be a lawyer to know that."

"We ain't got no cell just for women, so she's goin' to have to stay here for a while." Proxmire closed the door on the cell, locked it, and he and the other deputy returned to the front of the jail.

The woman sat down on her bunk, leaned her elbows on her knees, and dropped her head in her hands.

"I'm sorry about this," Luke said. "It's not right, them bringing you in here."

She looked up at him. "Thank you for speaking up for me."

"I'm only doing what's right, Miss McCoy."

"Have we met?"

"No, we haven't. But I've wanted to meet you for some time now. I just wish it could have been under better circumstances, for both of us."

"I'm not a whore, by the way."

"No, ma'am. I know you aren't." Luke stuck his hand through the bars that separated their cells. "I'm Luke Shardeen. I own a ranch just north of town."

Jenny crossed her cell and shook his hand. "Luke Shardeen. Yes, I know who you are. You own Two Crowns. I read about your case in the paper. Everyone I know says that they don't believe you are guilty."

"I'm not. Oh, I killed Gates, all right, but he and Sheriff Ferrell were trying to hold me up."

* * *

"What are you doing putting this poor girl in jail?" a woman demanded. "You let her out this very instant, or I will go to the newspaper with the name of everyone who has visited the Social Club in the last six months. Do you understand what I'm saying, Deputy Proxmire? Everyone!"

"I can't let her out until the judge says I can," Proxmire replied.

"Really? Would that be the same Judge Briggs who was with," Adele took a piece of paper from her pocket and started reading from it, "Sandra, Sara Sue, Kate, and Ella Mae?"

"Uh, all right, I'll let her out. But she has to be present for her hearing tomorrow, and if she ain't, I'll hold you responsible."

"She'll be there."

Proxmire returned to the cell area and unlocked Jenny's cell.

"Looks like you're getting out," Luke said. "I'm glad."

"I hope everything goes well for you, Mr. Shardeen," Jenny said as Proxmire opened the door. "Good night."

"Good night."

Proxmire escorted Jenny to the front. "You just make sure you have her there for the hearing tomorrow," he demanded as Adele left with Jenny.

"I told you, you had no business bringing her here," Luke called out after hearing the door closed behind them.

"I don't need you tellin' me what is, and what

isn't my business," Proxmire replied with a low growling snarl.

"Your honor, Jenny McCoy is not a prostitute," Adele said at the closed hearing the next day.

"Does she, or does she not work for you?" Judge Briggs asked.

"Yes."

"And do you run a house of prostitution?"

"I run the Colorado Social Club."

"Which is a whorehouse."

"I don't like to think of it in quite those terms."

"Regardless of how you like to think about it, it is a whorehouse. And if you deny that, I will lock you up for perjury."

"All right I admit, Your Honor, that I do have, uh, ladies of that profession in my employment. But Mrs. McCoy certainly isn't one of them. Her only function is that of a hostess, not as a prostitute."

"But you do employ prostitutes?"

"You know that I do, Your Honor. I might even add that you have, let us say, personal knowledge of that fact."

Briggs cleared his throat and rapped his gavel on the bench. "I am not the one on trial, Miss Summers. Jenny McCoy is on trial. Unless you want me to extend the charges to you as well."

"No, Your Honor."

"Then we will continue the hearing, and you will add nothing except your responses to my questions."

"Very well, Your Honor."

"Would you say that Jenny McCoy is a hostess in your establishment?"

"Yes, that is exactly what she is. She is a hostess and nothing more. She is guilty of nothing."

"That's where you are wrong, Miss Summers. Mrs. McCoy was soliciting to provide sexual acts for money. Maybe she wasn't soliciting for herself, but she certainly was for others. And the penalty for solicitation for prostitution is the same as it is for prostitution itself."

"All right." Adele finally had enough. "If you are unable to see the difference, I won't argue with you. How much is her fine? I'll pay it."

"I'm afraid that won't work. This is far beyond having one of your women caught with a cowboy. You see, the gentleman she was with is the sitting governor of a neighboring state."

"I know that, Judge. Governors, congressmen, senators"—she paused—"and judges—have all visited the Colorado Social Club. And the more cultured of these gentlemen want to spend some time with Jenny, not as a sexual partner, but as a conversationalist.

"And why not? Jenny is the most educated and intelligent person I know, man or woman. And you can see with your own eyes how beautiful she is. It is no wonder that such people find her interesting."

"Nevertheless, if it gets out that the governor was with Jenny McCoy, it could have far-reaching consequences. Therefore, my sentence for you, Mrs. McCoy, is that you leave Pueblo."

"What?" Jenny asked with a gasp. "Where will I go? What will I do?"

"Like Miss Summers said, you are an uncommonly beautiful woman, Mrs. McCoy. I'm quite sure you will be able to find some means of supporting yourself. I just don't intend for you to do it here."

"I will not be a prostitute!" Jenny said resolutely.

The judge's only response was to bang his gavel. "This hearing is adjourned."

Adele walked back to the Colorado Social Club with Jenny, comforting her as best she could.

"I have never been so embarrassed and humiliated in my life," Jenny said.

"Nonsense, my dear. You have nothing to be humiliated for, or embarrassed about."

"But what will I do? Where will I go?"

"You can go to Red Cliff," Adele suggested. "I have a brother who owns a nice store there. I'll write to him, and ask him to give you a job."

"Would you? Oh, Adele, you have been such a wonderful friend."

Colorado Springs—December 17

Bob Ward was meeting Felix Parker, a man he had served time with in the Colorado State Prison in Cañon City. Also present at the meeting were three men Parker brought with him: Roy Compton, Gerald Kelly, and Melvin Morris.

"Michael is still in jail in Kiowa. From what I've

learned, he'll be transported on the Red Cliff Special, leaving Pueblo at nine o'clock at night on the nineteenth," Ward said.

"What day is that?" Parker asked.

"That will be Monday, day after tomorrow."

"How are we going to work this?" Morris asked.

Ward gave out the first set of instructions. "You four will board the train in Pueblo. The train will have to go through Trout Creek Pass. It is 9,000 feet high, so by the time the train gets to the top of the pass, it won't be goin' any faster than you can walk."

"That's when I'll go to work," Parker continued. "I'll go up front and stop the train."

"And while everyone is distracted by the train being stopped, Compton, you, Kelly, and Morris, will take care of the deputy escorting Michael, then come to the front with him."

"I'll disconnect the train from the engine, and we'll go on over the pass, leaving the rest of the train behind," Parker said.

"I'll meet you in Big Rock with horses," Ward continued. "After that, we'll go get the money."

"Are you sure the money is there?" Morris asked.

Ward smiled. "Let's put it this way. The money damn well better be there, because Michael knows what will happen if it ain't there."

"He's your brother."

"Yeah? So was Abel Cain's brother," Ward said.

Chapter Eight

Claro, Nevada

Matt Jensen opened his eyes and looked around his hotel room. The shade was pulled, but a small hole in the shade projected onto the wall a very detailed image, not a shadow but a photographic image of the winter-denuded cottonwood tree growing just outside the hotel.

He sat up in the bed and swung his legs over the side, remaining there for a long moment before padding barefoot across the plank floor toward the chest of drawers. He picked up the porcelain pitcher and poured water into a basin. The water was just short of freezing, but it had an invigorating effect as he washed his face and hands, then worked up a lather that enabled him to shave.

It was already mid-morning, but the heavy green shade covering the window kept out most of the light. Not until he was dressed did he open the shade to let the morning sunshine stream in.

He stood at the window for a moment, looking out onto the street below.

Across the street, an empty wagon with one of its wheels removed sat on blocks. Another freight wagon was just pulling away while a third was being loaded. That Claro was an industrious town was well demonstrated by the painted signs and symbols used to make the various mercantile establishments known to the citizens as well as the farmers and ranchers who came into town to buy their supplies. The apothecary featured a large cutout of a mortar and pestle. Next to that, a striped pole advertised the barber shop, and next to that a big tooth led patients to the dentist. Directly across the street, Matt could see the painted, golden mug of beer inviting customers in to the Red Dog Saloon.

Matt turned away from the window, pulled his suitcase from under the bed, and began packing. Nothing in particular had brought him to Claro, and nothing was keeping him there.

When his suitcase was packed, he took it to the depot and bought a ticket to Denver, figuring it was time he got back to Colorado. He decided to send a telegram to his friend and mentor, Smoke Jensen, informing him of his plans.

DEPARTING CLARO NEVADA 10 AM DEC 17 STOP ARRIVING DENVER 2 PM ON 19 STOP REPLY BY TELEGRAM TO CENTRAL PACIFIC DEPOT IN CLARO STOP MATT

Matt checked his suitcase in, then went over to the Red Dog Saloon to have his breakfast. He had made friends in the Red Dog and thought to tell them good-bye.

He took a seat at a table halfway between the piano and the potbellied woodstove that sat in a sandbox. Roaring as it snapped and popped, the fire put out too much heat if one was too close to it and not enough if one sat some distance away from it. Matt knew exactly where to sit to get just the right amount heat to feel comfortable.

Trebor von Nahguav was sitting at the next table, drinking coffee. An Austrian, he was a pianist who had studied under Chopin.

"Matthew, is it true you are actually leaving today?" Trebor asked.

"I am."

"I will not like to see you go. You have brought a bit of *bekanntheit* to the saloon, and to the town."

"Bekanntheit?"

"*Ja.* It means"—Trebor struggled for the word, then smiled as it came to him—"Fame. It is not every day that one gets to meet a character who has stepped from the pages of a book." He was referring to the Beadles Dime Novels, specifically those written by Prentiss Ingram and featuring Matt Jensen as the protagonist. Matt's friend Smoke had long been a character in the novels and, through him, Prentiss was made aware of Matt.

Matt chuckled. "Just remember, Trebor, the operative word there is *novel.* By definition, novels are fiction. I do not claim any of the accomplishments Colonel Ingram has written about."

"That is only because you are too modest," Trebor said. "I know about your exploits in Wyoming where you single-handedly eliminated the Yellow Kerchief gang and saved the young nephew of Moreton Frewen. What was his name? Winston?"

"Yes, Winston Churchill. He was quite an impressive young man."

Lucy Dare, a buxom blond with flashing blue eyes and an engaging smile, walked over to join the conversation. So far, the dissipation of her trade had not diminished her looks.

"Lucy, our friend is leaving us today," Trebor said.

Lucy leaned over Matt's table, displaying her cleavage. "Are you sure I can't talk you into staying with us?"

Matt laughed. "No, but you can sure make it damn tempting."

"I will play something for you before you leave," Trebor said. "I will play Tchaikovsky's Piano Concerto Number One. It is not something the average saloon patron would like but you, *mein freund*, I know, will enjoy it."

"Thank you," Matt said. "I am sure I will enjoy it."

Trebor moved over to the piano and played the piece, losing himself in the sweep and majesty of the concerto. Matt enjoyed it, but knew Trebor enjoyed it more. He used any excuse to play the classical music he loved, rather than the simple ballads he was forced to play night after night.

After his breakfast Matt told his friends good-bye and left the saloon. He'd walked about a block when a man suddenly stepped in front of him and pointed a gun.

"Give me all your money," the armed man demanded.

"Now why would I want to do that?"

"Why? Because if you don't, I'll blow a hole in your stomach big enough to let your guts fall out." To emphasize his threat, the man thrust the pistol forward until the barrel of the gun was jammed into Matt's stomach.

That was a mistake. Matt reached down and clamped his hand around the pistol, locking the cylinder tightly in his grip.

His assailant tried to pull the trigger, but it wasn't possible with the cylinder locked in place. He looked down in surprise, and Matt brought his left fist up in a wicked uppercut. The man relaxed his grip on the pistol as he went down, and it wound up in Matt's hand.

Bending down to check the robber's pulse, Matt saw the man was still breathing. He waited until the man came to, then walked him, at gunpoint, down the street to the office of the Claro City Marshal.

"Well, now, hello Percy," the marshal said when Matt turned his prisoner over to him. "It didn't take you long to get back in jail, did it? I just let you out this morning."

"What was I supposed to do?" Percy complained. "I didn't even have enough money to buy breakfast."

"If you had asked me for enough money to buy breakfast, I would have given it to you," Matt offered. "But pointing a gun at me doesn't put me in the sharing mood."

When Matt went to the depot later that day, he found there was, indeed, a telegram waiting for him.

DUFF MACALLISTER AT SUGARLOAF STOP COME SPEND CHRISTMAS WITH US STOP SMOKE

Matt had to pay for only two words in his return telegram.

WILL DO

He smiled at the thought of spending Christmas with Smoke, Sally, and Duff. Sally was a very good cook, particularly bear claws, an almond flavored, yeast-raised pastry that was the best Matt had ever tasted. He turned his thoughts to Christmas, which was supposed to be spent with family. But he had no family.

His parents and sister had been murdered when he was a boy. After spending some time in a brutal orphanage, he ran away in the dead of winter and would have frozen to death if Smoke Jensen hadn't found him and taken him in. Smoke was the nearest thing to a family Matt had, so much so that he had taken Smoke's last name as his own.

It would be good to spend Christmas with his old friend, and Sally's home-cooked meals would make it even nicer.

Matt extended his ticket from Denver to Pueblo, putting him in Pueblo at eight o'clock in the evening on the nineteenth, just in time to connect with the last train to Big Rock. That trip would require going through Trout Creek Pass over the Mosquito Range, a part of the Rocky Mountains.

He boarded the train at ten o'clock on the morning of the 17th of December for what the schedule said would be a two-and-a-half-day trip to Pueblo.

Pueblo—December 19

Jenny McCoy entered the train station at seven o'clock in the evening and bought a ticket on the Red Cliff Special, due to leave at nine. The judge had given her one week to settle her affairs and leave town, but it had taken her only three days.

That didn't leave time for Adele to write to her brother and receive a reply, so she wrote a personal and impassioned letter she gave to Jenny.

"Show my brother this letter. He's a good man with a good heart. When he reads this he and his wife will take you in, and if he can't find work for you in his own store, I've no doubt that he will help you find employment."

"Thank you, Adele. I don't know what I would have done in this town if it hadn't been for you. I don't know how I would have made a living."

"It is I who should thank you. You were a wonderful and classy addition to my business. I'm just sorry things turned out as they did. The judge had no right to order you out of town."

"I have made some good friends here, you especially, and I'm sorry to leave them."

"Someday you may come back, and when you do, remember that I will always count you as a dear friend." Adele hugged Jenny and left the station.

With Adele's letter secure in her purse, Jenny bought a newspaper, then settled in a seat near one of the roaring potbellied stoves and began to read the *Pueblo Chieftain.*

Another Cold Wave

MOUNTAIN TOWNS REPORT CONTINUAL SNOWFALL

Reports from the mountains show a snowstorm has been in progress several days, thus far without serious or unusual results. The storm is most severe in Eagle County, where snow is several feet deep and drifting. So far all passes are still open for trains.

At nine o'clock of the morning, the temperature was two below zero and growing colder. Those who watch the weather say Christmas Day will be very cold. That Christmas will be white is surely to be a joy to the children of the city, who will hope to see "Santa Claus" and his sleigh.

Michael Santelli to Pass Through Pueblo

OUTLAW IS ON HIS WAY TO BE HANGED

Michael Santelli, the notorious gunfighter who is said to have killed seventeen men, met his match when he was confronted by Deputy Sheriff Ben Mason and well-known Western figure Matt Jensen in the town of Kiowa. Santelli was tried for the murders of George and Elaine Rafferty while robbing Rafferty's Grocery in Red Cliff. Convicted of the crime, he is being transported to Red Cliff, where he will be hanged. He is expected to pass through Pueblo, where he will be put on the train to Red Cliff.

Deputy Sheriff Braxton Proxmire, who will escort the prisoner, says that he does not expect any trouble.

Senator Daniels to Visit Red Cliff

WILL SPEAK AT REPUBLICAN CHRISTMAS EVE DINNER

Senator Daniels has made no statement as to whether or not he will run for governor of Colorado in 1894. He has, however, been a frequent speaker at political gatherings such as the Republican Christmas-Eve dinner being held in Red Cliff on the 24th, thus giving rise to speculation of his future plans.

Senator Daniels is known to be a vocal opponent of the procedure of paying coal miners in "company script" that can only be redeemed in company stores. He has proposed a bill in the state legislature which would prohibit that practice. He has also proposed that mine owners be responsible for building shoring and other such means of ensuring miners' safety. As it now stands, all safety improvements are paid for by the miners themselves.

Chapter Nine

As Jenny continued to read the paper she heard a few gasps and comments from others in the waiting room and, looking up, she saw Deputy Sheriff Proxmire coming into the depot with two men in handcuffs and shackles. One of them she recognized as Luke Shardeen, the man she had met during her brief time in jail. She had no idea who the other man was until she heard someone point him out.

"That's Michael Santelli!" The stranger's voice was filled with awe. "They say he's killed more 'n thirty men."

"He's only killed seventeen," another man corrected.

"Yeah, well, they're goin' to hang him, and he'll be just as dead whether he killed thirty or seventeen men."

The first man chuckled. "You got that right."

"That's Luke with him. What's he there for?"

"He's goin' to serve his four years in jail."

"He's goin' to Cañon City?"

"No, he's goin' to be put in the Eagle County Jail at Red Cliff."

The two prisoners were either unaware of the conversation about them or were ignoring it as they kept their eyes straight ahead. Deputy Proxmire prodded them toward the bench where Jenny was sitting. "You two men sit right there while I get the tickets," he ordered.

Jenny started to get up, but Proxmire looked at her. "No, you stay there. You are being run out of town, so you are as much under my authority as these two men are."

Jenny, with her cheeks flaming in embarrassment, sat back down.

"Hello, Miss McCoy," Luke said. "It's good to see you again."

Jenny appreciated the calm and respectful greeting, and it helped her overcome some of the embarrassment she had felt at Proxmire's harsh words to her. "Hello, Mr. Shardeen."

"You remember my name. I'm flattered."

"Of course I remember your name. I also remember that you are a rancher."

"I *was* a rancher. Now I'm a prisoner." Luke made the comment with a disarming smile.

"Oh, I'm so sorry."

"I am too. I have finally met you, a most attractive and very pleasant young lady, and now I must leave."

"Lady?" Santelli scoffed. "She ain't no lady. You heard what the deputy said, didn't you? This here woman's bein' run out of town. What did you do, girlie?"

Jenny didn't answer.

"Cat got your tongue?" Santelli laughed.

Several women came hustling into the depot, drawing his attention. They unfurled a big, hand-painted sign.

HARLOTS WILL FIND

NO WELCOME

IN PUEBLO

"Whoa!" Santelli said, holding his handcuffed hands out toward the women. "Did they bring that sign in here for you? Are you being run out of town because you're a whore?"

Still, Jenny didn't answer.

"That's it, ain't it? You're a whore. Well, I'll tell you what, darlin', I'm about to go get myself hung. And if you had any kindness in you, why, you'd let me enjoy this almost last night I'm goin' to have on earth. What do you say that me 'n you go over there in the corner and have us a little poke?"

"Please," Jenny said. "I'd rather not talk."

"I'd rather not get hung, too. But we don't always get what we want," Santelli said.

"Santelli, why don't you leave the lady alone?" Luke couldn't stay silent any longer.

"Lady? Ha! I told you, she ain't no lady. She's bein' run out of town because she's a whore, and you're calling her a lady?"

"Yes, I'm calling her a lady."

Santelli stared at Luke for a moment, then turned his attention back to Jenny. "Tell me, darlin', what if I—?"

Smack! With both hands cuffed together, Luke brought his fists around in a powerful stroke. The blow knocked Santelli out.

"I'm sorry, Miss McCoy," Luke said to Jenny. "I apologize for his rudeness."

"You have no need to apologize for him. You have nothing to do with him, and you have been most kind to me. I appreciate your coming to my aid."

At that moment Proxmire returned. "All right, I have the tickets here. We can board as soon as—" He stopped his comment in mid-sentence and frowned.

Santelli was sitting with his head thrown to one side, his mouth open and his tongue sticking out. He was totally unconscious.

"What happened to him?" Proxmire jerked his head toward Santelli.

"Oh, he went to sleep," Luke said.

The deputy stroked his chin. "He went to sleep, huh? Did you help him?"

"I might have sung a lullaby or something to him to get him in the mood," Luke suggested.

Jenny choked back a giggle over Luke's comment, and his smile showed that he appreciated her reaction.

"I don't know what's going on here, but it's not going to go any further. Luke, you sit on the other side of the girl, I'll sit on this side of her, and Santelli will be on the other side of me. That ought to keep the two of you apart.

Santelli came to a moment later and he stared straight ahead as if trying to orient himself. He reached up to touch his black eye and winced.

"What happened?"

"You fell out of your seat," Proxmire said. "You should sit up straighter."

It was obvious that Santelli didn't remember being hit by Luke, and when Jenny saw him adjusting his position in the seat so as "not to fall out again," she couldn't help chuckle a second time.

"Say," Luke said. "When I come back here four years from now, would you like to have dinner with me?"

"Oh, I"—Jenny started to say that she had no idea where she would be in four years, but found the idea of having dinner with Luke Shardeen a very pleasant one—"would be glad to have dinner with you." Besides, it would obviously make him feel better if he had something to look forward to, whether it ever happened or not.

"Good. Now, don't you be backing out on me. I plan to hold on to that thought for the next four years. That's what's going to get me through it."

State Senator Jarred Daniels stood before the checkout desk at the Victoria Hotel.

"We've been just real proud to have you as our guest, Senator," the desk clerk said. "Yes sir, being as you were one of the people most responsible for getting the Colorado Mining Museum here, why, it's an honor to have served you."

"Thank you. My wife and I sent our luggage down a while ago. Was it transported to the railroad depot?"

"Yes sir, it was, and it's all checked and ready to go onto the Red Cliff Special."

"Good man." Daniels paid the bill, then walked over to an upholstered sofa where his wife Millie and their daughter Becky were waiting for him. Millie was holding her hand to Becky's forehead.

"What is it?" Daniels asked.

"I don't know," Millie replied. "She feels as if she has a slight fever."

"It's probably from the heat here in the lobby. It's very cold outside, and I think they go overboard a little on the heat. How do you feel, Becky?"

"I don't feel good, Papa."

"Well, you'll feel better after we get out of this

lobby. A little cool air will do you good. Come on, the trolley will be here directly."

Millie made certain her daughter was well bundled up, then they stepped out into the frigid night air. It was so cold it nearly took Millie's breath away. She put her arms around her daughter and pulled her closer as they watched the approaching trolley, sparks flying from the wand connected to the overhead wires.

The trolley stopped and the motorman opened the doors. He smiled when he saw the statesman, who was easily recognizable because of his girth and his muttonchop beard. "Senator Daniels. Welcome aboard my car, sir."

"Thank you." Daniels turned to help his wife and daughter onto the car.

"Where are you going on this cold night?" the motorman asked. "I would think on a night like this, one would want to stay home before a warm fire."

"That might be true, young man. But, like you, I have work to do, work that calls me out on cold nights." Daniels sat next to Millie as the trolley started forward.

"I'm worried about her," Millie said. "She's being very quiet. You know she isn't normally like this."

"Naturally you are worried. You are her mother, and mothers tend to worry. But I'm sure there is nothing wrong with her. Once we get on the train she'll be warm, and she can sleep. Why, I'll bet she is fit as a fiddle come morning."

"I hope you are right."

"I know I'm right. You'll see." Daniels reached over to pat his wife on the knee.

Millie put her arm around her daughter and pulled her closer.

Just down the street from the depot, Parker, Compton, Kelly, and Morris were having a beer in the Lucky Strike Saloon.

"Are you sure he is going to be on this train?" Compton asked.

"That's what we were told," Parker answered.

"Besides which, it's in the newspaper today," Kelly added. "I seen the story myself."

"Yeah, but newspapers ain't always right."

"He'll be on the train," Parker said.

"Do you really think Santelli has enough money to give us five hundred dollars apiece?" Morris asked. "That's two thousand dollars."

"Ward says he does. And he prob'ly has a lot more 'n that," Parker insisted. "There's no tellin' how much money he has stole over the last three or four years. I would be surprised if he didn't have four or five thousand dollars hid away somewhere."

"Which ain't goin' to do him no good if he's hung," Kelly added.

"Exactly right," Parker replied. "So as soon as we get him away, he'll take us to where he's got the money hid."

"What if he don't do it?" Morris asked.

"You heard what Ward said. If he don't do it, we'll kill 'im." Parker snorted.

"Yeah, that's what he said, all right," Morris agreed. "But what if he just told us that to make sure we come in with him?"

"It's a little late to be thinkin' about all that now, ain't it?" Parker asked. "I mean we're already here. The train will be comin' tonight, and I say we go through with it. Unless five hundred dollars don't mean nothin' to you."

"No, no, I didn't say I wasn't goin' to go through with it." Morris quickly changed his tune. "I was sort of thinkin' out loud, is all."

"Well, don't think," Parker instructed. "There's no need to be thinkin'. Ever'thing's already been thought out for us."

"It's gettin' pretty close to time," Compton reckoned. "I expect we'd better get on down to the depot."

As soon as the four men left the saloon, they were hit by an icy blast of wind.

"Damn, that's cold!" Kelly shivered as they walked to the depot.

"Feels like it's goin' to snow," Morris surmised.

"What difference does it make how cold it is?" Parker asked. "We'll be on the train. They got heatin' stoves in all the cars, and they keep the cars nice and warm. Otherwise, they wouldn't have nobody ridin' the trains in the wintertime."

Once inside they moved to the stove for a moment, then stepped up to the ticket window.

"We want four tickets to Big Rock."

"Yes, sir, four tickets to Big Rock," the ticket agent said.

Parker pointed to Santelli. "What car is he going to be in?"

"Oh, sir, I don't know. Unless someone buys a ticket specifically for a Pullman car, I never have any idea where they will be. This is a narrow-gauge railroad, so there are no Pullman cars on this run. But I'm sure if you don't want to be in the same car as a murderer, you will be able to avoid him."

"We want to be—" Parker stopped mid-sentence. He'd started to say they wanted to be in the same car as Santelli, but thought that might make the ticket clerk suspicious. "That is, I really don't care what car we get put in."

"Well, I will say this, sir. Normally the Red Cliff Special is pretty much filled. But it being nearly Christmas, it seems there aren't as many passengers as normal, so you can probably sit just about anywhere you want."

After the four men received their tickets, three of them went over to the farthest side of the depot waiting room, but Parker went over to the prisoners. "Santelli, Bob Ward is an old friend of mine. He said if I saw you, I was to tell you hello."

"Really? You've met with him recently?"

"Just a couple of days ago."

"Well, thank you. And thank you for bringing the message," Santelli nodded indicating he understood.

"Here," Proxmire fussed. "Get away from my prisoner."

"I was just passing on a greeting from a mutual friend," Parker replied.

"You have no business with my prisoner. I'm going to ask you again, sir, to move away."

Parker held his hands out. "Whatever you say, Deputy. I'm not one to cause trouble." He turned away and went over to join his partners.

Jenny continued to watch the four men for the next few minutes. She was sure the man who'd spoken to Santelli had exchanged some sort of signal with him. She wondered if she should mention it to Deputy Proxmire. After a moment's consideration, she decided not to say anything about it. There was no law against exchanging glances, and though Jenny was of a suspicious nature, she convinced herself there was nothing significant about the way the men had looked at each other.

An overweight well-dressed man, a woman, and a child came into the depot then. The man pointed to one of the long wooden bench seats. "Millie, you and Becky wait there for me. I'll get the tickets."

"All right." The woman hustled the little girl to the bench.

"Mama, I still don't feel good."

"I know, dear. There's room on the seat, and you can lie down and put your head in my lap."

"What about when we get on the train?"

"I'm sure there will be room enough on the train, too, for you to lie down."

"Senator Daniels! Senator Daniels, I'm with the *Pueblo Chieftain.* Will you stand for an interview, sir?" a young man asked the girl's father as he started toward the ticket counter.

"Certainly, my good man, as soon as I secure the tickets for our travel."

So, Jenny thought, *that's Senator Daniels.* She looked over toward the senator, remembering the article she had just read about him. If he was going to give a speech in Red Cliff, they would be on the same train.

At that moment the depot began to shake and rumble as a train came into the station.

"Is that our train?" Santelli asked.

Proxmire shook his head. "No, that's the south-bound. We'll be on the Red Cliff Special, going west."

Chapter Ten

Matt was on the train pulling into the Pueblo Station. He would leave that train and board the one going toward Red Cliff. Big Rock was on that line, being the first stop on the other side of the Mosquito Range of mountains. He was anxious to get to nearby Sugarloaf Ranch, where he planned to enjoy Christmas with his friends.

"Pueblo!" the conductor called, coming through the cars. "This stop is Pueblo. This is where you're getting off, isn't it, Mr. Jensen?"

"Yes, it is."

The conductor reached out to shake Matt's hand. "Well, sir, let me tell you it has been a real privilege having you aboard. I can't wait until I tell my son. He has read all about you. Oh, and I thank you for the autograph."

"It's quite all right," Matt said. "Tell your son I said hello."

"I'll do that, Mr. Jensen. Yes, sir, I will certainly

do that." He continued on through the cars calling out the stop. "Pueblo! This stop is Pueblo!"

Matt had been a little embarrassed at being asked for his autograph. He was always self-conscious about being connected with the literary work of Prentiss Ingram.

"It's hardly literature," Sally had said once, scoffing at the books Ingram had written, not only about Matt, but about Smoke and Falcon MacAllister, as well as books about and plays starring Buffalo Bill Cody.

Matt looked out the window as the train drew close to the Arkansas River, then passed several houses, the windows gleaming gold from the inside electric lights. Like Denver, Pueblo had been electrified. Maybe he was old-fashioned, but he preferred the soft, golden glow of gas lanterns to the harsh white of the electric lights.

Matt saw a buckboard, a young boy on the seat beside the driver. In the back of the buckboard was a freshly cut evergreen tree, no doubt soon to be sprouting tinsel and Christmas ornaments.

That turned his thoughts to Christmas with Smoke and Sally, and Matt realized it had been a long time since he had seen his friend. He was looking forward to seeing him again and renewing his acquaintance with Duff MacAllister. It was fitting they would be meeting at Christmas as he had first met him five years ago, during Christmas of 1888, when he helped Duff and Smoke deliver a herd of Abner cattle from Wyoming to Texas.

The train rolled into the station and rattled and rumbled to a halt. It was almost eight o'clock in the evening. Matt helped a young woman get her grip down from the overhead rack, then reached up for his suitcase. Carrying his coat, he followed the young woman through the car and down onto the depot platform. Immediately, he was hit by a blast of cold air. Shivering, he hurried across the brick platform and into the inviting warmth of the station as the train's overheated journals and bearings popped in the cold air.

Inside, he saw two men talking, or rather, one man talking while the other man was busy recording their conversation in a small notepad. Matt wondered what was so special about the man that everything he said had to be recorded. Then, he heard the man with the small, narrow notepad ask a question and he knew what it was.

"Senator Daniels, are you aware of the claim being made by the coal mine owners that paying in company script is the most efficient way to run their businesses?"

"I know it is what they say. But consider the miner, how he sweats and toils beneath the earth to mine coal, only to see that his remuneration is in paper that is worthless to spend anywhere except in a company store."

"Which provides all the necessities for living," another reporter said. "Food, furniture, clothing. What more does someone need?"

"In my opinion, that is nothing more than a form of slavery," Senator Daniels answered.

"But, according to the mine owners, this actually helps the miners' families as it prevents the miners from spending money on whiskey or gambling it away."

"Of course slave owners could justify their actions as being best for the Negro," Senator Daniels replied. "But we all know they weren't. Besides, who are the mine owners to make such decisions for someone else? No, sir, it is wrong. Wrong, I say, and I intend to fight against it, and I intend to fight with every ounce of my being."

"There are some who say you have no real interest in your bill, other than as a way to generate publicity for yourself," the reporter suggested.

"To what end, sir?" Daniels replied, obviously irritated by the question.

"Why, so you could run for governor during the next election. What about that, Senator? Do you have aspirations to run for governor? Or perhaps even a higher office?"

Senator Daniels reached up to stroke his muttonchop whiskers before he responded. "Right now, I just want to be a very good state senator. But I have chosen politics as my profession, and anyone who enters into any profession would want to reach the top, would they not?"

"So you do want to be governor?"

"No, no, I didn't say that. And you can quote me on that."

The reporter looked at him in confusion. "I can quote you on what, Senator?"

"You can quote me on saying I didn't say that." With that rather convoluted comment, Senator Daniels left the reporter scratching his head as he walked over to join his wife and their nine-year-old daughter.

"How is Becky? Is she doing any better?"

"No, Jarred, I don't think she is doing well at all," Millie replied. "Maybe we should stay here and find a doctor for her."

"Nonsense. Do you really want to spend Christmas in Pueblo? You know how important it is that I be in Red Cliff for that dinner. Besides, I've no doubt the doctors there are just as skilled as the doctors here in Pueblo."

"Is the dinner more important than the health of our daughter?"

"Of course not," Senator Daniels replied. "But I don't think it is any more than a childhood malady of some sort, and I'm sure she will be over it soon enough."

Parker saw Matt come into the depot, and leaned over to speak to Compton. "Do you know who that fella is?"

"No, I can't say as I do."

"His name is Jensen. Matt Jensen."

"Damn! You sure?"

"Yeah, I'm sure. I've seen him before."

"You think he might be goin' on the same train we are?"

"It looks likely that he is."

"So, what do we do?"

"If he is in the same car as Santelli and the deputy, we ain't goin' to do nothin'."

"You mean we ain't goin' to get Santelli free?"

"That's exactly what I mean."

"If we don't get Santelli away from the deputy, we won't get paid."

"Is your life worth five hundred dollars? 'Cause if we go up against Jensen, we're likely to get ourselves kilt."

"Hell, there's just one of him."

"Yeah, but he's carryin' a gun with six bullets," Parker pointed out.

"So, what do we do now?" Compton asked.

"We wait and see. If he goes to a different car from Santelli, then we'll do just what we planned to do."

Matt checked the schedule board and saw that he had at least half an hour remaining until the westbound train was due. He hadn't eaten since lunch, but he didn't think he would have time to order a regular dinner. So, stepping up to the depot lunch counter, he ordered a piece of apple pie and a cup of coffee.

As he ate, he looked round the waiting room of

the depot, appraising as best he could the people who would be his fellow travelers.

The first ones he checked were the senator and his family. The little girl didn't look well and Matt was struck by the expression of concern on the mother's face. He saw considerably less concern reflected in the face of the young girl's father.

Matt noticed the two men in handcuffs and shackles, and was surprised to see one of them was Michael Santelli. He wondered why there was an attractive young woman sitting with them, then he saw the banner and could tell by her demeanor it was directed at her.

"Hey"—the reporter looked over toward Matt—"you're Matt Jensen, aren't you?"

Matt took a swallow of his coffee.

"Yes, you are. You are the one who took down Michael Santelli. He's here, you know, on his way to Red Cliff to be hanged. He's sitting right over there, right now." The reporter pointed toward the bench occupied by Santelli, Luke, Proxmire, and the young woman.

"Yes, I saw him."

"You know what would be good? If I could get a picture of you with Santelli. We use the half-tone method of reproducing photographs."

"No, thank you."

"Is Santelli the reason you are here in Pueblo?" The reporter kept hounding.

"No, I'm just passing through Pueblo. And by the

way, I didn't take him down. He was arrested by Deputy Sheriff Ben Mason. He is a fine officer."

"Yes, but everyone knows if you hadn't been there, Santelli would more than likely have killed Mason. You were the hero of that event."

"I don't agree," Matt said. "The fact that Mason took Santelli on, knowing that he could be killed, makes him the *real* hero."

"Yes, I guess you have a point there. But say, would you mind if I interviewed you for a story?"

At that moment a whistle sounded and a bright light illuminated the darkness outside as the beam from the great, mirrored headlamp announced the approach of another train. Everyone in the depot started getting ready to board the westbound train.

"Sorry," Matt said as he finished his coffee. "But that's my train."

As the others began gathering their belongings and getting ready to board, Matt walked over to the telegraph office and wrote out a quick telegram to Smoke.

> IN PUEBLO BOARDING TRAIN NINE PM STOP ARRIVE BIG ROCK SIX AM TOMORROW STOP MATT

Matt paid the telegrapher, then, grabbing his small case, he hurried outside to join the others in boarding the train.

Just before they boarded, Proxmire looked over at Jenny. "Now look here, Mrs. McCoy. You ain't goin' to jump back off the train before we get started, are you?"

"Don't worry, Deputy. I have no intention of remaining in this town."

"Good. Because after I get these prisoners delivered, if I come back and find you are still here, it'll be more than just askin' you to leave town."

"Leave the lady alone, Deputy," Luke said.

"Mr. Shardeen, seein' as you're goin' off to jail yourself, it don't seem to me like you're in any position to be a' tellin' me anything. This here woman's bein' run out of town, and I'm charged to see to it that she leaves."

At Jenny's assurance she would stay on the train, Proxmire turned and steered his prisoners toward the train. Matt watched them shuffle to the next to last car. The four outlaws quickly followed.

From in the line behind them, Becky asked, "Mama, why are they telling that lady she has to leave town?"

"Hush, darling. I don't know, and it is none of our business," Millie replied.

Again, Matt saw the young woman's cheeks flame in embarrassment and watched as she climbed into the last car. He didn't recognize her, but at least knew he had seen her somewhere before. He just couldn't remember when or where. Without that information, he wasn't able to put a name to the face.

Matt and the Daniels family followed Jenny into the last car, illuminated by kerosene lanterns, three on each side, mounted on gimbals. Two coal-burning stoves—one at each end—were in the car, and the smoke was carried outside by chimneys, which passed through the roof. The stoves were well stoked and burning briskly so the car was comfortably warm, despite the brutal outside temperature.

Matt took the very last seat in the car, which was exactly where he wanted to be. From his position at the back, he could observe without being obvious. He looked at the woman the deputy had called Jenny McCoy. It was not a name he recognized, and if she was a prostitute as the sign had indicated, she was certainly unlike any prostitute he had ever seen before.

She was very attractive, but not garishly so as was the case with so many prostitutes. She was quiet and noncombative, and, even in her obvious embarrassment, there was a sense of bearing about her he would describe as regal.

Just as the train whistle blew, a man came flying out of the depot and ran up the steps of the last car. He sat down quickly in the front seat.

The train started forward then, jerking a few times until all the slack was taken from the couplings. It gradually and smoothly increased speed until it reached approximately twenty miles per hour, the speed at which it would run for as long as it was on flat ground. After a few hours, it would start on a long upgrade, and the speed would decrease sharply.

"I'm cold, Mama," Matt heard the little girl say.

"Don't be silly," Senator Daniels replied. "It's not cold in here. If anything, it is too warm."

"I'm cold," Becky repeated.

"Darling, she is ill," Millie objected. "She is probably having chills."

"Can I have a blanket?"

"I'm sorry, honey. We don't have a blanket," Millie explained.

Jenny, overhearing the conversation, got up and walked back to the seat where the senator and his family were sitting. She held out a long coat toward the little girl's mother. "Your little girl is certainly welcome to use my coat as a blanket," she offered with a smile.

"Madam, I saw the sign in the depot, and I heard the deputy address you, so I know who and what you are," Senator Daniels barked. "Just what makes you think I would want my daughter to use something from someone of your kind for a blanket?"

The smile left Jenny's face to be replaced by an expression of hurt.

"Jarred! Don't be rude!" Millie said sharply. Then, smiling at Jenny, she reached out for the coat. "How gracious of you to offer your coat. Yes, thank you. I think that would work quite nicely. But, I wouldn't want you to get cold."

"I'm close enough to the stove, I don't think I will get cold," Jenny answered, obviously grateful her offer had been accepted.

"It's a very pretty coat," Becky said.

"It will be even prettier when it's covering a pretty little girl like you." Turning, Jenny walked back to her seat.

"Did you hear what she said, Mama? She said I was pretty."

"Yes, darling, I heard it. And she was only telling the truth. You are a very pretty little girl."

"I think she is pretty," Becky said.

"Yes, I think so, too. Try and go to sleep now."

Matt saw Jenny McCoy smile at the little girl's words, and was glad.

Chapter Eleven

Sugarloaf Ranch

The Denver Pacific, the Denver and Rio Grande, the Kansas Pacific, the Colorado Central, the Burlington, Rock Island, and Missouri Pacific railroads had all laid tracks into Colorado. Those railroads linked the state with the rest of the nation's economy, bringing in the nation's manufactured goods and shipping out Colorado's minerals and cattle.

One of those taking advantage of the network of railroads was Kirby Jensen, known by everyone as Smoke Jensen. Since marrying his wife Sally and settling down, he had built one of the most successful ranches in Colorado. His ranch, Sugarloaf, was located near the town of Big Rock, just west of the south end of the Mosquito Range. Big Rock would be the first stop on the Denver and Pacific Railroad after the train had traversed Trout Creek Pass coming north and west, and the last stop before climbing the pass when going east and south. And, because that train could carry his cattle to the eastern markets, Smoke Jensen had become a very wealthy man.

At the moment, Smoke and his friend, Duff MacAllister, also a cattleman who owned a ranch in Wyoming, were in the parlor, decorating a Christmas tree. The tree was strung with red and green ribbons as well as brightly painted ornaments.

Underneath the tree was an exquisitely, hand-carved crèche. Duff picked up one of the sheep and examined it closely. "Whoever did this, did mighty fine job."

"That whole thing was carved by Preacher," Smoke said.

"An artist, was he?"

"Yes, he was an artist," Smoke agreed. "But he was much more than that."

"Aye? Well, I'll tell you lad, sure 'n if 'twas only for his art he was known, he would have a well-deserved reputation. I've never seen finer work done."

The smell of freshly baked pastries wafted into the parlor from the kitchen. "What is that wonderful aroma?" Duff asked, looking toward the kitchen.

"If I don't miss my guess, that would be Sally's bear claws. Come, let's go try out a couple."

"Aye, 'tis a good idea." Duff followed him willingly and eagerly into the kitchen.

Both of the men grabbed a bear claw from the table where several of the pastries lay.

"Smoke!" Sally scolded. "You aren't supposed to eat any of those now."

"Well, now, surely you'll want Duff and me to try them out, just to make certain they are good enough to serve at Christmas, won't you?" Smoke teased as he took a bite.

Sally smiled. "And how is it?"

"I'm not sure I can tell with just one. It'll take at least two, I think, before I'll know whether or not they are any good." Smoke finished the first one, then reached for a second. Duff followed suit.

"Uh-huh," Sally said with a condescending smile. "If you and Duff don't quit eating those bear claws, there won't be any left for Christmas."

"Sure there will be." Smoke he took a bite of the second pastry, then wiped his mouth with the back of his hand. "It's a few more days till Christmas. All you have to do is make a couple dozen more."

"I've already made two dozen. This isn't a bakery, you know."

"Just be glad Pearlie and Cal decided to spend Christmas in Denver. Otherwise you'd have to make about three dozen more. With them gone, you probably don't need more than another one or two dozen. Although, you could make three dozen more, just to be safe."

Sally laughed. "You're impossible."

"Of course I'm impossible. You wouldn't love me any other way. You know that," Smoke teased. Looking through the kitchen window, he saw a rider approaching. "Looks like we have another telegram. Here's Eddie again."

"Oh, Smoke, take a bear claw out to him," Sally said. "Bless his heart, having to ride out here in the middle of the night when it is this cold."

"It's only nine o'clock. It isn't the middle of the night. Besides, I thought you said we weren't going to have enough."

"You know I'm going to make some more."

Laughing, Smoke put on his coat, then grabbed one of the pastries and went outside to meet Eddie, the fifteen-year-old telegraph messenger.

"Another telegram?"

"Yes, sir."

"Hope there's no trouble with Matt getting here."

"No, sir. He's just tellin' you he's gettin' on the train, is all," Eddie said. "'Course, that don't mean there ain't goin' to be no trouble."

"Why, what do you mean?"

"We're gettin' reports from all over about snow. I know it ain't started snowin' here yet, but it's acomin' down just real heavy in the mountains, they say. I'm surprised they even let the train leave."

"Eddie, would you like to come inside and warm up a bit before you start back to town?" Smoke invited.

"No, sir. Thank you very much. If I come in and get warm, it'll be that much harder to come back outside again."

Smoke chuckled. "Young man, you are wise

beyond your years." He gave the boy a dollar and the pastry.

"Thank you!" the boy said with a broad grin. "There can't nobody make bear claws as good as Miz Sally can."

"Well, if you're going, you'd better get on back into town before you freeze to death," Smoke pushed. "It's really cold, and I have a feeling it's going to get a lot colder before this night is out."

"Yes, sir, I do believe it is goin' to do just that," Eddie agreed as he turned his horse and started back into the night.

Smoke looked toward the mountains, thinking of the train traveling through Trout Creek Pass. It had snowed quite a bit in the last several days, and he could see the white, almost luminescent, snow-capped mountain peaks against the dark sky.

Once back inside the house, he opened the yellow envelope and read the message aloud. "In Pueblo boarding train nine p.m. Arrive Big Rock six a.m. tomorrow."

"What time does that mean Sally will have to get up to go meet him?" Duff asked.

"I'd say about four-dark-thirty in the morning would get her there on time," Smoke teased.

"What? Not on your life, gentlemen. I'll have you know I will be warm in bed when you two go to town to meet him."

"Is that the way it's going to be? And here, I thought that being it is so close to Christmas, you'd have a little more compassion in your heart,"

Smoke teased some more. "All right, if that's the way it is, you can stay home. But there's no sense in Duff and me both going to pick him up. I'll go by myself."

"I'll be for goin' with you, lad," Duff offered. "I'd be glad to."

"Did you hear that, Sally? He's not only going to go with me, he'll be glad to go. That's what he said. He would be glad to go."

"I heard."

"Well, I think you should know it's good to see that I can count on some people," Smoke said pointedly.

"Try not to wake me when you leave," Sally taunted.

"What do you mean, don't wake you? Aren't you even going to get up to make coffee for us?"

"Nope."

"You are one cruel woman, do you know that?"

"So I've been told," Sally replied with a laugh.

"Eddie said there's been a lot of snow up in the mountains. I hope the train has no trouble getting through the pass," Smoke said.

"Don't they keep the tracks clear?" Duff asked.

"Well, yes, when they can."

Sally walked over to the window and looked up toward the mountains. "I don't know, Smoke, it looks like there might be a big storm brewing."

"Could be," Smoke agreed. "Sally, what was that poem about snow that Preacher liked so much? You remember, he was always asking you to say it to him. It was by . . . some poet. I can't remember."

"Ralph Waldo Emerson. 'The Snow-Storm.'"

"Yes, that's the one. Can you still say it?"

"Of course."

"Say it for us. Listen to this, Duff. I swear, you could hear this poem in the middle of the summer and start shivering."

Sally began to recite the poem, speaking with elegance, flair, and with all the proper emphasis.

"Announced by all the trumpets of the sky
Arrives the snow, and, driving o'er the fields
Seems nowhere to alight: the whited air
Hides hills and woods, the river, and the heaven,
And veils the farm-house at garden's end.
The sled and traveller stopped, the courier's feet
Delayed, all friends shut out, the housemates sit
Around the radiant fireplace, enclosed
In a tumultuous privacy of storm."

"That was beautiful, Sally. You have quite a way with words," Duff said.

"Thank you, but I only spoke the words. Emerson wrote them, and it was a loss to literature when he died."

Smoke chuckled. "Until I married Sally, I had never heard of him. One of the advantages of marrying a schoolteacher is that you get an education."

"I like to say I didn't educate him, I trained him." Sally grinned.

"Whoa, now. I wouldn't go that far," Smoke protested.

Sally and Duff laughed.

"I will say this, though. What Preacher didn't teach me, Sally did."

"Who is Preacher? You mentioned him before. He was the one who carved the crèche, I believe."

"Yes," Smoke said. "Preacher didn't exactly raise me, but he almost did."

"He gave you your name, too," Sally pointed out.

"That's right. I was called Kirby until Preacher changed it to Smoke. Did you know that he killed a bear with just a knife when he was only 14 years old?"

"Och, 'twould take quite a man to do such a thing."

"You've got that right. He was quite a man. You probably wouldn't like him, though. He fought against the English at the Battle of New Orleans. He was just a boy, then."

"I've no real love for the English, laddie, I can tell you that for sure," Duff declared.

"But you are English," Smoke argued.

"I'm a Scotsman, lad. We may be part of Great Britain, but there be no love lost between the Scots and the English, that I can tell you. 'Twill be another hundred years or more before the Scotts forgive the English for Flodden, and then forgiven it will be, but never will it be forgotten."

"Flodden? Yes," Sally said. "I think I once read a poem about Flodden."

Duff cleared his throat and began to speak.

"From Flodden ridge,
The Scots beheld the English host
Leave Barmoor Wood, their evening post
And headful watched them as they crossed
The Till by Twizell Bridge.
High sight it is, and haughty, while
They dive into the deep defile;
Beneath the cavern'd cliff they fall,
Beneath the castle's airy wall.
By rock, by oak, by Hawthorn tree,
Troop after troop are disappearing;
Troop after troop their banners rearing
Upon the eastern bank you see."

"Yes!" Sally said. "That is the poem."

"There's a song about the battle called 'The Flowers of the Forest'," Duff said. "If you'd like, I'll play a wee bit of it on m' pipes."

"I would love for you to," Sally said.

Duff went into his room then returned a moment later with his bagpipes. After filling the bag with air, he began playing the piece, the melody, with its poignant strains, re-creating the tragedy of the terrible event. When he finished, the last note lingered as a haunting echo.

"That was beautiful, Duff. Sad, but beautiful," Sally commented.

"Thank you," Duff acknowledged with a nod of his head.

"Uh-oh," Smoke remarked.

"What?" Sally asked.

"Look out the window."

Outside the snow was falling thick and fast. Huge, heavy snowflakes were quickly covering the ground.

"This can't be good," Sally said.

"Maybe, maybe not," Smoke said. "Just because it is snowing here, doesn't mean it is snowing in the pass."

"But it probably is, right?" Sally asked.

Smoke was silent for a moment, before he answered. He nodded. "Yeah, it probably is."

Chapter Twelve

Big Rock

Cephas Prouty had on woolen long johns under his clothes, and a wool-lined sheepskin over his clothes. He had a scarf around his neck, a stocking cap over his head, and heavy gloves on his hands. Thus attired, he set out in a handcar for the purpose of inspecting Trout Creek Pass. For the first eight miles the track was relatively flat and pushing the hand pump up and down was easy. But it got harder when he started up the long grade that would take him to the top of the pass.

Prouty was used to it, though, as he made the trip several times a week. And tonight, he didn't even mind the pumping. The extra exertion helped keep him warm in the subzero temperatures.

It took him an hour and a half to reach the summit. He set the brake on the car, then stepped down to have a look around. He checked the track, then examined the cut on either side. If he found any reason why the train couldn't make it through, he'd wire the station at Buena Vista, warn them the pass wasn't safe, and have them hold the train there.

Prouty walked along the track from its most elevated point to where it started back down on the west side. He turned around and walked up to the summit, continuing on to where it started back down on the east approach. Occasionally he would stick a ruler into the snow to measure its depth. Nowhere did he find the snow over two inches deep, and even then it wasn't accumulating on the rails. He didn't see any reason why the trains couldn't continue to come through the pass.

It wasn't only during the snow season that he would come up to check. He made frequent trips during other seasons as well, to ensure the rails were whole and unobstructed. On a clear night in the summer. he could look one way and see the lights of Buena Vista or look the other way and see the lights of Big Rock.

Tonight, though, the night was so overcast that when he looked out to either side of the pass he saw nothing but darkness.

His inspection done, Prouty got on his handcar and started back toward Big Rock. His trip up the grade to the top of the pass had been difficult, requiring hard pumping. Going back down was easy. No pumping was required until he reached the flat. In fact, he had to apply the brake to keep from going too fast. He was certain that he was doing at least forty miles per hour on the way down. He began pumping when he hit the flats, making his total trip down the mountain in less than an hour. He coasted into the station at about nine-thirty, moving the cart onto a side track before going inside.

"Well, Cephas, I see you made it back," the stationmaster said. "I figured you would be turned into an icicle by now."

"I damn near am one," Prouty replied as he stood shivering by the stove. "You got 'ny coffee, Phil?"

"Yes, stay there by the stove and warm yourself. I'll get it."

"Thanks."

"What about the pass?" Phil asked as he handed Prouty the cup.

Prouty took a welcome sip before answering. "I think it's all right."

"You *think*?" Phil chuckled. "That's not very reassuring. What do you mean you think? Don't you know? You were just up there, weren't you?"

"It's open now, but the next train isn't due through there until midnight. I believe that the pass will still be open, but I can't guarantee it."

"Should I stop the train at Buena Vista?"

"The next train through is a freight train, isn't it, Phil?"

"Yes."

"No, don't stop it. I think we should let the freight come on through. The Red Cliff Special isn't due through the pass until about five in the morning. When the freight pulls in here just after midnight, the engineer will have a more up-to-the-minute look at it, and a better idea as to the condition of the pass. We can get a report from him and make our decision about the passenger train then."

"Good idea," Phil agreed.

Prouty smiled. "You're a good station manager, Phil, offering a track inspector a hot cup of coffee after he's been out in the cold."

"Oh, I can do better than that. How about a cruller to go with your coffee?"

"Phil, you are indeed a gentleman," Prouty said gratefully.

On board the Red Cliff Special

On the other side of the Mosquito Range from where Phil and Prouty were having their discussion the Red Cliff Special was rumbling through the cold night. Matt kept repositioning himself, trying to get as comfortable as he could in the backseat. He had been on a train for over two days and was getting a little tired of the travel. The night before he had been in a Pullman car and had been able to sleep. But there were no Pullman cars on this run, so he had to make himself as comfortable as he could in the seat.

Fortunately, he had the seat to himself and was able to stretch out somewhat. He wadded up his coat and placed it against the cold window to use as a pillow. The kerosene lamps inside the car had been turned way down so that, while the car was illuminated just enough to allow someone to move about, it wasn't too bright to keep anyone from sleeping.

Falling into a fitful sleep, Matt dreamed.

An early snow moved in just before nightfall of the sixth day and the single blanket Matt had brought with him did little to push away the cold. It was also tiring to hold the blanket around him while walking. He considered cutting a hole in the middle but decided against it because he thought it would be less warm at night, that way.

As the snow continued to fall it got more and more difficult to walk. At first, it was just slick, and he slipped and fell a couple times, once barking his shin on a rock so hard the pain stayed with him for quite a while.

The snow got deeper and he quit worrying about it being slick, concerning himself only with the work it took just to get through it. His breathing came in heaving gasps, sending out clouds of vapor before him. Once he saw a wolf tracking him and wished he had his father's rifle.

He found a stout limb about as thick as three fingers and trimmed off the smaller branches with his knife. Using the limb as a cane helped him negotiate the deepening snowdrifts.

Just before dark he sensed, more than heard, something behind him. Turning quickly, he saw that the wolf, crouching low, had sneaked up right behind him. With a shout, and holding the club in both hands, he swung at the wolf and had the satisfaction of hearing a solid pop as he hit it in the head. The wolf yelped once, then turned and ran away, trailing little bits of blood behind it.

Matt felt a sense of power and elation over that little encounter. He was sure the wolf would give him no further trouble.

As the sun set he found an overhanging rock ledge and got under it, then wrapped up in the blanket. When night came, he looked up into the dark sky and watched huge, white flakes tumble down. If it weren't for the fact that he was probably going to die in these mountains, he would think the snowfall was beautiful.

"Here, try some of this."

Opening his eyes, Matt saw that he was no longer outside under a rock, but inside on a bed. How did I get here? *he wondered. A man was sitting on the bed beside him, holding a cup. Matt took the cup and raised it to his mouth, but jerked it away when it burned his lips.*

The man laughed. "Oh. Maybe I should have told you it was hot."

Matt tried again, this time sipping it through extended lips. It was hot and bracing and good. "What is it?"

"Broth, made from beaver," the man said.

"Don't know that I've ever tasted beaver, before," Matt said calmly.

The man laughed again.

"What's so funny?"

"I'll say this for you, boy, you do have sand. I found you damn near dead out on the trail, and now you are

telling me that you don't think you've ever eaten beaver before."

"I don't think I have," Matt answered as calmly as before. "Who are you?"

"The name is Jensen. Smoke Jensen."

Matt was awakened when the train ran over a rough section of track. He sat up and rubbed his eyes, bringing himself back from dreaming about the first time he ever met Smoke, or, more accurately, about the time Smoke had saved his life. Not surprised by the dream, he was sure the cold and snow had triggered an old memory. In addition, Smoke had been on his mind as he thought about spending Christmas with his friend and mentor.

It was dark in the passenger car, and pleasantly warm. According to the schedule he had read at the Pueblo depot, they weren't due into Buena Vista until two in the morning. That was a few hours away, so Matt repositioned himself in the seat and went back to sleep.

On board the Freight Number 7

Several miles ahead of the Red Cliff Special, a freight train was approaching the top of the pass.

"Better take it easy through here, Joe," the fireman said. "That snow is comin' down pretty good now."

"Yeah," the engineer said. "But it looks clear ahead. Look out your side. If you see anything, sing out."

The engine, which was pulling a string of ten freight cars, slowed until it was barely moving. Finally it reached the crest, topped it, then started down the other side.

"All right!" Joe cried. "Let's get out of here!" He opened the throttle, and aided by the fact that it was going downhill, the train reached fifty miles an hour. He started slowing it down three miles before they reached Big Rock, where they would have to take on water.

Big Rock station

Phil heard Freight Number 7 approaching, put on his heavy coat, and walked out to the water tank. He needed to talk to the engineer about the pass. He glanced up where a fire was kept burning in the large, cast-iron stove in the vertical shaft just below the tank to keep the water from freezing. When the train ground to a stop, the fireman climbed out to swing the huge water spout over to replenish the water in the tender.

The engineer leaned out the window of the cab and looked down toward the station manager. "What are you doing out here in the cold, Phil?"

"The Special will be coming through the pass about five in the morning. What do you think? Will they have any trouble?"

"We didn't have any trouble," Joe said. "The track and the pass are clear."

"There's a lot of snow higher up, though," the

fireman added. "If it don't come down, I don't see no trouble."

"What do you mean if it doesn't come down? Is that likely?"

"I don't think so," Joe answered. "I saw it too, and it looks like it's pretty solidly packed."

"All right, thanks," Phil said. "I'll send the word on back."

The fireman finished filling the tank, then swung the spout back. "Merry Christmas, Phil," he called out.

Phil smiled back at him. "Merry Christmas to you, Tony. And you, too, Joe." He started back toward the warmth of the depot, even as Joe opened the throttle and Freight Number 7, with ten cars of lumber, continued on its journey.

CHAPTER THIRTEEN

On board the Red Cliff Special

Matt awakened a second time when the train stopped. It was about two o'clock in the morning, which meant they had been under way for five hours. Looking through the window, he saw a small wooden building, painted red. A sign hung from the end of the building, but he couldn't see enough to read it.

"Folks," the conductor said when he stepped into the car. "This is Buena Vista and we'll more 'n likely be here for about half an hour. If any of you want to, you can get off the train and have a cup of coffee or maybe a bite to eat."

The porter went through the car, turning the lamps up brighter, and the other passengers started moving about, collecting coats, mittens, scarves, and caps.

"I don't want to go outside, Mama," Becky said. "I want to stay here and sleep."

"That's all right, darlin'. You won't have to go outside if you don't want to. You and I will stay here in the car, but we'll have to give the lady her coat back so she won't freeze when she goes outside."

"Your daughter can use this as a blanket," Matt said, handing his sheepskin coat to the girl's mother.

"Why, thank you, sir."

"And I thank you as well, Mr. Jensen." Jenny smiled as she retrieved her own coat.

"I was right," Matt said with a smile. "I knew that I had seen you before. I just can't remember where."

"It was a few years ago, on board a riverboat on the Mississippi. The boat was the *Delta Mist.*"

"Of course! You were the hostess for the Grand Salon. But, McCoy wasn't your name then. It was"—Matt hesitated for a moment, then he recalled the name—"Lee, wasn't it? Jenny Lee."

"Yes, I'm flattered you remember. I was married soon after that. Now I'm widowed."

"I'm sorry for your loss," Matt said automatically. Then, as they approached the door of the car he added, "I sure hope they have a warm fire going in the depot."

"I'm sure they will."

They stepped down from the train, and Matt figured the temperature was at least ten below zero. The wind was blowing so hard it cut through him, right to the marrow of his bones. By the time he crossed the platform and got inside, he felt half frozen to death. Moving immediately to the stove, he stood for a long moment with his arms out, circling the stove, as if embracing the fire. Finally, when the feeling gradually began to return to his extremities, he left the stove and stepped up to the counter to buy a cup of coffee, nodding to the man he'd seen board the train just before the train pulled out of the station. The man was leaning against the counter warming his hands around a cup of steaming coffee. Matt paid for his coffee and stepped aside. As he stood there drinking it, he looked around the room and saw that Deputy Proxmire had come into the depot with his two prisoners. The shackles had been removed from the prisoners' legs. Evidently, they were no longer a threat to run away, once on the train.

Santelli looked directly at him, the expression on his face registering surprise, as if seeing him for the first time. Evidently he had not noticed Matt back at the Pueblo Depot.

"Well if it isn't Matt Jensen. What are you doing here, Jensen?" Santelli called over to him. "Have you come to watch me hang? 'Cause if you have, you may have to wait around a while."

"I just happened to be on the same train with you, Santelli, that's all. You can damn well hang without me."

"Ha! Well, I got news for you, Jensen. I ain't goin' to hang. So what do you think about that?"

"I don't think anything about it one way or the other," Matt replied. "This may come as a surprise to you, Santelli, but you aren't important enough to even be on my mind."

"I told you one day that me 'n you would meet again, didn't I? Do you remember that?"

"I do remember that." Matt smiled. "And here we are, met again. I'm on my way to have Christmas with friends, and you are on your way to, what is it? Oh yes, to get your neck stretched."

"Yeah? Well don't you be counting on me gettin' hung, Jensen. No, sir, don't you be countin' on it, 'cause that ain't goin' to happen. And this here meetin' ain't the one I was talkin' about neither. There will be another time for the two of us to, let's just say, work out our differences."

"Santelli, why don't you shut up now?" Proxmire complained. "You've blabbered enough."

Santelli glared but said nothing more.

The man standing beside Matt at the counter had witnessed the exchange between the two men. Turning toward Matt, he stuck his hand out. "How do you do, sir? The name is Purvis, Abner Purvis."

"Matt Jensen." He shook Purvis's offered hand.

"I saw you talking with Santelli. Do you know him?"

"Not exactly, but I did run across him when he was arrested. Tell me, Mr. Purvis, do you know the other prisoner? Who is that with him?"

"I can't say that I actually know him, but I know who he is. His name is Luke Shardeen and I understand he used to be a sailor and has been all over the world. He's seen places the rest of us have just read about or heard about. Hawaii, China, India, Australia, but he gave all that up when he inherited some land from his uncle. He calls the ranch Two Crowns and he's been working it ever since, quite successfully, I'm told."

"Why is he a prisoner?"

"He killed the deputy sheriff from Bent County."

"He killed a deputy sheriff? That's pretty serious."

"I guess it would be if it was the way it sounds. But he claimed that the deputy and Sheriff Ferrell were trying to rob him. Of course, the sheriff said they were only stopping him to ask him a few questions."

"Evidently, the jury believed the sheriff," Matt said.

"Not entirely. It seems Shardeen had just sold a bunch of cows and had quite a bit of money with him. Naturally, he'd be worried if a couple armed men suddenly come up on him, wouldn't you think?"

"I could see that."

"You also have to wonder what a sheriff and a deputy sheriff from Bent County were doing stopping someone in Pueblo County. Why didn't they just go to Deputy Proxmire? Or to Sheriff McKenzie?"

"That's a good question. Evidently, though, it was answered to the satisfaction of the jury."

"The thing is, the jury pretty much had their hands tied."

"What do you mean, they had their hands tied?"

"If you ask me, Amon Briggs—he's the judge—sort of forced them into finding Shardeen guilty. Briggs is as crooked as they come, for all that he is a judge. He likes to do things his own way, and I'm not the only one that thinks this. Most of the folks think he browbeat the jury into finding Shardeen guilty." Purvis chuckled. "He didn't entirely get it his own way, though. He wanted Shardeen found guilty of first-degree murder, but the most he got was involuntary manslaughter and four years."

"Four years isn't all that bad."

"Ordinarily, I would agree with you, but I'm afraid in Shardeen's case it is. He won't have a ranch left when he gets out. He won't have anything left at all, so I don't have any idea what is going to happen to him."

Matt looked over toward Luke Shardeen and saw him sitting calmly beside the deputy sheriff and talking quietly to the girl.

"What about Miss Lee?"

"Who?"

"I mean Mrs. McCoy."

"Oh, yes, that's another example of the judge sticking his nose into everyone's business. Jenny McCoy worked for Adele Summers at the Colorado Social Club."

"Colorado Social Club? I take it the women there are . . . just real sociable?" Matt asked with a chuckle.

"Yes, they are. I'm not going to lie to you, Mr. Jensen, the Social Club is a whorehouse, pure and simple. But Jenny McCoy, now, she wasn't actually a whore. She was a hostess. I never heard of her going to bed with anyone, for all that they tried. But even if she wouldn't go to bed with anyone, she was very popular. Well, you can see how pretty she is. She's also very smart, and they she has a way of making people feel like they are someone important, no matter who they are. They also say that you could tell her anything you wanted, and know it wasn't going to get spread all over town. And if anyone was having troubles, why, she had a way about her of making them feel good. You know, making them think that everything was going to come out all right. But from all I've heard, she didn't whore with anybody."

Matt was glad to hear that. He remembered her from the *Delta Mist,* as well as her supportive testimony at his hearing in Memphis.

"I saw the sign back in the Pueblo depot. Someone thought she was a whore."

"Yes, well I guess she hasn't made friends with many of the women in town, that's true. But that isn't what got her run out of town. The thing that got her run out of town was having her picture taken when she was naked and sitting on the sofa with Governor Crounse."

"Naked?"

"She claims, and so does the governor, that some men broke in to the sitting room and forced her, at gunpoint, to take off her clothes so they could get a picture of them together like that. The governor thinks some of his political enemies were behind it. Nobody has said so, but I'd be willing to bet Judge Briggs was in on it from the beginning. Briggs is the kind of crooked no-good that can be bought off. Everyone knows that."

"If everyone knows that, why is Briggs still the judge? Isn't that an elective position?"

"Elections can be bought, and there's no doubt in my mind but that Briggs bought the election that got him there in the first place, and now just keeps on buying them. I wouldn't be surprised if Briggs doesn't find some way to take over Shardeen's ranch while he's gone."

Matt smiled. "You seem to have your fingers on the pulse of the town. Are you a newspaper reporter? Or are you just well connected?"

Purvis laughed. "Well connected? I wouldn't say that, exactly. But I do hear things."

"What do you do in Pueblo?" Matt asked. "Not that it's any of my business," he added quickly. "I'm just making conversation, here."

Purvis paused for a moment before he answered. "I suppose I'm what you might call a jack of all trades. I've done a bit of everything since I've been here, but I've seen the elephant now, and I'm going back to the ranch my family owns just outside Red Cliff."

One of the other passengers called out to Purvis, and he excused himself, leaving Matt standing alone. Matt continued to observe Luke Shardeen and Jenny McCoy, finding the study more interesting, now that he knew a little something about each of them.

Chapter Fourteen

At the far end of the depot, Matt saw the conductor and a man he assumed was the locomotive engineer talking to the depot agent. Their conversation was quite animated, so Matt moved closer to see if he could hear them. He gave a quick smile, thinking about using the trick Smoke had taught him, a trick Smoke had learned from Preacher, who had learned it from the Indians.

"In order to better hear what you want to hear, you have to systematically eliminate every other sound, so that nothing competes with what you want to hear," Smoke told him.

"How do you eliminate all the other sound?"

"You just sort of think about each sound for a moment, then, one sound at a time, put it out of your mind."

Outside the depot, the fireman was still on board the locomotive, still keeping the steam pressure up. As a result the water in the boiler was gurgling and hissing. But the real noise was coming from the pulsating relief tube, opening and closing rhythmically, making loud rushing noises as as if the train itself was breathing.

Matt quickly eliminated that sound and concentrated on the loudest remaining sound, which was the buzz and chatter of those conversationalists congregated in the waiting room. Their noise was punctuated by periodic outbreaks of laughter and the sound of small shoes on the floor as a couple young boys ran about in play.

After eliminating the many conversations and the children at play, Matt heard only the sound of the clacking telegraph and the ticking of the large clock on the wall nearby. He pushed those sounds aside as well, and could finally concentrate on the conversation between the engineer, the conductor, and the station agent.

"Look," the station agent was saying. "Last night a track inspector went up to the pass and checked it out. He said it was all right then, and a freight train went through after that, so the latest word we have, by telegraph, is that the pass is open."

"What if we get up there and we are blocked? What if we can't go ahead and we can't come back?" the engineer asked.

"I don't think that is likely to happen, at least not in the next twelve hours," the station agent said. "On the other hand, if you don't go now, and it does get blocked, you could be here for a month."

"I can tell you right now, Don, if that happens, we are going to have a lot of very upset people," the conductor said to the engineer. "Nearly everyone on this train wants to get somewhere for Christmas, and we don't have that much time left before Christmas is here."

"You're the conductor, Mr. Bailey," Don said. "So the decision as to whether to go on or stay here is up to you."

Bailey looked at the station agent. "Mr. Deckert, what is the latest time you received a report on the condition of the pass?"

"Well, like I said, a freight train went through no more 'n two hours ago, and the pass was open then. Do you want to hear the telegram?"

"Yes, read it to me," Bailey said.

Deckert pulled the telegram from his pocket. "Midnight. Trout Creek Pass open. No difficulty." He handed the telegram to the conductor who read it again.

"Hmm, 'no difficulty.' I find it interesting he says that specifically," Bailey commented. "That's a good sign, I would think."

"There has been no new snow since I received this telegram so my guess would be that the pass is still open."

"Your guess," Don quipped.

"It's not just a wild guess," Deckert reasoned. "It's based upon that telegram and the fact that there has been no new snow."

Bailey nodded, then stuck the telegram in his pocket. "All right, Don, I say we go."

"Like I said, you're the boss. How much longer before we leave?"

Bailey pulled out his pocket watch and examined it, even though he was standing right under the clock. "We shouldn't stay here too long. I would think the sooner we get to the pass, the better off we will be. I'll give 'em about fifteen more minutes, then I'll get them back aboard."

"All right, I'd better go tell my fireman." The engineer went outside to return to the locomotive and the station agent went back to his position behind the counter. Having heard what he wanted to hear, Matt let the other sounds start drifting back in, and turning toward the waiting room, he saw that Jenny and Luke were engaged in quiet conversation.

Their conversation looked to be private, so he made no effort to overhear them. Instead, he concentrated on the cup of coffee he was drinking.

Don Stevenson hurried across the brick platform and through the cold to the big 4-6-2 engine sitting on the track, wreathed in its own steam. Reaching up to grab the ladder, he climbed up and into the cabin.

His fireman, Beans Evans, reached down to give him a hand in. "So what's the story? Are we goin' on?"

"Yep."

"Then the pass is open?"

"They think so."

"They think so? You mean they don't know?"

"Nobody knows for sure," Don said. "But the last report they got was a telegram from Big Rock. Freight Number Seven passed through at midnight, and said that it was open."

"That was two hours ago, and it'll be another three hours before we get there," Beans pointed out.

"Yes. Well, if the pass isn't open, we can always back down the hill."

"Yeah, that is if there ain't another train comin' up behind us."

"Well, you know what they say, Beans. Ours not to reason why, ours but to do or die."

"Yeah? Well, who says that? Not the people who have to do or die, that's for damn sure," Beans replied.

"You've done a good job keeping the steam up."

Beans smiled. "I wasn't keeping the steam up, I was keeping myself warm."

Inside the depot, Jenny and Luke were still engaged in conversation.

"Nobody in town thinks you are guilty," Jenny said. "I've heard them talking."

Luke smiled. "Unfortunately, none of the people who thought I was innocent were on the jury. The men on the jury thought I was guilty."

"No, they were just too frightened of the sheriff and the judge to go against them, that's all. That's why they said it was involuntary manslaughter instead of murder."

"It wasn't even that. It was self-defense. The two men who accosted me were armed. Sheriff Ferrell and his deputy, Gates, tried to rob me."

"Ha!" Santelli had been listening in to their conversation. "People like you are never guilty. Why don't you own up to it? Take my advice. If you've done somethin', admit it."

"Santelli, the last thing I need is advice from you," Luke remarked.

"All right, don't pay me no never mind, I'm just tryin' to be helpful, is all."

"Would you like to move closer to the stove?" Luke asked Jenny.

"Yes, that would be nice."

Luke stood, then reached down with his handcuffed hands to help her up.

"Where do you think you're goin', Shardeen?" Deputy Proxmire asked.

"To get warm," Luke replied "You may have noticed, it's cold outside, and I left my coat on the train."

"Just don't try and run away."

"Where would I go without a coat on a night like this?"

Luke and Jenny found a place to sit near the stove that also afforded them a modicum of privacy.

"We have something in common," Jenny said with a smile.

"You mean because we are both under Proxmire's watchful eye?"

"Well, yes, I suppose there is that, but that's not what I'm talking about. I'm told that you used to be a sailor."

"Aye. That I was. I've crossed the Pacific eleven times. Wait, are you telling me you were a sailor?"

"Of sorts."

Luke laughed. "How can you be a sailor of sorts?"

"The difference is in the water we sailed. You were on the Pacific; I was on the Mississippi River. I worked for my uncle. I was a hostess on board the *Delta Mist* riverboat."

Luke nodded and smiled. "You're right. River, ocean, it makes no difference. We were both sailors."

"How long have you been in Pueblo?" Jenny asked.

"Three years. And you?"

"Not quite a year. I started teaching school, but when the school board learned I had been married to a gambler, they decided I was a bad influence on the children."

"Why, that's ridiculous," Luke said. "I can't think of anyone who would have a better influence on the children than you."

"Thank you," Jenny said with a small smile. "That is very nice of you to say."

"It takes no extra effort to tell the truth," Luke insisted.

"You are a very nice man. It makes me wonder

why we couldn't have—" Jenny interrupted her comment in mid-sentence.

"You mean why we couldn't have met before this?" Luke concluded.

"It doesn't seem fair." Jenny's eyes welled with tears. "I finally meet someone nice and where do I meet him?" She managed a weak laugh through the tears. "I meet him when we are both under the care of a deputy sheriff, you, going to jail, and I being run out of town."

Luke reached up with his manacled hands and, sticking a finger out, caught a tear as it slid down her cheek.

"It was almost different," Luke said.

"Oh? What do you mean?"

"I had heard about you. I went to the Colorado Social Club, just to meet you."

"Really?" Jenny had a questioning look on her face. "I don't remember meeting you. I'm sure I would remember."

Luke smiled. "You didn't meet me, because I didn't stay."

"Oh."

"I wish I had stayed."

"No, I'm . . . I'm glad you didn't stay. I don't think I would have wanted to meet you that way."

"I understand. I think that is probably why I left. But at least we have met now," Luke said. "And I'm thankful for that."

"Yes," Jenny agreed. "At least we have met."

"All right, folks!" the conductor called. "Let's get back aboard!"

Luke stood first, then helped Jenny up. They stood there for a moment, just looking at each other, then, with a smile, Jenny spontaneously gave Luke a kiss on the lips.

Luke raised his arms, then realized that, because his hands were cuffed together, he couldn't easily embrace her. "That's not fair. You took advantage of me when my hands are cuffed, and I can't put my arms around you."

"Under the circumstances, it is probably best," Jenny said.

Those passengers who had come into the depot house hurried through the brutal cold back onto the train. Fortunately, the cars had been kept warm.

Walking toward the back of the car, Matt shook off the chill. His coat was still drawn over the sleeping daughter of Senator Daniels. He stopped and asked Mrs. Daniels, "How is she?"

"I'm worried about her."

Matt reached down to feel her forehead. "It feels as if she has some fever."

"Yes. I wish we had stayed in Pueblo so she could see a doctor."

"There are some fine doctors in Red Cliff. At this point we are much closer to Red Cliff than we are to Pueblo."

"Yes, I was thinking that as well. Do you want your coat back?"

"No, I'm doing just fine. Let her keep it. She needs it more than I."

"Thank you. That is most kind."

During the entire conversation, Senator Daniels had been sitting in the seat facing his wife and daughter, staring out the window at the bleak and empty depot platform. He paid no attention to the conversation between Matt and his wife.

The train started forward with a jerk so severe Matt reached out and grabbed a seat back to keep his balance, then moved quickly to his seat and sat down. He had told Mrs. Daniels they were closer to Red Cliff than to Pueblo, and in terms of distance, that was true. But Trout Creek Pass was between them and Red Cliff, and though the consensus of the conversation he had overheard was that the pass was open, in the final analysis they had proceeded on toward the pass based upon the stationmaster's belief that the pass was open and the conductor's call to proceed.

Matt wasn't all that convinced.

Across the aisle from Matt's seat and in the very front, Jenny sat quietly, looking down at her hands folded on her lap. She was thinking of Luke Shardeen, and trying to analyze her feelings for him.

She wasn't feeling the same way she had felt about Nate McCoy when first she'd met him. At that time, she had thought Nate was the most handsome man she had ever seen. After spending eighteen months with him she realized what she had felt was little more than infatuation. And it was childish infatuation at that, for all that she was an adult at the time.

She wasn't feeling childish infatuation for Luke. In fact, she didn't think it was something she would even call infatuation, though she was certainly interested in him. What would have happened if he had come in to see her the night he visited the Social Club? Would she have felt the same interest? Or would she have put any such feeling aside as she did for all the other customers who had come to visit with her?

She shook her head a little. The best time to have met him would have been while she was still teaching school, before she got involved with the Social Club and before he got into trouble with the law. If she had met him then, they might have fallen in love and gotten married. She smiled.

Then suddenly, reality set in, and the smile left her face. What was she doing? She shook her head again. These thoughts were getting her nowhere. The best thing was to get such thoughts out of her mind. She settled back into her seat, let her head rest against the seat back, and drifted off to sleep.

Chapter Fifteen

In the car just ahead, Luke and Santelli were sharing a seat. Deputy Proxmire sat facing them so he could keep an eye on both at the same time. Luke sat closest to the window, looking outside. It had begun to snow again, the snow coming down in big, tumbling flakes, a swirl of white against the darkness.

"You know what I'm thinkin'?" Santelli said, his words interrupting Luke's contemplation.

"I don't really care what you were thinking," Luke said.

"I think you are fallin' for that whore."

Luke didn't answer.

"Yes, sir, that's what I think. You seen yourself a pretty woman and you fall for her. But here's the funny thing. You're goin' away to jail, and more 'n likely the girl is goin' to wind up in another whore-house somewhere." Santelli laughed. "Tell me, how does that make you feel, knowin' your girl will be layin' with anyone who has the price?"

"You talk too much, Santelli," Luke muttered.

"Yeah? Well, talk is cheap. And right now, talk is all I've got. So I reckon I'll talk as much as I want."

"If you don't shut up talking about Jenny, I'll shut you up."

"Really? How are you going to do that?"

"I'll do it the same way I did it before."

"What do you—" Santelli stopped in mid-sentence, lifted his cuffed hands to touch his still-sore, black eye, and realized what had happened back in Pueblo. "Did you do this?"

Luke smiled, then turned to look back outside.

Parker, Kelly, Compton, and Morris were sitting across from each other in the front two facing seats, three rows ahead of the deputy and his prisoners.

"When do we make our move?" Kelly asked.

"Just before we reach the top of the pass," Parker said. "The train will be going slow enough that it will be easy to get it stopped."

"Who's going to go up on top?" Compton asked. "'Cause I'm tellin' you right now, you ain't goin' to get me on top of a movin' train. Most especially in weather like this when it's snowin' and the tops of the cars is likely to be slippery and all."

"Don't worry about it, I'll go. I've stole a lot of rides on freight trains, and I've run on top of a lot of cars in good weather and bad. It won't bother me none a' tall to run along the top of these cars." Parker went over the plan once again. "I'll get the engineer's attention, and as soon as I get the train stopped, you three take care of the deputy. Once we have Santelli, we'll cut the engine free, then go on down the other side of the mountain, and leave the rest of the train sitting up here on the track."

"I know you said you've stole rides on a lot of trains before," Morris said. "But are you sure you can drive this thing?"

"Drive it? Who said anything about drivin' the train? I don't have to drive it. All I have to do is stick a gun in the engineer's gut and he'll do all the drivin'. Yes, sir, he'll be more than glad to take us anywhere we want to go." Parker smiled. "At least, he'll take us anywhere we want to go as long as there is track to run on."

"I know Ward says Santelli has the money, but seein' as we're the ones that's actually takin' a risk here, I'm going to ask you again. What do you think? Do you really think he has the money to pay us?" Kelly asked.

"I wouldn't be doin' all this if I didn't think there was some payoff in it," Parker said. "I sure ain't doin' it 'cause me 'n Santelli is tight."

One hour after they left Buena Vista depot, Matt could feel by the angle of the car that they were starting up the long grade taking them to the top of the pass. The train also began to slow, going from a rapid twenty miles per hour down to no faster than a brisk walk.

The Denver, South Park and Pacific Railroad first laid tracks through Trout Creek Pass in 1879, and Matt had traversed the pass many times since then. He knew it well. The pass climbed to 9,300 feet at its highest elevation, and he knew they were coming very close to the top of the pass because he felt the train slow down even more.

Looking out through the window and into the darkness, he could see whirling white flakes and knew the snow had intensified since leaving Buena Vista. He shook his head, thinking the engineer and conductor were probably having second thoughts. If the track was closed ahead, they would have to back all the way down to Buena Vista, and backing at night, in a heavy snowstorm, down a steep grade, couldn't be a very good thing.

And still the snow came down.

In the engine of the train, Beans Evans was scooping up coal from the tender, then throwing it into the open door of the firebox. Inside the box, the flames leaped and curled around the added fuel, and even above the noise of the engine, Beans could hear the fire roaring. He closed the door and stood up. "That ought to keep us goin' till we reach the other side of the pass. Then we can damn near coast into Big Rock."

"Why don't you take a breather, Beans?" Don

said. "You've got enough fire to keep the pressure up for quite a while.

"Yes, sir, I think I will." Beans pulled a big red bandanna from the chest pocket of his overalls and wiped the sweat from his face. "You wouldn't think a body could get hot enough to sweat on a cold night like this."

"Why not?" Don answered. "We've got a fire going, and you've been working hard."

Beans chuckled. "I have to confess that I like standin' by the firebox a heap more in the wintertime than I do in the summertime."

"I agree," Don said. "Trouble is, I've got to keep my face in this window lookin' ahead all the time, and that lets the cold wind on me."

"It's funny, ain't it? I mean, what with both of us no more 'n five feet apart and here you are near 'bout freezin' to death, and I'm burnin' up, I'm so hot."

"Yeah," Don agreed. "Tell me, Beans, what did you get the missus for Christmas?"

"I bought her a cookstove."

"A cookstove?" Don laughed. "A cookstove? That's what you bought her for Christmas?"

"Yeah. She keeps tellin' me she don't have the right kind of stove to bake a cake, so I bought her one."

"Come on, Beans, what were you thinking? Women don't like things like that as Christmas presents. I mean, yeah, buy her a stove if you want, but women like pretty things."

"Oh, it's pretty all right. You should see it, Don. That stove is just real pretty."

Don laughed. "I don't think that's the kind of pretty women think of, when they think pretty."

"What about your kids?" Beans asked. "Are they excited about Christmas?"

"Oh, yes. They're wanting to see what Santa Claus will bring them." Don chuckled. "I know one thing he better not bring them. Not if I want to stay on the good side of Doreen."

"What's that?"

"Donnie wants a drum. Ha! Can you see him running around the house, banging on a drum? Well, it wouldn't bother me none. I mean when you stand here all day listenin' to all the noise this makes. But it would more 'n like drive Doreen crazy. Now Little Suzie, all she wants is a doll. Girls are a lot easier than boys. They don't seem to get into as much trouble. When you and your missus start havin' children, try 'n make 'em all girls."

"Ha!" Beans said. "Like you can choose."

"I know a witch that'll put a spell on your wife to make her have girls or boys. It only cost ten dollars."

"And it works?"

"Sure it works. Anyhow, you can't lose no money 'cause if she puts the hex on and it don't work, then she don't charge you nothin'."

"Ha. Sounds to me like she's got a real game goin' there."

"What do you mean? What kind of game?"

"If her hex works, she gets paid. If it doesn't work, she doesn't get paid. Is that what you said?"

"Yeah. So you can't go wrong, that way."

"Well, think about it, Don. All she's doin' is bettin' that you're goin' to have a boy or a girl. Only she ain't exactly bettin', 'cause she don't put up no money. She's just collectin' if she wins."

Don stroked his jaw for a second as he considered what Beans said. "I'll be damned." He smiled as he suddenly realized the truth of it. "You're right."

In the next to the last car of the train, Parker and the other three men were finalizing their plans.

"Remember"—Parker gave instructions once more—"make your move as soon as I get the train stopped."

"Yeah," Kelly said. "More 'n likely, Proxmire and ever'one else on the train will be tryin' to figure out why we're stopped."

"You can get the train stopped, can't you?" Morris asked.

"Yeah, don't you worry about that. I'll get the train stopped all right."

"All right," Compton said. "We're all ready, so let's do it."

With a final nod, Parker got up and left the car, passing through the front door and onto the vestibule. Crossing the vestibule, he went into the next car and then the next, proceeding through the cars until he walked through the dining car and started out the front door.

One of the dining car porters came up to him. "You can't go no farther, Mister. There ain't nothin' up there but the baggage and express car, and there ain't no passengers that's allowed in it."

Without a word in reply, Parker pulled his pistol and brought it down hard on the train crewman's head. The porter collapsed to the floor. Nobody else in the dining car saw it, and Parker went on without any more interference.

From the front vestibule of the dining car, he climbed up onto the top of the express car, ran across it, then jumped down onto the tender and moved toward the engine. He saw the engineer with his hand on the throttle and the fireman standing alongside, leaning on his shovel. Neither of them saw him because they were engaged in conversation.

"Hey! Engineer! Stop this train!" Parker shouted, but there was too much noise for him to be heard.

"Hey! Engineer!" Parker shouted again.

When neither the engineer nor the fireman heard him, Parker fired two shots into the air, which caught the attention of both the engineer and the fireman, and they looked around in surprise.

"I want you to—"

A deep and very loud roar interrupted what he'd intended to say.

Looking up, Parker saw an avalanche of snow cascading down the side of the mountain, set in motion by the sound of his gunshots. He barely had time to open his mouth in a scream before tons of snow swept him from the top of the tender, burying him, the engine, the tender, and most of the baggage car under hundreds of feet of snow.

The train to come to an immediate and jarring stop, causing many of the sleeping passengers to tumble out of their seats. A few shouted out in alarm.

"All right, boys, he's got it stopped. This is it!" Kelly shouted, and he and the other three advanced toward the rear of the car. Proxmire's back was to them as they approach, and he was sitting next to the window, trying to figure out what had caused their sudden stop.

"Hello, Santelli," Kelly said.

"Do not speak to the prisoners." Proxmire turned away from the window and was shocked to see a gun pointed directly at him.

"What are—"

Kelly pulled the trigger. The bullet hit Proxmire between the eyes, forming a fan-like spray of blood on the window behind him.

The other passengers in the car were either trying to recover from the sudden stop or staring out the window when they heard the shot fired. In alarm, they all looked around and saw Proxmire's bloody head leaning against the window. A woman screamed.

"Shut up!" Morris shouted, turning his pistol toward the other passengers. "I'll shoot the next person who makes a sound!"

Cowed by the threat, the others in the car grew quiet as they watched through wide, frightened eyes. A little girl started crying.

"Shut that brat up!" Morris shouted.

The father clamped his hand over the child's mouth.

Santelli held his hands up, showing his cuffed wrists. "The deputy has the keys in his jacket pocket."

Morris dug out the keys and opened Santelli's cuffs.

"What about him?" Morris indicated Luke Shardeen. "Should we take off his handcuffs?"

"No," Santelli said as he rubbed his wrists. "Just shoot him and be done with it. Better yet, give me a gun and let *me* shoot him."

Acting quickly, so quickly it caught the others by surprise, Luke stood up from his seat and shoved Santelli back into Morris, causing both men to struggle to maintain their balance. With them distracted, he dashed out the back door, then leaped off the vestibule into a pile of snow nearly as high as the railcar itself. He disappeared at once.

The three armed men rushed out the back of the car and onto the vestibule. Kelly fired into the snowbank where Luke had jumped. They heard a rumble up above the pass, and more snow came sliding down.

"Don't do that!" Compton shouted, reaching out to stay Kelly's hand. "Don't shoot again! You could bring the whole mountain down on us!"

Kelly swore. "Where did he go?"

"It don't really matter much. Hell, it's below zero and he ain't wearin' no coat," Morris noted. "Like as not he'll be froze to death in no more 'n ten minutes or so. What I'm wonderin' is, what happened to Parker?"

"I expect he's up in the engine, keepin' the engineer and the fireman covered till we get up there," Compton reckoned.

"So, what is the plan now?" Santelli asked.

"Soon as we get you free, we're goin' to go up to the front of the train," Compton answered.

"Yeah," Kelly added. "We're goin' to unhook the engine and go on down the pass, leavin' the rest of the train up here."

"Ha! Good plan," Santelli agreed. "By the time anyone figures out what has happened, we'll be long gone."

The four men started forward then, tracing the same route Parker had taken, earlier.

Passing through the cars they saw that the other passengers were in a state of confusion and worry as they gathered by the windows, looking out to see what had brought them to such a sudden and unexpected stop.

"Can you gentlemen tell us what has happened?" one of the passengers asked. "Why was there such a sudden stop?"

"Have we had a train wreck?" another asked.

"Just stay here in your seats and keep calm," Kelly said. "We're goin' up to the front of the train now to find out what happened. We'll let the rest of you know as soon as we know."

"Thank you."

Nobody noticed that the man who had been a prisoner when the train left the depot was now as free as the others. And nobody noticed that all four had pistols in their hands, Santelli having taken Proxmire's weapon.

When the four men reached the dining car they saw the kitchen staff gathered around a man who had obviously been injured.

"What happened here?" Kelly asked.

"Some man came through and hit Pete over the head with his gun," a staff member answered.

Kelly smiled and looked at the others with him. "Looks like Parker left his calling card."

"The man who did this. Where did he go?" Santelli asked.

"As far as I know, he's dead, along with the engineer and fireman."

"He's dead? What do you mean he's dead? And what do you mean the fireman and the engineer are dead? What are you talking about?" Santelli exclaimed.

"Where you been, Mister? Didn't you notice the train come to a sudden stop?"

"Yes, of course I noticed it."

"Well, what do you think stopped it?"

"I would think the engineer."

"The engineer didn't have nothin' to do with it. The front end of this train is under about three hundred feet of snow. We been hit by an avalanche. We're stuck here."

Moving quickly to the front of the car, Santelli opened the door and discovered an impenetrable wall of white. "What the hell?" He slammed the door and turned around. "What happened?"

"What happened is the mountain collapsed on us. That's what happened. Like I told you, we're trapped here."

Chapter Sixteen

The sudden stop of the train jarred Matt, and he looked over toward Becky to see if she was all right. Fortunately, Becky's mother was sitting in the seat in a way that sufficiently braced her and the little girl, so the sudden stop caused no problem.

It had tumbled a sleeping Jenny out of her seat, though, and Matt hurried over to help her up. "Are you all right?"

"I'm fine," Jenny answered. "I wonder why we stopped so suddenly. You don't think we hit anything, do you?"

"No, I'm sure that the engineer must have seen something on the tracks ahead and brought the train to a stop. We weren't going very fast, so it was fairly easy to stop."

"What are they doing up there?" Senator Daniels asked, irritation in his voice clearly evident. "Is this some puerile stunt? I intend to find the conductor and give him a piece of my mind."

"Why would you pick on the conductor, dear? He wasn't driving the train," Millie said.

"No, but he is supposed to be in charge." Senator Daniels fumed in anger.

"Senator, I'm quite sure this is not some childish stunt," Matt said. "No doubt there is a perfectly good reason for the sudden stop."

"There may be a reason for the stop, but I guarantee you, it isn't a good reason," Daniels complained. "I simply must get to Red Cliff in time to prepare for my speech on Christmas Eve. Don't people realize a speech requires preparation?"

Luke sunk down several feet into the large bank of snow. Snow got into his ears, his eyes, and his nose, and he realized he couldn't breathe. Frightened that he might suffocate, he began to flail his arms about until he was able to open up a little pocket of air in front of his face. Still unable to breathe through his nose, he opened his mouth and took in a deep, gasping breath. The air that went into his lungs was so cold he felt a sharp pain in his chest, and for a moment he feared he might be having a heart attack.

Taking in the cold air with deep, painful gasps, he finally managed to work his way out of the snowbank and brush snow off his face. Opening his eyes, he saw a narrow gap right alongside the cars and pushed his way to it. Keeping his hand on the cars to steady himself, he stayed on that band of relatively clear path, hurried to the back of the train, and climbed up onto the vestibule.

Matt had just returned to his seat, when, unexpectedly, the rear door opened, and he felt a blast of frigid air. Looking toward the door he saw what appeared to be a snowman. He had to look a second time before he realized it was Luke Shardeen covered in snow and nearly frozen to death. His hands were still cuffed.

"Luke?" Matt asked, the tone of his voice mirroring his curiosity.

Luke moved away from the back door and stumbled into the car, his sudden and unexpected appearance startling all the other passengers. Without so much as a word to anyone, he moved quickly to the stove to warm himself.

Jenny was the next person to recognize the intruder under all the clinging snow. "Luke!" She hurried to him. As he shivered, she began brushing the snow away from him.

"What are you doing in this car?" Senator Daniels demanded. "You are getting snow over everything, and you are frightening the people."

"I'm . . . s-s-sorry," Luke stammered. He was shaking almost uncontrollably.

"Wait a minute! You are one of the prisoners, aren't you?" Daniels insisted when he saw the handcuffs. "What did you do, attempt to escape?"

Luke was still shaking too much to reply.

"Answer me!" Senator Daniels snapped sharply. "Did you attempt an escape?"

"Please, Senator, can't you see that he is nearly frozen to death?" Jenny asked.

"He's going to be worse than that when he is returned to custody. I'm going up to the next car, right now, and tell the deputy that his prisoner is back here." Daniels pointed to Luke. "I'll have you returned to his custody."

"You c-c-can't do that," Luke managed to say.

"And just what is going to keep me from doing it?"

Luke paused for a moment before he answered, this time managing to speak without stuttering. "You can't do it because Proxmire is dead."

"He's dead? Good heavens man, did you kill him?"

"No. Some men in the car were in league with Santelli. One of them, I expect, is responsible for getting the train stopped. The remaining three killed the deputy and set Santelli free."

"And you?"

"They were going to kill me as well," Luke answered. "But I jumped off the train into a deep snowbank and got away."

"I don't believe you," Senator Daniels uttered.

"I believe him," Jenny affirmed.

"Yes, I am sure someone like you would believe him," Daniels grumbled.

"I believe him, too," Matt agreed. "Hold your hands out, Luke. I'll get those cuffs off of you."

"You have a key?" Luke asked in surprise.

"Of sorts," Matt said with a smile as he held up his penknife.

"What?" Senator Daniels sputtered angrily. "What

are you doing? Don't you dare set this prisoner free! Why, I'll not allow you to do such thing!"

Ignoring the senator, Luke held his hands out. Opening the penknife Matt stuck it in where the handcuffs closed, wedging the ratchet down so he could pull the lock arm out. He did the same thing with the other side and within a moment, Luke was free.

"That's a good trick to know." Luke smiled as he rubbed his wrists. The severe shaking had stopped as the heat of the stove was beginning to take effect.

"What happened, Luke? Why did we stop, do you know?" Matt asked.

"Yes, I know. At least, I'm pretty sure I know. The entire front of the train is buried under snow."

"What do you mean *buried in snow*?" Senator Daniels snapped.

"I mean buried. You can't even see the engine or the tender."

"Will we be able to dig out?" Matt asked.

Luke shook his head. "I don't see how we can. It looks like the entire mountain came down on the engine; at least two hundred feet of snow. More than likely, the engineer and fireman are dead by now.

"Oh, my God! You mean we are trapped here?" Millie Daniels cried.

"Don't listen to a word this man says," Daniels prompted. "Can't you see he is merely trying to justify his escape? I don't believe we are trapped."

"Then why aren't we moving?" Purvis asked.

"I don't know. You'll have to ask the engineer why he stopped," Daniels answered.

Purvis stepped out of the car onto the vestibule, then leaned out so he could look toward the front. When he came back into the car, there was a look of shock on his face.

"It's too dark to tell, but I think Shardeen is right. It sort of looks like the whole front of the train is under snow."

"Oh! Then we *are* trapped!" Millie moaned.

"I wouldn't worry about it so much. I'm sure they will send another train up to get us," Senator Daniels informed her.

At that moment the porter came into the car, the expression on his face reflecting his concern.

"Porter, this man tells us that the front of the train is buried under an avalanche of snow," Daniels barked. "Is he correct?"

"Yes, sir, he is. And it's worse than that," the porter answered.

"What do you mean it is worse than that? How can it be worse?"

"This wasn't no accident," the porter said. "And the men that caused it are up in the dinin' car right now. They've taken it over."

"So they've taken over a car. What good is it going to do them if the train can't move?" Daniels asked pointedly.

"Well sir, that's where all the food is," the porter said.

"If they've got the dining car that means we are

likely to get awful hungry before this is over," Luke added.

"What's your name, porter?" Matt asked.

"My name is Julius, sir. Julius Kerry."

"Julius, do you know where the conductor is?"

"Yes, sir, he's in the car just ahead. His name is Mr. Bailey."

"Would you please tell Mr. Bailey to come back here?"

"I'm just the porter, sir," Julius replied. "I can't tell the conductor anything. I can ask, but that don't mean he'll come back here."

Daniels spoke quickly. "Tell him Senator Daniels has requested his presence. Do you understand that? Senator Daniels wants to speak with him."

"Yes, sir, I can do that." Julius left the car, then returned a moment later with the conductor.

Bailey approached Daniels. "Senator, Julius said that you wished to speak with me,"

"Mr. Bailey," Daniels jumped right in with his complaints. "I want you to know that I will hold the Denver and Pacific, and you, personally responsible should I be unable to fulfill my speaking engagement. Furthermore, I will also hold you responsible for any harm that may befall my family."

"I'm glad to see the welfare of your family is almost equal in concern to your speaking engagement," Matt said dryly.

"Of course it is," Senator Daniels answered, not perceiving the sarcasm.

"Is that why I was summoned back here?" Bailey questioned.

"It is indeed."

"Senator, I assure you, what happened here was entirely beyond our control, and certainly beyond my control."

"Really? Are you telling me you had no idea the pass could be blocked in with snow?"

"The latest telegraph information we had indicated the pass was clear," the conductor replied.

"Mr. Bailey, I'm glad you came back, because I would like to speak with you as well," Matt interrupted. "But I have no intention of making any accusations." He glared at Senator Daniels.

"Thank you, sir. What can I do for you?"

"It is our understanding that the engine is completely buried under a lot of snow. And that armed men have freed the prisoner Santelli and are now occupying the dining car."

"I'm afraid that is true, sir."

"How many are on this train?" Matt asked.

"When the train left Buena Vista we had forty people on board, counting the crew," the conductor said. "That is also counting the sheriff and his two prisoners. But the sheriff is dead, and I fear that the engineer and fireman are also dead. I don't know about Fred, Troy, and Pete."

"Who are they?"

"The three who work in the dining car. I haven't heard from any of them since the train stopped, and I am afraid they may be dead as well."

"That leaves thirty-seven people still aboard, but even if the dining car porters are still alive, no doubt they are being held by Santelli and the others so we may as well discount them. We must subtract the five bad guys, which leaves twenty-nine of us."

"That makes it twenty-nine to five," Daniels said, changing his tune. "We ought to prevail."

"Are you traveling with a gun, Senator?" Matt asked.

"A gun? No, of course not. What makes you think I would be traveling with a gun?" Daniels looked at Matt, perplexed.

"You can be sure all five of the men who took this train will have guns," Matt said. "That tilts the odds in their favor."

"Yes, if you put it like that, I suppose I can see what you mean." Once again, Daniels back-pedaled.

Matt took a count of the passengers in his car, all seven of them. In addition, the conductor and the porter Julius had come into the car. "There are nine in here, leaving twenty more in the other three cars. Mr. Bailey, do you know how many of the remaining passengers are men and how many are women?"

"We have three more woman passengers," Bailey said. "There are also six more children—four girls, the oldest about eleven and two boys, both about nine. The youngest child is about five."

Chapter Seventeen

Even as Matt and the others were discussing the situation, five of the remaining male passengers were huddled in the first passenger car, making plans of their own. Leading the discussion was Paul Clark, a deputy city marshal from Red Cliff. "I know these kind of men. I deal with them all the time. Basically they are cowards and get their way by bluffing. If we go into the dining car armed, like as not they won't even put up a fight. And if they do, we'll have the advantage of surprise."

"You can count on me," Dennis Dace said. "I was a sergeant in the army. I've fought Indians from Wyoming to the Dakotas."

"I'm in." Patterson was a teamster from Denver.

The other two men also agreed to be a part of the team. All five pulled their guns and checked the loads.

Clark looked back over the car at the other passengers, who were looking on with obvious anxiousness.

"You folks. I think you'd best go back to the next car. You'll be in less danger back there."

"What are you going to do?" one of the passengers asked.

"What's it look like we're goin' to do? We're going to take back the dining car. Unless you folks are ready to go hungry."

"There are at least four of them in there."

"And there are five of us," Clark replied. "Now, go on back into the next car. I wouldn't want any of you hurt when the shootin' starts."

Quickly, the passengers left the car.

Clark and Dace led the other three men out onto the vestibule between the passenger car and the dining car. Signaling them to stay low, Clark raised up to look in through the door window. The car was well lit inside, and he could see the four armed men sitting at one of the tables drinking coffee. The three dining car workers, easily identified because they were wearing white uniforms, were sitting at a table between the armed men and the front of the train, effectively being held prisoners. Because the front of the train was under snow, there was nowhere for them to go.

Inside the dining car, Santelli spoke quietly. "Boys, I think we are about to have a few visitors."

"What are you talking about?" Compton muttered.

"I just saw someone peek in through the window, then he ducked his head back down. I wouldn't be surprised if there weren't four or five men out there about to rush us. You'd better get ready."

Unaware he'd been seen, Clark turned to the other men with him. "All right. They are all sitting at a table at the other end of the car. None of them will be expecting us, so that gives us the advantage. Are you ready?"

"We're ready," Dace insisted. The other three men nodded, but said nothing.

"Let's go!" Clark shouted. Pushing the door open, he led the rush into the dining car.

"Here they come!" Santelli shouted, alerting the other three gunmen, and all four turned their guns toward the men coming through the doorway.

The attackers could only come through the door one at a time. Before they could even bring their guns to bear, Santelli and his men were shooting.

Clark went down first, then Patterson, then Dace. The last two men, who hadn't even made it into the car, withdrew quickly when they realized the attack had failed. One of them was nursing a wounded arm.

Compton and Morris started after them, but Santelli called them back. "Let 'em go! They can't do anything."

Outside they heard another rumbling sound.

"What's that?" Kelly called out in fright.

They felt the train shake as snow came down on

the dining car, but it stopped rather quickly, not covering the car completely.

"We'd better be careful about any more shooting," Santelli said. "I think that's what's causing all the snow to come down."

"Tell me, Santelli, how are we going to get out of here?" Kelly asked.

"What do you mean?"

"We was supposed to disconnect the engine from the rest of the train and take it on down the other side of the pass. We sure can't do that now, can we? I mean what with the engine under all that snow."

"We're all right here. We'll just wait it out."

"How are we goin' to do that?"

"Easy." Santelli made a waving motion with his hand, then smiled. "We've got food. They don't."

When Kelly realized what Santelli was saying, the expression on his face changed from one of concern to a broad smile. "Yeah. Yeah, that's right. We do have food, don't we?"

"But how long will it last?" Morris asked, a bit concerned.

"Quite a while, I expect. You know there is enough food to feed thirty or more people, and they always pack a bit extra. But there's only four of us that will be eatin' it. Yes, sir, we are in fine shape."

"What about the three men we just killed?" Kelly asked.

"What about them?" Santelli replied.

"I don't care to stay in this car with three dead men."

"That's no problem. Just push 'em off. The cold won't bother 'em none," Santelli added with an evil chuckle.

Matt learned of the aborted attack from one of the participants, a man named Turner. He had made his way to the last car.

"There was three of us that got killed." Turner had been shot in his left arm and was being attended to by Jenny, who had tied a bandage around the entry and exit wounds of the bullet. "Clark, he was the first one to go down. He was the one that talked the rest of us into doin' it. Then Dace went down, and after him, Patterson got kilt. Me 'n Simpson was still out on the vestibule, hadn't even made it into the dining car yet, but when them other three got shot, well, we turned and run off."

"Was Simpson hit?" Matt asked.

"No. He was just scared is all." Turner chuckled. "I was, too, to tell the truth."

"Well, there is certainly no need for shame," Senator Daniels said rather pompously. "To try and rescue the rest of us was a noble and brave thing."

"It might have been noble and brave, but it wasn't very smart." Matt let out a sigh.

"What do you mean it wasn't very smart?" Senator Daniels asked all in a huff. "What is your proposal? That we just sit here and do nothing while we starve to death?"

"I propose that, as much as possible, we do not shoot a gun nor incite them into shooting one. Any more shooting and the entire train could be buried under hundreds of feet of snow."

"Heavens!" Millie exclaimed. "We certainly don't want that!"

"Well, just what do you propose that we do?" Senator Daniels asked again.

"I think we should just sit tight. When the train doesn't reach the station in Big Rock, the station agent will telegraph back to Buena Vista, and they'll send another train after us."

"Yes"—Senator Daniels cheered up a bit—"I suppose that is true, isn't it? Unless . . ."

"Unless what?" Millie asked.

"Well, if the pass is buried under hundreds of feet of snow, the telegraph poles will be as well. They won't be able to get a telegram through. How will anyone know of our plight?"

"That's not a problem," the conductor said.

"What do you mean, it isn't a problem?" Once again Senator Daniels questioned what had just been said.

"We are used to lines being down for one reason or another," Bailey explained. "If they can't send a telegram directly through the pass to Buena Vista, they will send it where the wires are up. The telegram will be sent from station to station, going all the way around the pass, perhaps even as far as New York and back."

"To New York?" Millie repeated. "Oh, my, if it has to go that far it will take so long they'll never know about us."

Bailey chuckled. "How long do you think it takes to get a telegram signal to New York?"

"I don't know."

"As fast as you can blink an eye."

"He's right, Mrs. Douglas. It doesn't make any difference how far away it is, the telegraph signal gets there instantly. Why, a telegram can come all the way from London to New York, then by telegraph wire across the United States to San Francisco. It is so fast a message from London can reach San Francisco before it was even sent from London."

"What?" Millie gasped.

Luke smiled. "Well, maybe I am joking with you just a little. But you needn't worry if the telegraph has to go to other places before it reaches Buena Vista. Believe me, that won't slow it down."

Millie smiled. "Well then, we have nothing to worry about, do we?"

"Nothing at all, my dear," Senator Daniels said, putting on a brave front for his wife and daughter.

Up at the front of the train, the engine had withstood the avalanche. Don and Beans sat unharmed in the engine cab within what amounted to an air bubble. They'd been stuck there for several hours. Realizing they were beginning to run out of air, they were trying to decide their best course of action.

"You know what? I've got a shovel," Beans said. "There's no need to be trapped here like this. We can shovel our way out of here."

"Good idea," Don agreed.

Beans stepped to the edge of the steel plate between the tender and the engine and began shoveling. Within fifteen minutes his shovel hit something and he stopped. "I'll be damned."

"What is it?" Don stood and called out.

"It's a body. I think it's the fella that tried to stop us."

"He did more than try. He did stop us . . . but I don't think this was quite what he had in mind."

Chapter Eighteen

Sugarloaf Ranch—December 20

When Smoke woke up he got out of bed and looked through the window. "Woowee."

"What is it?" Sally asked groggily.

"We had some kind of snow last night. I'll bet we had at least twelve inches."

"Um, I'll bet it's pretty."

Smoke raised the window then scooped up a little snow from the windowsill. "You want to see how pretty it is?" He dropped the snow onto Sally's head.

"Smoke! Have you gone crazy?" Sally shouted, though her shout was ameliorated with laughter.

"Poor Duff, he must think we are having a big fight in here," Smoke said.

"We are."

"Then I think the least you could do is get up and see us off this morning."

"Ahh. That was the whole idea of dropping the snow on my head, wasn't it?"

"You don't have to fix breakfast. We'll get something in town. Maybe just some coffee and warm up a couple of the bear claws."

Sally got out of bed and dressed, and soon the house was permeated by the rich aroma of coffee and warm pastries. Sally joined the men at the table. "How are you going into town? With this snow, I don't think a buckboard would be a good idea."

"I was thinking we might hook up the sleigh," Smoke said.

"Yes," Duff agreed. "That's a good idea."

Warmed and full of coffee and bear claws, it took only a few minutes to get the horses in harness and attached to the sleigh. Then, wrapped in buffalo robes, and taking an extra robe for Matt when they met him, the two men started into town.

The horses quickly found their footing, and the runners of the sleigh made a swishing sound as they slid quickly and easily through the snow. Reaching the depot a little before six o'clock, Smoke and Duff went inside to warm themselves as they waited for the train.

"Smoke, are you here to catch the train?" Phil Wilson, the station agent asked.

"Hi, Phil. No, I'm here to meet a friend who is going to spend Christmas with Sally and me." Smoke introduced Duff.

"I hope it gets through."

"Why do you say that? Have you heard something?"

"No, I haven't heard anything. It's just that, if it snowed so hard here, what must it have done in the pass?"

"Why don't you send a telegram to Buena Vista and see if they have anything to report?"

"I was going to wait until six-thirty, and if the train didn't arrive, contact them then. But there's really no sense in waiting, is there?"

Smoke and Duff followed Phil back to the corner where the telegrapher had his office.

"Johnny, contact Buena Vista for me, would you? See if they have any information on the train."

Johnny nodded, then reached out to the telegraph key. He clicked out the code for BV, or Buena Vista. He tried it several times, then looked up at the men gathered anxiously around his desk.

"I'm not getting a response. Their line must be out."

"Can you go around?"

"Yes. I can go south to Del Norte, and they can go through Pueblo. Pueblo should be able to reach Buena Vista."

Johnny keyed the instrument again, then it was answered with a series of clacks. Smiling, Johnny sent his message. "It'll take a moment for them to forward the message on," he said, looking up from the telegraph key. "I made some coffee if you fellas would like some."

They were drinking coffee and talking when, a

few minutes later, the telegraph instrument started clacking.

Johnny held up his finger, then hurried to the key to respond. After that, the instrument emitted a long series of clicks while Johnny listened and recorded. When it was finished, he read the message to the others. "The train left the station at Buena Vista on time last night. It has not returned to the station, and we have no further word."

"How do you interpret that, Phil?" Smoke asked.

"If it didn't return, then I think it is probably still en route. Even if the snow didn't close the pass, there is no doubt it would slow it down quite a bit. I suspect they are still on the way, just that it is coming very, very slow. I wouldn't be surprised if it didn't get here until sometime around noon, or maybe even later than that."

"All right. We'll wait for it," Smoke said.

"Where will you be if I get any further word?" Phil asked.

"We'll be in Longmont's Saloon." Smoke turned at the door. "Oh, Phil, is it all right if I leave the team and sleigh here for a while?"

"Certainly it's all right," Phil replied. "Tell Louis I said hello."

"Will do."

Smoke and Duff started toward Longmont's saloon, which was four blocks away. They passed several business establishments where the owners or employees were out front, shoveling snow off the boardwalk. As a result, less than half of their walk was actually through the snow. One large, lumbering wagon pulled by four mules was the only traffic on the street. The snow was so high it was an impediment to the wagon's forward progress.

Longmont's was on the opposite side of the road, so Smoke and Duff had to make their way through the knee-deep snow, too. Once they gained the walk in front of the saloon, they stomped their feet on the shoveled boardwalk to get rid of the snow clinging to their boots and the lower part of their trousers. When they had sufficiently divested themselves of the snow, Smoke pushed on the solid doors that had replaced the batwings to keep the cold out and they went inside.

Longmont's was one of the nicest establishments of its kind. The place would have been at home in San Francisco, St. Louis, or New York. It had a long, polished mahogany bar, with a brass foot rail that Louis kept shining brightly. A cut-glass mirror hung behind the bar, and the artwork was truly art, not the garish nudes so prominent in saloons throughout the West. Longmont's collection included originals by Winslow Homer, George Catlin, and Thomas Moran.

Louis Longmont was in the bar alone, sitting at his usual table in a corner. He was a lean, hawk-faced man, with strong, slender hands, long fingers, and carefully manicured nails. He had jet-black hair and a black pencil-thin mustache. He always wore fine suits, white shirts, and the ubiquitous ascot. He wore low-heeled boots, and a nickel-plated pistol with ivory handles hung low in a tied-down holster on his right side. If anyone thought the gun was an affectation, he would be foolish to call him on it. Louis was snake-quick and a feared, deadly gun hand when pushed.

He had bought the saloon with winnings at poker, and could make a deck of cards do almost anything, but had never cheated at cards. Possessing a phenomenal memory, he could tell you the odds of filling any type of poker hand, and was an expert at the technique of card counting.

"Smoke, good morning," Louis called. "Ah, I see you brought Duff with you. What are you doing here so early? Not that I'm not pleased to see you, just a little surprised, is all. Especially on a day like today."

"We're meeting the Red Cliff Special."

"Really? You mean even with all the snow we had last night, there will still be a morning train?"

"Yes, well, that is the question, isn't it? We were just over at the depot and as far as we know, it is still on the way."

"My cook's on duty, if you'd like some breakfast," Louis suggested.

"Well, yeah, that's why we came in here. You didn't think we were going to start drinking this early, did you?" Smoke teased.

"I thought you came in here out of genuine friendship, just to visit me," Louis said, feigning hurt feelings.

Smoke laughed. "Did the cook make any biscuits this morning?"

"Of course she did. Can you really have breakfast without biscuits?"

As Smoke and Duff waited for their breakfast, they carried on a conversation with Louis Longmont.

Four blocks down the street, Bob Ward went into the depot, approached the stove, and stood there for a moment, warming himself.

"Have you come to catch the train, sir?" Phil asked.

Ward stared at him, but didn't answer.

"Because the train hasn't arrived, and may not arrive."

"Why not?"

"The mountain pass is blocked with snow. It may be that the train can't get through."

"It *may be* that it can't? Or it can't?"

"I don't know. It might get here, but if it does, it will be very late."

Ward nodded, then walked back outside and mounted his horse. He rode down to the far end of the street, to an area known as the red light district, where the seedier saloons were, and where women were available for a price. He dismounted in front of Hannah's—a step above the cribs and the girls in the saloons, it made no secret of being a brothel—and went inside. "Where the hell are they?" he asked a middle-aged woman sitting behind a counter.

"I beg your pardon?"

"The women. Where are they? Isn't this a whorehouse?"

"That's such a harsh word." The woman smiled. "I much prefer to say that we have ladies who will cater to your pleasure."

"Well?"

"Well, what?"

"The whores. Where are they?"

"Oh, I suspect most of them are sleeping. They do work nights, you know. And it is so cold and awful outside I'm quite sure nobody was expecting a client on a day like this."

"I'm a client. So, roust one of 'em up."

"Very well, sir. Which one?"

"Which one? How the hell do I know which one? I ain't never been here before. It don't make no never mind to me. Just choose one. Choose the one you like the best."

Hannah laughed a deep, throaty laugh. "Well, now, honey, I like men, not women . . . so I don't have a favorite. But they are all fine-looking ladies. I don't think you will be disappointed no matter who I select. Come to think of it, I think I saw Midge up a few minutes ago. Just a moment, and I'll find her for you."

On board the Red Cliff Special

Matt slept fitfully during the remainder of the cold night, but had fallen into a more sound sleep just before dawn. The sun streaming in through the window awakened him and he sat up, rubbed his eyes, and looked around the car.

Luke Shardeen and Jenny McCoy were on the front seat, asleep and cuddled together for warmth. Becky was asleep under Matt's coat, her head on her mother's lap. Mrs. Daniels was asleep with her head leaning against the window. Senator Daniels was snoring in the facing seat across from them.

Since stopping in the middle of the night, it was the first opportunity Matt had to actually see anything out the window. The snow had stopped, but it was piled up on the side of the train as high as the bottom of the windows.

He decided to see for himself how badly the front of the train was snowed in. Standing up, he stretched, then opened the back door, climbed up to the top, and looked forward. What he saw wasn't very reassuring. The front end of the train disappeared into a huge mountain of snow. They were fortunate the entire train had not been buried under the avalanche. Taking in everything around him, he realized they were totally locked in. Even if the engine had been clear, they go could not forward. And the snow was such that they could not go back down the track, either. That meant no rescue train would be able to come for them.

They were trapped at the top of the pass . . . under extraordinary circumstances.

It grew too cold for Matt to stay outside any longer. Once he was back inside the car, he saw that the coal supply for the heating stove was running low and realized that they would soon be facing a second danger. In addition to not having control of the food on board, they would soon run out of coal for the two stoves. When that happened, the temperature in the car would quickly drop below freezing.

That's just great, Matt thought. *It's not enough that we have no food; we are also facing a situation where we have no heat.* Matt picked up the half-full coal scuttle sitting beside the stove at the rear of the car and carried it up to the front where he set it beside the other scuttle.

"What are you doing?" Purvis asked.

"If we try and keep both stoves going, we are going to run out of coal in no time. I think it might be best if we just keep a fire going in one."

"Yeah," Purvis said. "I see what you mean."

The eight other people in the car moved to the front.

"Do you think they will send someone after us?" Millie Daniels asked after settling Becky back in her lap.

"I'm sure they will." Bailey took out his pocket watch, opened it, and examined it. "We were due in Big Rock over an hour ago. When they learn back in Pueblo that we haven't made it into Big Rock yet, why, they'll send a relief train after us."

Matt knew no train could get through, but didn't say anything, figuring it would be best if they thought help was coming.

Chapter Nineteen

Big Rock

When Smoke and Duff returned to the depot, Phil was talking to a customer, so Smoke waited for the conversation to finish.

But seeing him, Phil called out. "Hello, Smoke. I'm afraid there is still no word from the train."

"No word means they haven't gone back to Buena Vista, doesn't it?"

"Yes. If the train had gone back, we would have been informed by now."

"So what you are saying is that the train is still up there, possibly trapped in the pass so it can go neither forward nor backward."

"That's a possibility." Phil nodded his head.

"That's not good. If they are up there too long, they'll run out of food, won't they?"

"I wouldn't worry too much about anything like that happening. A couple winters ago we had a train get snowed in up on top of the pass, and it was a week late getting here," Phil said.

"A week without food?"

"It wasn't anything all that significant. These trains carry enough food with them so that, by rationing, they could survive for two weeks or longer. I've no doubt, within two weeks enough snow will melt and the train will be able to proceed, or at worst be relieved by a rescue train."

"All right, Phil, you've been through this before," Smoke said. "I guess the best thing Duff and I can do now, is go back to the ranch and wait it out."

"You may as well," Phil agreed.

Smoke walked over to the telegraph office, where Eddie sat in the corner, reading. "Eddie, when the train comes in, I want you to meet a man named Matt Jensen. Tell him to wait here for me, and I'll come get him." Smoke gave the boy a five-dollar bill. "Then, I want you to come tell me that he is here."

"Yes, sir, Mr. Jensen!" Eddie smiled broadly as he took the equivalent of a week's pay.

Down the street, Hannah brought one of her girls into the parlor. The girl was in her early twenties, but looked younger. It was early in the day and she had not yet painted her face and lips, nor had she donned the garish costume of her profession. The dissipation of the trade had not yet worked its evils on her, and she looked like any young woman you might see on the street or in a shop.

Ironically, Ward found that much more appealing than if she was in full garb. It made her look innocent, and he was aroused by the idea of taking a young girl's innocence. "How much?"

"It will be three dollars, sir," Hannah said.

"Three dollars?" Ward replied. "What do you mean? There ain't a place in Colorado where you can't get a whore for two dollars."

"This isn't just anywhere in Colorado. This is Hannah's," the owner said proudly. "If you want one of my ladies, it is going to cost you three dollars. If you think I am charging you too much, you might try one of the saloons."

Ward ran his hand through his thin, blond hair and looked at the girl. She had dark hair and large, brown eyes.

"How long can I stay?"

"You can stay all day if you want. At least, until we get busy tonight."

"Yeah? Well if I leave to go get somethin' to eat, can I come back?"

Hannah smiled at him. "Why would you have to leave to get something to eat? We have a kitchen."

Ward chuckled. "So, I can stay here all day and eat here besides? All for three dollars?"

"I told you, there is no other place in Colorado like Hannah's."

Ward took out three dollars, handing the bills to Hannah. "You've got yourself a deal."

"This way," the girl said, turning and walking away from him.

Returning to the sleigh, Smoke and Duff drove back to the ranch house. When they arrived at the house they were met by a smiling Sally, though the smile faded when she saw that Matt wasn't with them.

"The train never made it to Big Rock," Smoke explained. "Or, perhaps I should say the train hasn't arrived *yet.*"

"What happened to it?"

"It's probably hung up in the pass somewhere, blocked by snow . . . from coming through and maybe even from going back."

"Oh, my, Smoke! Do you mean those people are trapped up there?"

"It's not as bad as all that. Phil says this has happened before, and the train probably has enough food for them to survive."

"Probably? That doesn't sound all that good."

"We may be imagining the worst. The train may yet get here today. If it does, Eddie will come tell us."

"Oh, I certainly hope it gets here before Christmas." Sally looked out the window at the depth of snow.

"We have a few days yet. We'll just wait and see."

On board the Red Cliff Special

By late afternoon everyone was beginning to get hungry. One of the dining car porters came hustling into the rear car with a message for the conductor.

"Troy!" Bailey called out. "I thought you were trapped in the dining car!"

"Yes, sir, I was. But the men with guns let me go so I could bring a message."

"What is the message?"

"Don't be mad if I say a bad word in front of the ladies, but it's the message they told me to say."

"Go ahead," Matt said. "We know it's not your words."

"Yes, sir." Troy nodded and took a deep breath. "Here is the message. The men with guns say, send them the whore, and they'll let the rest of the folks on the train have some food."

"What?" Luke shouted angrily.

Troy drew back. "I tol', you, sir, that's not my words. That's the words of the men with guns."

"And that's what they said?" Bailey asked. "Send them the whore and they'll give food to the rest of the passengers?"

"Yes, sir, that's what they said all right."

"Just who is the whore they would be talking about?" Bailey asked.

"I don' know, Mr. Bailey. All I know is what they said."

"We all know who the whore is." Daniels looked directly at Jenny.

"Jarred!" Millie scolded.

"I'm just saying what everyone else knows," the

senator insisted. "They're talking about you, miss." He pointed to Jenny.

She was sitting in a seat with Luke. He put her arm around her, drawing her close to him.

"It's up to you now," Senator Daniels continued. "You could do something good with your life. If you go to them, we'll all get to eat."

"No," Jenny said in a quiet, frightened voice.

"What do you mean, *no*?" Daniels shouted. "Good Lord, woman, it's what you do! It's who you are! Instead of doing it for money for yourself, do it for others. For my wife and my little girl. It can't have escaped your notice that my daughter is sick. Perhaps all she needs is a little food. And you can make that possible. Is that asking too much? It isn't as if you are the total innocent in such things."

"You don't understand." Once more, Jenny tried to explain. "You have the wrong idea about me. I'm *not* a prostitute and I've *never been* a prostitute."

"Don't lie to us, woman. We all saw that sign back at the depot," Senator Daniels said sharply. He pointed toward the front of the train. "I am a sitting state senator, which makes me an officer of the state government. And as an officer of the state government, I am ordering you to go to those men . . . for the good of everyone on the train."

"I won't do it."

"Oh, yes, you will." The senator moved toward her.

Luke stood up and stepped in between Daniels and Jenny. "If you so much as touch her, I'll throw you off this train," Luke said in a cold, intense voice.

"What?" Daniels barked. "You, a jailbird, are threatening a state senator?"

"It's not a threat, Senator," Luke said calmly. "It's a promise."

"You, conductor!" Daniels looked toward Bailey. "You are in charge of this train. What are you going to do about this?"

Bailey looked at Luke, then back at Daniels. "Senator, I clearly am not in charge of this train at the moment. It has been taken over by armed brigands."

"What?" Daniels sputtered. He pointed at Bailey. "The Denver and Pacific is going to hear about this. We should never have left the station in the first place. Now we are trapped in the mountains for who knows how long, and armed men, which you allowed to board this train, have taken us all hostage. And you stand by and let this man threaten me, but do nothing about it. Yes, sir, the Denver and Pacific will most assuredly hear about this."

"Jarred, you are frightening Becky." Millie tugged on the senator's arm. "Please, calm down."

"How can I calm down when our very lives are at stake? And this . . . *harlot* has the means to save us all."

Matt had heard enough. "Senator, even if the girl did go to the dining car, do you think they would let her live?"

"I don't know," Senator Daniels ranted. "But that's the chance you take when you become a prostitute."

"I told you, I am not a prostitute!" Jenny screamed.

"Then what are you doing on this train, can

you tell me that? You were run out of town, were you not?"

Jenny didn't answer.

"I thought so."

The senator made a move toward her, but Luke stepped between them again, and with a vicious backhand blow, sent the senator reeling back. The blow cut the senator's lip and it began to bleed.

Daniels pulled a handkerchief from his pocket and held it over his lip, glaring at Luke. "Young man, you have just made a huge mistake. Whatever your sentence is, you have just added fifteen years to it for striking a government official."

"Oh, Luke!" Jenny said anxiously.

Luke smiled. "Well, Senator, if I'm going to get fifteen years just for hitting you one time, I might as well make it worth my while. If you don't go back to your seat, sit down, and shut up, I'll beat you to within an inch of your life."

"What?" The word was filled with fear.

"Jarred, for heaven's sake, get back over here and sit down," Millie ordered.

Senator Daniels pulled his handkerchief away from his lip, looked at the blood, then glared once more at Luke. He neither made a move toward Luke and Jenny, nor did he speak again. Instead he acquiesced to his wife's demand and returned to his seat.

Matt watched the drama play out before him, but made no move to interject himself into the situation when it was obvious Luke had things well in hand. When he saw Senator Daniels return to his seat, and Luke and Jenny sit back down, he knew it was over.

"Troy," Bailey said, "you can go back and tell the gentlemen who have taken this train that the young lady will not be joining them."

"Yes, sir," Troy answered. "That's exactly what I would tell them if I was goin' back to the diner car." He shook his head. "But I ain't goin' back."

"What do you mean you aren't going back?" Bailey asked. "Good Lord, man, don't you understand the situation? We have no food here. All the food is in the diner. At least you would get to eat."

"No sir, it wouldn't do me no good to go back. The men with the guns, they had themselves a fine breakfast and a fine lunch, but me 'n Fred 'n Pete, we didn't have nothin' to eat at all. And if it's all the same to you, I won't be goin' back."

"All right, you can stay here in the car with us," Bailey conceded.

"Mr. Bailey, you may have noticed that he and the porter are colored," Senator Daniels felt the need to point out.

Bailey made an exaggerated point of looking at Julius and Troy. Then he hit his forehead with the palm of his hand. "By golly, Senator, now that I look at them, I believe you are right. They *are* colored."

Matt and Luke laughed out loud.

"Are you ridiculing me?" Daniels snapped.

"No, Senator, you are ridiculing yourself. Of

course I know they are colored. What is your point?" Bailey frowned.

"My point is, they can't stay here in the car with us."

"Just where do you think the porters stay when the train is under way?"

"I don't know. I never see them until I need something done, and then they just sort of appear. I'm just saying it doesn't seem right that they are in the same car with us. But I suppose, if they stay to the back of the car, it would be all right."

"The back of the car is getting pretty cold," Matt said. "With only one stove going, just the front half of the car will be heated. These two men will stay in the front of the car with us."

Senator Daniels glared at Matt, then he sat back down.

Julius stood up then. "Thank you, Mr. Bailey, and thank you, sir, for speakin' up for us."

"It's only common decency," Matt replied. "No thanks are needed."

Chapter Twenty

"We ain't gettin' nowhere," Beans said, sitting down on the floor of the engine, breathing heavily. His body gleamed gold from the single kerosene lamp illuminating the inside of the cab, as well as from the exertion of digging through the snow. "We've dug a tunnel forty feet long or longer, and all I see is snow and more snow. Besides, workin' this hard we're just breathin' harder and usin' up more air."

"We don't have any choice." Don frowned. "We have to keep digging, no matter how far we have to go. If we don't get from under all this snow, we will eventually run out of air."

"You're right there. But I tell you true, I don't see how we are going to do it."

Don took the shovel for his turn at digging. Then he turned back toward Beans with a smile on his face. "Whoa, I just thought of something. We're digging in the wrong direction!" He pointed down. "We need to dig down to the ground."

"Why? What good would that do us? That would just put us under more snow, wouldn't it?"

"Not if we get under the train. We'll dig down to the ground, then crawl under the train all the way to the back."

"What if the whole train is under snow?" Beans questioned.

"We'll just pray that it isn't."

For most of the day, one stove had kept the front part of the car bearable, if not comfortable. But by nightfall it became much colder in the car, so cold that sheets of ice covered the inside of the windows. The situation was made worse by having to use as little coal as possible, in order to save fuel.

"The irony," Bailey pointed out, "is that there is enough fuel in the tender to keep every stove on the train going until summer."

"You can't get to it," Troy said, shaking his head. "The engine, tender, and the baggage car are all under a pile of snow as high as a mountain."

"We've got to do something, or it's going to get very, very cold in here."

Suddenly the back door opened and two men blew in. As Luke had been earlier, they were covered with snow.

"Don! Beans!" Bailey shouted excitedly. He went to the two men and embraced them happily.

"Who are these people?" Senator Daniels demanded.

"The engineer and the fireman," Troy explained. "Praise be the Lord, they ain't dead!"

Moving quickly to the stove, Don told the others about the man who had attempted to stop the train and how shooting the gun had brought the avalanche down. Matt reported the current predicament, how four armed men were holding the entire train hostage by occupying the dining car and commandeering the only food.

"Who are these men anyway?" Don asked. "Why did they stop the train?"

Luke explained it had all been planned as a means to free Michael Santelli.

"But it backfired on them," Bailey added.

"Actually, it backfired on all of us." Luke muttered glumly.

Buena Vista

Deckert stroked his chin as he read the telegram from the station agent in Big Rock.

TRAIN FROM BUENA VISTA NOT ARRIVED STOP
FOURTEEN HOURS OVERDUE STOP PHIL WILSON
STOP STATION AGENT BIG ROCK.

"Where do you think the train is?" Ticket Agent Garrison asked.

"Like as not it's stranded at the top of the pass."

"If they can't get through goin' forward, why don't they come back here and wait it out?"

"I don't know. Maybe they can't go either way." Deckert drummed his fingers on the desk.

"So, what are we going to do?"

"If we haven't heard anything by tomorrow morning, we'll send a relief train up after them."

"Good idea," Garrison said.

"I shouldn't have let them go."

"It's not your fault, Mr. Deckert. The conductor makes the decision as to whether or not to go . . . doesn't he?"

"Yes, and Mr. Bailey seemed hell-bent to go."

"Then it's not your fault."

"Yeah, that's what I keep telling myself."

"What about the people here in town? People who have relatives and such on the train?" Garrison asked. "When are you going to tell them?"

"I reckon I'll tell anyone who comes to ask about it. And no doubt it'll be in the newspaper soon enough."

"I'm sure glad I'm not up there." Garrison shook his head. "They might be there all the way through Christmas. I'd sure hate to spend Christmas stuck on the top of the pass."

"Ah, it won't be all that bad," Deckert pointed out. "They'll be warm enough, I reckon. I mean if they had to, there's enough coal in the tender to keep all the heating stoves going until next summer. And food enough for a week or two."

On board the train

Luke and Jenny were sitting together, as much for warmth as anything else. Suddenly, Luke stood up. "I'll be right back. I'm going into the next car for a moment."

"Luke, must you? What if those men are there? They tried to kill you, remember?"

"You heard the porter. They're in the diner. I'm sure they haven't come back into the train. When I jumped from the train, I left my coat up there. I'm going after it."

"All right, but please be careful."

"I will."

Luke glanced over toward Matt. He was sitting in a seat with his arms folded, staring at the stove as if by sheer willpower he could cause it to generate more heat. His coat was still spread over Becky.

Luke squatted down beside him. "I left my coat in the other car. I'm going after it. If Deputy Proxmire's coat is still there, I'll bring it back for you. I warn you, though, it may have some blood on it."

"A little blood won't matter," Matt said. "And thanks, I would appreciate that."

Luke left by the front door, crossed the vestibule, then stepped into the other car. He counted eight people in the car, and didn't see either coat. "Hey. Did any of you see the two coats that were left here?"

"That other fella, the one who was a prisoner with you?"

"You mean Santelli?"

"Yes. He come back and got both of them."

Luke noticed both stoves were still burning. "If I were you, I'd stop feeding this stove and just keep one of them going. That way your fuel will last longer."

"Good idea. What about food? Have you folks got any food back there?"

"None," Luke said.

"If them fellas don't let us have anything from the diner, we're goin' to get powerfully hungry," the passenger said.

Luke smiled and rubbed his stomach. "I'm already hungry."

"Yeah, I am, too."

"Ain't no need in worryin' about food," one of the others said. "We're likely to freeze to death before we starve to death."

Luke returned to the rear car and told Matt the coats were gone. "I'm sorry. It looks as if you and I are going to get pretty cold tonight."

Matt nodded. "I'm afraid so."

Luke returned to his seat beside Jenny, and Matt joined the engineer and the fireman close to the stove, fighting the urge to feed more coal into it.

"You know," Don said. "In a way, I'm almost glad this happened."

"What?" Beans asked, surprised by the comment. "What do you mean, you are glad this happened?"

Don chuckled. "I didn't say I was glad, I said I was *almost* glad."

"Why?"

"Tell me, Beans, when we are up there in the

engine, driving the train, do you ever think about the people we are hauling around the country?"

"Think about them?"

"Yeah, you know, wonder about them."

"I don't know as I have thought about them," Beans said. "Mostly the only thing I think about is keeping the steam up."

"Well, I think about things like that, too, but I'm always wondering about who is back here, and where they are going. Are we taking some soldier boy home to see his mama and daddy for the first time since he left home? Maybe some young woman is going to meet the man who's going to be her husband."

"Or maybe some folks goin' to see their grand-baby for the first time," Beans suggested.

Don smiled. "See, you do wonder about the people we carry."

"I reckon I do. It's just not somethin' I think about very much."

"So, here we are sittin' back here with 'em," Don said. "I've been drivin' a train for over twenty years, and this is the first time I've ever got to actually meet any of them."

"So, what do you think, Mr. Stevenson?" Matt asked. "I mean now that you have met some of the people."

"Some of 'em I like"—Don glanced over toward Senator Daniels—"and some of 'em, I don't like."

"But the little girl is sweet," Beans said. "Bless her heart, I hope she gets better."

"I'm surprised they haven't sent a rescue train after us," Don continued. "Come six o'clock tomorrow morning, we'll be twenty-four-hours overdue."

"Ha! What do you bet Doodle will be the engineer?" Beans asked.

"Oh, yeah, Doodle would love to be the one to come to the rescue. And to tell the truth, I'd love to see him pulling up behind us right now, for all that it'll give him a head bigger 'n a watermelon."

Abner Purvis couldn't sleep. He could hear the conversation going on by the stove, but that wasn't what was keeping him awake.

Purvis had told Matt he was going back home to the family farm just outside Red Cliff. What he hadn't told Matt was that his parents may not even let him back into the house. He had not written to his father to tell him he was coming back, because he was afraid his father would tell him he wasn't welcome.

Purvis had left home two years ago, to the great disappointment of his father, who had wanted and had planned for him to take a greater role in running the farm.

"Abner, someday, this will be yours, and your mother and I will live out the rest of our lives quietly and comfortably," his father had told him.

"If someday the farm is to be mine, how about just giving me enough money to get started on my own somewhere else? You can give my part of the farm to Aaron. He is more suited to it than I am, anyway."

Purvis's father had been very disappointed, but he borrowed a thousand dollars against the farm and gave it to Abner to go out into the world and make his mark.

Purvis invested the entire one thousand dollars in a gold mine claim, a claim that proved to be worthless. When all of his money was gone, he went through a series of jobs—mucking out stalls in a livery, emptying spittoons and mopping the floors of saloons, and tending pigs for a butcher.

Not once during the two years he was gone had Purvis ever written to his parents. They had no idea where he was, or if he was still alive. The longer he went without contacting them, the more difficult it became to reach out to them.

It was while he was tending pigs that he came to his senses. He had made a huge mistake in leaving the farm and the future his father had worked so hard to give him. He decided to go back home, confess to his father that he had been a fool, no longer worthy to be called his son, and beg to be allowed to return.

"I know that I have forfeited my right to any inheritance," he would say. "I ask only to be allowed to return and work as one of your hired hands."

Would his father take him back? That was the question keeping Purvis awake.

Chapter Twenty-one

December 21

The night had been long and cold, and Matt welcomed the sun. Bringing a little warmth with it had somewhat brightened his spirits. But it also ushered in another day without food. As Matt pondered the situation, he knew it was least ten more miles to the bottom of the pass and on in to Big Rock. Even if he could get through the mountain of snow, he couldn't attempt it without a coat. If he took his coat away from the little girl, she might die. His thoughts had come full circle, leaving him without a plan to improve the circumstances.

Troy had had a deck of cards in his pocket when he brought Santelli's message to Bailey. He'd started a card game the men, including Senator Daniels, had participated in at one time or another. The card game helped to pass the time. Facing another day with no food, another game was started while Jenny and Millie were engaged in conversation.

"My mother came to America from England. When the ship was halfway across the ocean it started taking on water. Fortunately, an empty cattle steamer was passing close by, and my mother's ship signaled they were in distress."

Jenny smiled. "And the captain of the cattle ship told the *Pomona* to launch the lifeboats and get as many women and children across as they could."

"The *Pomona*! Yes, that was the ship my mother was on! How do you know that?"

"My father was first officer on the *Western Trader*, the cattle ship that encountered the *Pomona* that day. I know the story, but only from my father's side. Please, do tell. I would like to hear the story from the other side."

Millie nodded and continued the story. "After all the women and children crossed, they sent across the older men, then finally the younger men and all the crew. All made it across safely, not one person was lost.

"The next day they could see the ship hanging at a list and within a few hours it went down. When my mother abandoned the *Pomona*, the only thing they let her take was a small handbag with thimble and scissors, a little money, and a few handkerchiefs. That was all she had when she first set foot in this country."

"What a wonderful story," Jenny said. "And what

a wonderful testimony to your mother's courage. You must be very proud of her."

"I am. And you should see her with Becky. Why, my mother thinks the sun rises and sets on this little girl. It would be awful if . . . if . . ." Millie's eyes pooled with tears.

Jenny reached out to take her hand. "I have a feeling Becky is going to be all right."

Wetmore, Colorado

Dewey Ferrell, Sheriff of Bent County, was in Custer County. He wasn't wearing a badge, and he was carrying a hood, ready to cover his face when necessary. Ferrell and Jeb Clayton were at the top of a long grade, waiting for the stagecoach. They could see the coach below them, still some distance away.

"He'll have to stop when he reaches the top of the grade, to give the horses a blow," Ferrell said. "That's when we'll hit them."

"How much money do you think he'll be carryin'?" Clayton asked.

"Judge Briggs said three thousand dollars would be in the strongbox."

Clayton smiled. "This is goin' to be a fine Christmas."

They could hear the driver's whistle and the occasional pop of his whip as the coach lumbered up the long grade.

"How much longer you plannin' on bein' the sheriff?" Clayton asked.

"What do you want to know for? You plannin' on runnin' against me?"

"No, I was just wonderin' is all."

"I got no plans on *not* bein' the sheriff. Things is workin' out just real good for me."

"Yeah." Clayton chuckled. "This has been real good for me, too. Only thing is, we got to be careful about how we spend our money, or folks is goin' to start wonderin' how we can do it on forty dollars a month. Well, forty for you. Thirty for me."

"No problem," Ferrell said. "We just need to go someplace like Denver, maybe even San Francisco, to spend it. That way, nobody will be the wiser."

On board the coach, Silas Cambridge took out a twist of tobacco and took a bite of it. He offered some to his shotgun guard, Jake Nugent.

"Thank you, no. I never took up the habit." Nugent broke down his double-barrel shotgun, checked the loads, then snapped it closed.

"You see somethin'?" Cambridge asked.

"Nothin' in particular. But the horses will be winded when we get to the top of this climb, and if someone is plannin' on hittin' us, that's more 'n likely where it'll be." Nugent set the shotgun down by his feet and pulled out his revolver to check it, too.

Dr. Grant, his wife, and three children were inside

the coach, wrapped up in buffalo robes against the bitter cold of the Colorado winter season. They were going to Yorkville, in Fremont County, to spend Christmas with Mrs. Grant's parents.

"Mama, will Grandma and Grandpa have Christmas presents for us?" Joey asked.

"I expect they will," Mrs. Grant said. "But don't you be asking for anything when we get there."

"I won't. But I wonder what it will be."

"Whatever it is, you will thank them for it."

"Yes, ma'am, I will."

The coach reached the top of the long grade, then it stopped. "Folks," Cambridge called down. "We're goin' to spend a few minutes here so the horses can rest up a bit. If you'd like, you can get out and walk around a bit."

"Mama, I want to go to the bathroom," Joey said.

"All right, as soon as we get out, you can go find a rock or a tree."

The entire family got out of the coach and the driver hopped down to check the harness on his team. Only Nugent stayed where he was, sitting up on the driver's box.

Joey hurried into the trees, then he saw two men tying off their horses. Forgetting the reason he was there, he started toward them to say hello.

"What about the passengers?" one of the men said. "Are we going to rob them, too?"

The other man chuckled. "Why not? As long as

we are robbin' the stage, we may as well get the whole hog."

Turning, Joey ran back to the coach, straight to his father. "Papa! Papa!" he said breathlessly. "There's two men in the woods, and they are going to rob us!"

"Whoa now, Joey," Dr. Grant caught him. "You aren't letting your imagination get away from you, are you?"

"No, Papa! I heard them. They said they were going to rob the stage and the passengers."

Nugent heard Joey and looked down toward the doctor and the others. "Dr. Grant, are you armed?"

"No, sir, I am not."

Nugent pulled his pistol, handed it down, and pointed to an outcropping of stones away from the trees. "Take your family over there behind those rocks and stay down. If anything goes wrong, use the gun."

"I'm not skilled with firearms," Dr. Grant advised.

"You don't have to be skilled. Just point it and pull the trigger. But let's hope you don't have to do that. Now, get over there fast before the robbers come up."

Dr. Grant nodded and shepherded his wife, whose face reflected her fear, and the three children to the relative safety of the rocks.

"Silas," Nugent called quietly from the box.

Cambridge looked up from the harness.

"Get over here on this side. Keep the team between you and the trees."

Cambridge, reading the seriousness in Nugent's voice, didn't waste time asking for clarification. He moved to the other side of the team as two men on horseback stepped out of the trees, their faces covered with hoods, their guns drawn.

"All right!" one called out as they approached the coach. "You know what this is. Put your hands up. Which one of you is the driver?"

"I am," Nugent answered before Cambridge could speak. Both men had their hands raised.

"Ha! Got your shotgun guard tending to your team, huh? Well, I reckon you're the boss and you can do that."

"I reckon so," Nugent replied.

"Call your passengers out."

"We ain't carryin' any passengers."

"What do you mean you aren't carrying any passengers? What kind of stagecoach makes a trip with no passengers?"

"A coach that carries only money and mail," Nugent disclosed.

"Good enough answer. All right. I want you to reach down and bring up the strongbox, then throw it down to us."

"I'll have to put my hands down to get to the box."

"Go ahead."

Nugent lowered his hands, then reached down toward his feet where the double-barrel shotgun lay. "Silas, where'd you put that box?"

"Don't you be giving them that box! Don't you dare give them that box!" Cambridge kept on shouting at the top of his voice, drawing the attention of both armed robbers.

That was exactly what Nugent wanted. The noise covered the cock of the shotgun and when he came up from the floor he fired off one barrel, then the other, and both would-be robbers were blasted out of their saddles.

Nugent jumped down from the driver's box and hurried over to them. "Doc! You'd better come take a look at these two."

"I want to see, too!" Joey shouted, running from behind the rocks.

"Joey! You get back here!" Mrs. Grant called.

The boy skidded to a stop and turned around. "Oh, Mama, why can't I see them? I've never seen anyone who was killed before."

"You just stay here," Mrs. Grant ordered.

Dr. Grant hurried over to the men and bent down to put his fingers on their necks to find the carotid pulse, though he could tell by looking at the massive wounds in their chests it wasn't necessary. When he didn't find a pulse in either, his suspicion was confirmed. "They're both dead."

Cambridge squatted down beside the two men and pulled their hoods off.

"I'll be damned! This is Sheriff Farrell from Bent County!"

"The sheriff? The sheriff was robbin' us?" Nugent sputtered in disbelief.

"Yes. That's sure some surprise, ain't it?"

"Maybe not as big a surprise as you might think," Dr. Grant replied.

"Why, what do you mean?"

"Back in Pueblo, a rancher there by the name of Luke Shardeen shot one of Ferrell's deputies. He made the claim the sheriff and his deputy had tried to rob him. Looks like he was telling the truth."

Chapter Twenty-two

On board the train

As the sun got lower that evening, the temperature in the car dropped again. Matt shivered, wondering how those who had no coat would get through the night. He looked down at the aisle for a second, and his eyes followed it all the way to the back of the car. He smiled. "Luke. I've got an idea."

Luke, who had been sitting with Jenny, came over to him. "I hope it's a good one."

Matt chuckled. "Yeah, so do I." He took out his penknife, opened it, then walked up to the front of the aisle and squatted down. He made a slice across the aisle carpet and pulled up the end.

"Help me pull up this carpet. We can make serapes out of it."

"Yes!" Luke said. "Yes, that *is* a good idea!

Bailey saw Matt and Luke pulling up the carpet. "Here! What are you doing? You can't do that! That carpet belongs to the Denver and Pacific!"

"We'll give it back when we are through with it," Matt said as he and Luke continued to pull up the carpet. When it was fully taken up, he cut it into long sections, then cut a hole in the middle of each section for a head to stick through.

The carpet made four serapes. He put his on first to demonstrate how to use it, then he gave one each to Luke, Julius and Troy. After a bit of good-natured teasing about how they looked, Matt walked over to the seat where the little girl was lying with her head on her mother's lap. "How is Becky doing?"

"Oh, Mr. Jensen," Millie apologized. "I'm so sorry you have to wear that."

"Don't worry about it. It's keeping me warm now. I just hope your daughter doesn't get too cold."

"I think that, with your coat, she is warm enough," Millie said. "In a way, I'm almost thankful she isn't feeling well. She has no appetite, so she isn't suffering from hunger the way the rest of us are."

"I'm sure it won't be too much longer before they send a relief train after us." Matt didn't believe that at all, but he thought it would be better to give her some hope.

"Yes. I'm sure you are right."

Conductor Bailey was also without an overcoat, so he maintained a position nearest the stove. With what heat the stove was putting out, Matt was reasonably sure he would be able to pass the night in relative comfort.

Chapter Twenty-three

Sugarloaf Ranch

That evening, Smoke, Duff, and Sally sat in the keeping room, drinking coffee, looking out at the snow-covered ground, and basking in the warmth of the fireplace.

"Tell me, Duff, how did you fare during the great die-up?" Smoke asked. The question referred to the winter of 1887–88, when an enormous blizzard resulted in the death of almost half the cattle in the Northwest.

"I've got a natural shelter on my place, and I had enough hay stored, so for the most part I came through it without too much difficulty. But some of the English ranchers didn't fare so well. It completely broke Moreton Frewen. How did you do?"

"I had been through a few killing blizzards before, so I was ready for it as well." Smoke pointed toward the barn. "I've got enough hay laid by now that if this condition lasts, I'll be able to feed my stock."

"That's smart of you." Duff took a swallow of his coffee and was quiet for a moment as he recalled that winter.

"On the day after the storm, I rode out with a neighboring rancher to cut his fences so his cattle could drift on to shelter. We found hundreds of them frozen to death and others whose tails had cracked and broken off like icicles. Och, I don't think I'd ever seen a sadder sight, or heard a more heartrending sound than the moaning of cattle freezing to death. With the ice and snow so deep, they couldn't get to food, so many died of starvation. All we could do was to cut the fences and let any still alive drift, for if they stayed in place, they would have died, too. Later, when the snow was gone, you could ride for miles and not get away from the sickening sight of dead cows."

"Heavens," Sally said with a shiver. "It's nearly Christmas. Can't we talk about something more pleasant? Duff, tell us about Christmas in Scotland."

"Oh 'twas a fine time we had in Scotland. I remember that m' mither used to make a Black Bun cake."

"What is it? Maybe I could make one," Sally said.

"Na, for you have to prepare for it, gather a lot of fruit. The cake is filled with fruit of all kind, almonds, spices, and"—Duff smiled—"being as we are Scottish, it had to have plenty of whisky." He gathered the tips of his fingers, then opened them up. "Sure 'n 'twas quite a delight to eat."

"What other traditions did you have? Other than food," Sally asked.

"We had the *Oidche Choinnle,* which means the Night of Candles," Duff explained. "We put candles in every window to light the way for the Holy Family on Christmas Eve.

"Ah, but there was one custom that's for the rancher," he added.

"You have a Christmas custom just for the rancher?" Smoke asked.

"Aye. 'Tis called the Christmas Bull. A cloud in the shape of a bull crosses the sky early on Christmas morning. If the bull is going east, 'twill be a good year. If it is going west, 'twill be a bad year."

"Christmas morning, we'll have to remember to look for the bull in the sky," Smoke said.

"If we'll even be able to see the sky on Christmas morning," Sally mumbled.

"Aye, that's the question," Duff agreed. "For 'tis been an evil sky for some days now."

"Where will Matt be Christmas morning?" Sally wondered. "With us? Or will he still be on that train?"

"Either way, he will be all right," Smoke said. "He's on a train, after all, not stranded in the mountains. It may not be his most pleasant Christmas, but at least he will be warm, and well fed."

Big Rock

Inside Hannah's, Bob Ward stood at a window, looking out into the dark. He had been there for one night and two days, virtually the only customer because the weather had kept others away. So far his stay had cost him nine dollars, but he had been provided with food and a warm bed.

The bed had come with companionship, Midge the first day and Dora the first night. At the moment, he was in Annie's room.

"Honey, if you're goin' to be stayin' tonight, it's goin' to cost you another three dollars."

"All right. But bring me up something to eat, would you?"

Annie smiled. "I will, honey. You can count on me."

Ward had no intention of spending another night there, but he led Annie to believe that, so he could get another meal. As soon as he ate, he would tell her he was broke, and ask her if she could extend him credit. He knew she wouldn't, and would kick him out, which was what he wanted.

He drummed his fingers on the windowsill and wondered if the rescue of his brother had gone as planned. They weren't all that close, but Ward knew without Santelli, he would never be able to find the money.

On board the train

During the long, dark night, Luke and Jenny found a way to deal with the cold. Jenny took off her coat, and opening it up, spread it across the two of them like a blanket. Luke did the same thing with his "serape," and the two snuggled together. The arrangement kept them warm, but Jenny knew some of the warmth was coming from within, her reaction to feeling Luke's body pressed up so closely against her own.

Why was she feeling this way? She had just met him the night before. She knew he had a ranch outside Pueblo, and had heard about his trial from some of the "guests" who had visited the Colorado Social Club. For the most part, people had spoken well of him. And to a man, they said the verdict was a miscarriage of justice.

As she sat there, warm in his arms, she allowed herself the fantasy of thinking what it might have been like if she had met him earlier. Would he have courted her?

She expanded the fantasy, picturing them having dinner together in a fine restaurant, or going to a concert or show together in the Pueblo Theater. They would take walks together in the summertime, and—

Cold reality set in. She had been working at a whorehouse, and though it was the dream of every woman who was on the line to have a "prince" come to her rescue, marry her, and take her out of "the life," it rarely happened. Jenny wasn't naive enough to think it would have happened to her, even if she had met him earlier.

For his part, Luke was lost in his own reflections. He smiled as he recalled how he had gone to the Social Club for the purpose of meeting Jenny. At the last minute he had backed out. And then he was convicted of something he didn't do. Santelli made a break, the train got stranded by an avalanche, and in the middle of the night, he was sitting close to the most beautiful woman he had ever seen. He smiled as he realized he may be the only one on the train who was actually enjoying the current situation.

Luke put his arm around her, ostensibly for warmth, and he pulled her very close to him.

Jenny wasn't sure when it happened, but the embrace grew beyond one of warmth and comfort. She was aware of his muscular body against hers, and she leaned into him, enjoying the contact. They stayed that way for a long moment, then Luke turned toward her. She could see his eyes shining in the soft light of the dimmed lanterns.

Jenny wasn't surprised when he kissed her, but she was surprised by her reaction to it. She felt a tingling in her lips that spread throughout her body, warming her blood. When they parted, she reached up to touch her lips and held her fingers there for a long moment.

Luke backed away a bit. "I'm sorry. I had no right to do that."

"I'm not sorry," Jenny said, surprising herself

with her boldness in word and deed, for she leaned into him, lifting her head toward his.

Luke kissed her again, deepening the kiss as he pulled her more tightly against him. Then, gently, he tugged her head back to break the kiss. She stared up at him with eyes filled with wonder, and as deep as her soul. Her lips were still parted from the kiss, and her cheeks flushed.

"Jenny, this is doing you a great disservice. I'm going to jail. This isn't going anywhere. It can't possibly go anywhere."

Jenny felt a ragged disconnect, having allowed herself to come this far, only to be pulled back. *No,* she wanted to shout. *Not now, don't stop.* But she knew he was right. There could be no future between them.

She leaned her head against his shoulder, and he lowered his head so it rested on hers.

"Jenny," he said quietly. "Have you ever heard of the Samoans?"

"The Samoans? No, I don't think so. What are the Samoans?"

"They are natives to some South Pacific Islands. They are a very interesting and friendly people, wonderfully athletic."

"You have been to islands in the South Pacific?"

"Oh, yes, I've been there many times. And among the Samoan culture, there is a saying that applies to us right now, that is, to you and me. The Samoans say there is no difference in the heart of a flower that lives but a single day, and the heart of a tree that lives for a thousand years."

"That's a beautiful saying."

"Do you know what it means?"

"Yes," Jenny replied. "For us, it means we should live in the moment."

"Exactly." Luke kissed her again. Opening his lips on hers, he pushed his tongue into her mouth.

Involuntarily a moan of passion began in her throat. The kiss went on, longer than she had ever imagined such a thing could last, and her head grew so light she abandoned all thought save this pleasure. Realizing she was totally powerless before him, she made herself subservient to his will, totally surrendering to him.

Then the kiss ended, and he pulled away from her. Only then did Jenny's own willpower return, and she gave a silent prayer of thankfulness that Luke had been strong enough for both of them.

December 22

Santelli, Compton, Morris, and Kelly were enjoying a morning breakfast of bacon and eggs, still holed up in the dining car.

"What are we going to do, Santelli?" Compton asked.

"What do you mean, what are we goin' to do? We're sittin' fine here. We've got all the food we can eat, we're warm and cozy, and all we have to do is wait until some of the snow melts."

"This here is startin' our third day," Compton complained. "And we're still sittin' on this train. There's so much snow piled up on the engine and tender that it ain't likely to melt until August."

"It doesn't have to get all the way melted, just enough for us to get out of here," Santelli said. "In the meantime, we'll just enjoy our stay. Like I said, with just the four of us, we have enough food to last for a month, if need be."

"You know damn well the railroad people ain't goin' to leave us up here for a month," Morris put it. "I wouldn't be surprised if they come here tomorrow."

"How are they goin' to get here?" Santelli asked.

"Why, they'll come up in another train, I reckon."

Santelli shook his head. "No, they won't. I climbed up on top of the car to have a look around, remember? There's damn near as much snow behind us as there is in front of us. Certainly enough to keep any rescue train from making it here for quite a while."

"So we're trapped here." Compton voiced what the rest were thinking.

"No, we aren't," Santelli replied. "We"—he pointed to himself, then took in the others with a circle of his fingers—"are the trappers. The passengers are the trappees."

The others laughed at Santelli's comment.

"I wish that whore had come up here," Morris said, rubbing himself. "Hell, if we had her up here, we could have us a fine time just waiting it out."

"She'll come soon." Santelli smirked.

"How do you know?"

Santelli cut open a biscuit and slid a piece of bacon between the two halves. "Because"—he took a bite—"she's goin' to get damn hungry." He smiled as he chewed, and a few crumbs tumbled from his lips.

"Look at them," Fred whispered to Pete from the other side of the dining car. "Sittin' there, eatin' in front of us without so much as givin' us a crumb."

"There's no sense in ponderin' over it, Fred. There ain't nothin' we can do about it." Pete's stomach grumbled. He and Fred had been forced to cook for Santelli and the others, but had been denied anything to eat.

"Yeah, there is," Fred declared.

"What?"

"I aim to cut me off a piece of that bread. I'll get some for you, too."

"Fred, no. Don't do it."

"I'm goin' to do it," Fred said, picking up a knife, then getting a loaf of bread out of the breadbox.

Kelly saw Fred cutting off a piece of bread and shouted, "Hey!"

"What is it?" Santelli asked.

Kelly pointed to Fred. "That guy is stealing our food!"

"You, put that back!" Santelli ordered.

"It's only a bit of bread. Please, we ain't had nothin' to eat for two days," Fred begged.

"Throw him out of the car," Santelli said easily.

"No, sir! I don' have no coat!"

"You should have thought of that before you started stealin' food." Santelli nodded at the other three, and they grabbed the porter and dragged him toward the door. He put up a fight until Kelly hit him hard on the head with the butt of his gun.

"Fred!" Pete shouted as his friend went limp.

Morris nodded to Pete. "Get the door open. We'll drag him out."

"No, sir, don't take 'im out there now. He'll mos' like freeze to death out there without no coat, and him bein' knocked out an' all."

"He shouldn't have been stealin' bread," Compton justified.

"For the Lord's sake, mister, what kind of people would do somethin' like that?" Pete asked.

"If you're so worried about him, go join him," Santelli said.

"No, sir, I—"

Santelli pointed his pistol at Pete. "I said, go join him."

Compton and Morris walked over to Pete. "Are you going to go on your own? Or do we need to send you out the same way we did your friend?"

"No need to hit me. I'll go, I'll go," Pete conceded. He walked over to the door, looked back at the evil smiles on the gunmen's faces, opened the door, and stepped out into the snow.

Finding Fred, he grabbed him by the legs and

dragged him through the snow, far away from the dining car and the eyes of the four gunman. "Fred! Fred!"

Pete leaned down to examine his friend more closely. Fred's eyes were open and he wasn't reacting in any way to the snow on his eyeballs. Pete put his ear to Fred's chest, but couldn't hear a heartbeat. "Fred!" he called again.

But Fred couldn't hear him, because Fred was dead.

CHAPTER TWENTY-FOUR

Pueblo

City Undertaker Joe Ponder walked into the sheriff's office as John McKenzie was pouring himself a cup of coffee. "Sheriff, I just got a couple bodies in I think will interest you. You might want to come take a look at them before I get them ready to send back to Bent County."

"All right, Joe." McKenzie poured the coffee back into the blue metal coffeepot, put on his coat, and trudged through the cold to the mortuary.

"Murder victims?" McKenzie asked as they walked.

"No, sir, not exactly. Leastwise, I don't think so. According to Nugent, he killed both of them while they were trying to hold up the stage yesterday. The driver backs him up."

They entered the mortuary, where two bodies lay covered by shrouds.

McKenzie nodded to the bodies. "Who are they, do you know?"

"Yes, sir, I know both of them. That's why I come to get you. I think you're goin' to be mighty interested when you see who they are." Ponder pulled the shrouds back. The massive wounds in the chests were the first thing Sheriff McKenzie saw. Then he looked up at their faces. The faces were without color or any animation, but he recognized them at once.

"It's Sheriff Ferrell!"

"Yes, and the other fella is his new deputy. His last name is Clayton, but I don't know his first name."

"And you say Nugent killed them while they were holding up the stagecoach?"

"Yes, sir. That's what Jake Nugent and Silas Cambridge both say."

"Damn. You know what that means? It means Luke Shardeen was more 'n likely telling the truth. I'll tell Mr. Murchison. He'll for sure want to file an appeal. And I'll send a telegram to the Sheriff of Eagle County, telling him to have Proxmire bring Luke back for the new trial."

"After you see what I found, you may not be able to hold a new trial here."

"Why not?"

"Because it's likely we won't have a judge who can hold the trial."

"What are you talking about, Joe?"

"Well, sir, I found somethin' in Ferrell's pocket you might want to see."

"What is it?

"I slipped it back in his pocket so you could see where it came from. Seth Campbell was with me, and he'll back me up that it came from Ferrell's pocket."

"Are you going to tell me? Or are you just going to keep gabbing?"

"I don't have to tell you. I'll show you." Ponder reached into Ferrell's shirt pocket and pulled out a folded piece of paper. There was blood on the paper, but it didn't prevent the message from being read.

Stagecoach from Wetmore to Yorkville will be carrying three thousand dollars in cash. After you do the job, I shall expect one thousand as my cut.

Briggs

"Ha!" McKenzie slapped the note against his open palm. "We've got 'im! I've thought all along that damn so-and-so was crooked."

On board the Red Cliff Special

Julius was standing near the stove when he heard something at the back door of the car. Looking around he saw someone looking in through the window. "It's Pete!" Julius scurried to the back door and jerked it open.

Pete was covered with snow and shaking uncontrollably. Julius pulled him inside and he and Troy knocked the snow off him. Julius pulled his serape off and draped it over Pete.

"Come on up closer to the stove," Julius invited,

pulling him toward the front. "It's not puttin' out much heat, but it'll help some."

"Pete, where's Fred?" Troy asked.

"He's outside," Pete said, barely able to speak. "He's lyin' in the snow alongside the car."

"We can't leave him out there," Bailey said. "He'll freeze to death."

"He's already dead," Pete said bluntly. "Those men kilt him 'cause he tried to break off a piece of bread for me 'n him."

Julius, who had given up his serape, began to shiver. Troy took his off and gave it to him. "Here, Julius, you wear this for a while, then when I get too cold, give it back, and we'll swap it back and forth."

"You can do that, or we'll make another one," Matt suggested.

"How are we going to make another one? There ain't no carpet left," Troy said.

Matt smiled. "Not in this car."

Matt and Troy went into the next car. There were eight people in this car, a man, two woman, and five children. The body of Deputy Proxmire was slumped in a window seat.

"What do you want?" the man asked anxiously.

"We want to take up the carpet so we can make some more serapes, like this." Matt indicated the one he was wearing. "We have some people in our car without coats."

"All right," the man answered.

Matt looked at the firebox and saw there was

even less coal than remained in his car. "It looks like you don't have much coal left."

"No, sir, we don't."

"What's your name?"

"The name is Webb, Edward Webb. This is my wife Clara."

"My name is Timmy," said a boy about nine. Two younger girls sat next to him, but neither of them spoke.

"The two shy ones are Emma and Molly," Webb said.

"My name is Jensen—"

"Yes, sir. You are Matt Jensen," Timmy interrupted. "I've read about you."

"Have you now?" Matt asked with a smile. "Well, Timmy, I'm glad you are reading, but don't believe everything you read about me. Those are mostly made-up stories."

"I know," Timmy said. "But they wouldn't make them up about you if some of it wasn't true."

"Maybe," Matt granted.

He turned to the other woman. A girl and a boy sat in the facing seat. "And you, Mrs. . . . ?"

"My name is Anita Lewis. This is my daughter Barbara, she's eleven, and my son Steven."

"I'm nine, just like Timmy," Steven explained.

"Except I'm a month older," Timmy said quickly.

"Mr. Webb, Mrs. Lewis, I think you should take your families and the rest of the coal back into our car. We'll be able to consolidate the coal and make it last longer for all of us."

"That's a good idea," Webb said.

"All right," Anita agreed.

"Mr. Jensen, do you think we will be stuck here through Christmas?" Barbara asked.

"I don't know." Matt smiled, trying to put a good face on the situation. "But if we are, we'll just make the best of it. Why, we can have our own Christmas party."

"How can you have a party without food?" Steven asked.

"We'll just figure out a way," Matt said.

After the Webb and Lewis families left, with Mr. Webb carrying the scuttle of coal, Matt and Troy took up the carpet, then they returned to the rear car.

"That was a good idea, inviting them—and their coal—to our car," Luke said.

"Well, I would have just invited the coal, but I didn't think they would go along with that," Matt said. Webb stared at Matt for a moment, then when he realized Matt was only teasing, he laughed out loud.

It was good to hear laughter.

"Mr. Jensen, do you suppose there's more coal in the other car?" Troy asked.

"There may be," Matt said. "And good for you for thinking about it. We'll also cut up that carpet and make more serapes. We can't do anything about food, but at least we won't freeze to death."

Pueblo

Prosecutor Lloyd Gilmore was on the telephone in his office, talking to the governor. "Yes, Governor. Yes, I'm absolutely sure of it. Yes, sir, the sheriff and defense attorney are here with me now. Thank you, Governor. I will tell them. Yes sir. We will take care of it."

Gilmore listened for a moment, then looked over at Sheriff McKenzie.

"The governor wants to know if we have heard anything else about the stranded train."

"Nothing from the train itself, but I believe they are putting together a rescue train to go up and relieve them," McKenzie said.

Gilmore repeated the information to the governor, then hung up the phone. "There won't be any need for another trial for Luke Shardeen, Tom. I am dropping all charges."

"Thank you, Lloyd," Murchison said. "I've known Luke Shardeen ever since he came here, and I know he is a good man. You are doing the right thing."

"What are we going to do about Briggs?" Sheriff McKenzie asked.

"It has already been done," Gilmore said. "Governor Waite has just removed him from office. He wants you to inform him."

McKenzie agreed. "That is something I will do with great pleasure."

"May I come as well, Sheriff?" Murchison asked. "I very much want to see this."

"Sure, come along if you want to."

Accompanied by Gilmore and Murchison, Sheriff McKenzie walked to the courthouse. Inside, they climbed the stairs to the second floor, and stepped into the judge's outer office, where they were greeted by Arnold Rittenhouse, the judge's secretary.

"Gentlemen," Rittenhouse said. "Do you have an appointment with His Honor?"

"No appointment is necessary for what I'm about to do," Sheriff McKenzie declared. "And there is nothing honorable about him."

"I don't understand." The expression on the secretary's face reflected his confusion.

"Just stay out of the way and watch. You'll understand soon enough." McKenzie started toward the door to the judge's chambers.

"No, Sheriff, you can't go in there!" Rittenhouse shouted.

McKenzie jerked the door open and walked in.

"Here, what is the meaning of this?" Judge Briggs shouted, holding his pants up with one hand, while a young woman from the Colorado Social Club was busy trying to rearrange her clothes.

"You'd better leave, miss," Sheriff McKenzie said.

"What? Who are you to tell her to leave? If anyone is going to leave it will be you and this . . . this entourage you have with you." Briggs pointed at McKenzie with his free hand. "Get out! Get out of here at once, or by damn I will hold you in contempt of court!"

"I already hold you in contempt, you sorry excuse for a man," McKenzie said angrily. "Amon Briggs, you have been removed from the bench by order of the Governor of the state of Colorado. And you are also under arrest for stagecoach robbery."

"Stagecoach robbery! Are you out of your mind?"

"Tell him, Mr. Gilmore," Sheriff McKenzie said.

"Mr. Briggs—"

"You will address me as Your Honor or Judge Briggs," Briggs continued angrily.

"You are lucky I'm even addressing you as mister. You have been removed from the bench, Mr. Briggs, and I am filing charges with the Attorney General of the State, charging you with collusion with Dewey Ferrell and Jebediah Clayton for the attempted robbery of the Wetmore to Yorkville stagecoach."

"What do you mean attempted robbery?"

"It means they tried to rob it, but were killed," Sheriff McKenzie answered.

"What does that have to do with me?"

"We found a note in Ferrell's pocket—a note from you, Briggs—telling him the coach would be carrying three thousand dollars, and demanding one third of the money," McKenzie advised.

The expression of anger and defiance on Brigg's face faded, quickly changing to one of fear.

"Stick out your hands, Briggs," McKenzie said. "I'm going to cuff you.

"No, please," Briggs pleaded. "Don't parade me in handcuffs in front of the people! I'll lose all their respect."

"Tell me, Mr. Briggs," Gilmore said. "What makes you think anyone respects you now?"

Chapter Twenty-five

Buena Vista

Everyone in town had heard that the train was trapped at the top of the pass. About a hundred people were in the depot, most out of concern and curiosity. Those who had relatives and loved ones on the train had the greatest concern. Although they knew Deckert had no more information than they did, being at the depot made them feel closer to the people on the train.

The Chaffee County Times had put out a special edition extra, and they sold more copies than ever before.

Red Cliff Special Trapped in Pass

Word has reached this newspaper that the Red Cliff Special, which left the Buena Vista Depot at nine o'clock *post meridiem* two days previous, is now sitting at the top, or near the top of Trout Creek Pass. It is the normal procedure for a train unable to proceed farther through the pass to retrace its path and return to the station last departed. That the train in question has not done so is a disquieting indication it is probably entrapped.

There are forty people on board the train, not excepting the crew of engineer, fireman, four porters, and the conductor. State Senator Jarred Daniels, his wife, and daughter are said to be among the passengers. So too is Deputy Sheriff Braxton Proxmire with two prisoners, the infamous Michael Santelli and Luke Shardeen, a local rancher.

That Shardeen is aboard is an irony, for while he was found guilty of manslaughter and sentenced to four years confinement, the charges against him have been dropped. Though Shardeen did kill Deputy Gates, his defense was that Gates and Sheriff Ferrell attempted to rob him. Sheriff Ferrell was subsequently killed while he was in the act of robbing a stagecoach. That incident has provided sufficient veracity to Shardeen's defense claim to warrant the dropping of all charges.

Hodge Deckert, the Buena Vista stationmaster, says a rescue train has been assembled and will leave today.

* * *

An engine, a tender, and two passenger cars sat on the tracks ready to rescue the passengers stuck at the summit. The weather was fair, though it was exceptionally cold. By the time Deckert was ready to dispatch the rescue train, considerably over half those who had come to bear witness to the rescue effort had given up and returned home.

Although railroad personnel were confident the special had enough food, the rescue train was carrying food, anyway. In addition, they rightly figured fuel for the heating stoves would just about be exhausted, so they were also carrying a lot of blankets. Additional fuel for the heating stoves was not taken as the passengers would be returning on the rescue train.

The Buena Vista Fire Company band played as the rescue train got ready to leave. Finally, with salutes from the locomotive whistle and waves from the train crew, the throttle was opened and, amid chugs and great puffs of gleaming white steam, the engine got under way.

The departing whistle of the train was heard in every house and business establishment in the entire town. Those who had given up waiting breathed a prayer of petition that the train would get through and all on board would be returned safely.

Deckert watched the train leave, then he went back into the depot and walked over to the telegraph operator. "Send a telegram to Big Rock. Tell them the rescue train just got under way."

"I can't go directly to Big Rock. I have to go around."

"Send it however you have to do it, but just do it," Deckert ordered.

Big Rock

The telegraph instrument at the railroad depot began clacking. The telegrapher responded, then smiled as he began writing the message on his work pad. When he was finished, he signed off and took the message to the station agent. "Mr. Wilson, this just came in."

BV RESCUE TRAIN TO REACH STRANDED TRAIN NOON STOP WILL UPDATE STOP DECKERT AGENT BV

Phil read the article then nodded. "This is good to know. I'm not really worried about those people up there; they have enough food to have a comfortable wait until they are rescued. But they are bound to be more comfortable and less apprehensive if they are back in Buena Vista, even though that may not be where they want to spend Christmas."

"Mr. Wilson, do you think I should take word out to Mr. Jensen?" Eddie asked.

"Yes, I think that would be a very good idea. I'm sure he would like to know what's going on."

"All right, I'll saddle up and go right away." Eddie smiled. "I probably won't be back until after dinner."

Phil knew that, by dinner, Eddie was referring

to the noon meal, and he chuckled. "You're going to hit Miss Sally up for dinner, are you?"

"Why not? You know anybody that's a better cook?"

On board the stalled train

With the bright sun reflecting off the snow and pouring in through the windows of the car, the temperature in the car had risen so that, even with the smallest of flames, the stove was able to keep the car comfortably warm.

"Folks, I suggest that we put the fire out for now," Matt advised.

"Now, just why would we want to do a thing like that?" Senator Daniels protested. "We are all starving to death, but at least we are warm."

"Think about it, Senator," Matt said. "With the bright sun out, we're getting some heat in the car without the stove. But tonight, when the temperature drops several degrees below zero, we will need the heat the stove can provide. We have to save fuel to be certain that we will have it at night, when we need it."

"We've got extra coal now, and my daughter is ill," Daniels whined. "I'll not have you make it worse by putting out the fire in that stove."

"We've got some extra coal, yes, but I don't know how many more days we will be here. It's best to be as conservative as we can."

"Jarred, you know he is right." Millie laid her hand on her husband's arm. "You know how cold these last two nights have been. It will be worth being without heat in the daytime, if we can keep warm at night."

"We aren't going to be here much longer. Maybe not even tonight. I'm absolutely convinced a rescue train will reach us today," Senator Daniels said stubbornly.

"I certainly hope you are right, Senator. But I don't think we should take that chance."

"I don't, either," Luke put in.

"And you can count me in with Mr. Jensen," Bailey said.

"Mr. Purvis, what about you?" Senator Daniels asked.

"I'm sorry, Senator, but I'm going to have to go along with Mr. Jensen on this one."

"I'm not going to let my daughter get cold and get worse."

"I'm not so cold, Daddy," Becky said in a weak voice.

"All right, all right." Senator Daniels threw his hands up in frustration. "It is obvious I am the only sane one here. But I can't stand up to all of you. Put out the fire."

The fire was extinguished, and within fifteen minutes, the temperature began to drop.

"I told you it was going to get cold in here," Senator Daniels complained.

"It will be much colder tonight," Matt said.

During the discussion a man had come in through the front door.

Troy noticed him first and pointed. "It's one of them! It's one of the men who took over the dining car."

"Troy is right. This one's name is Morris," Pete said.

Morris reached out and grabbed Timmy, who was standing the closest to him.

"Mama!" Timmy called, trying to twist out of Morris's grip.

"Timmy!"

Morris tightened his grip and held his pistol to the boy's head. "You ain't goin' nowhere, boy."

"What do you want, Morris?"

"We want the whore. Give us the whore, and we'll give you somethin' to eat."

"If she didn't go before, what makes you think she is going to go today?" Luke asked.

"Because it's been two whole days since any of you have had anything to eat," Morris pointed out unnecessarily. "And if the whore will just come along with me, why, we'll feed the whole train."

"How you goin' to do that?" Pete asked. "There ain't no cooks left."

"Oh, we'll let one of you boys do the cookin'," Morris offered.

"She's not going," Luke insisted.

"Wait a minute," Abner Purvis interrupted. "The other day, I was on the woman's side. I figured she shouldn't have to go if she didn't want to. But now I'm thinkin', why not? I mean, we all know this is what she does anyway. So why not go ahead and do it again? Especially if it will get her and all the rest of us something to eat. There's no tellin' how long we're goin' to be sittin' here. You know if the rescue train coulda got through, it woulda come for us yesterday."

"She's *not* going," Luke repeated.

"Let me make it a bit easier for you to decide," Morris said. "If the whore comes with me, you all eat, and the boy lives. If she don't come with me, none of you eat, and I'll kill her, and the boy, and go back by myself."

"Morris, what makes you think you're going back with or without her?" Matt asked quietly.

"What do you mean?"

"I mean the young lady isn't going anywhere, and neither are you."

"Are you blind? You do see that I'm holding a gun to this boy's head, don't you? Now, I'm going to count to three. And if the whore don't say she's goin' back with me by the time I get to three, I'm goin' to kill this boy."

"I'm warning you, Morris, don't do that."

"Ha! You're warnin' me? One, two . . ."

Morris glanced over toward Jenny, and that was all the opening Matt needed. He drew and fired in one lightning-fast motion. The bullet hit Morris just above his right eye, and dropping the pistol, he was slammed back against the front door of the car.

The four women in the car screamed in shock and surprise.

"Wow!" Timmy cried. "Steven, did you see that?"

"Are you crazy?" Senator Daniels shouted. "You could have killed the boy!"

"No," Edward Webb said. "Morris could have killed my son, and I believe he would have, if it hadn't been for Mr. Jensen. Mr. Jensen saved Timmy's life."

"Wow!" Timmy said again. "Wait until I tell all my friends!"

"What difference does it make?" Purvis asked. "We're all going to starve to death anyway."

"Purvis," Matt said. "We may get hungry, but we aren't going to starve. I once went ten days without eating, and I've heard of people going for as long as a month without eating. In order to survive, first we need heat, so we won't freeze to death. Next, we need water, and with all the snow, we have plenty of that. The least important for our immediate survival is food."

"That might not be the most important, but my feelin' is we're goin' to get awful hungry before too long," Purvis complained.

"I'm hungry now," Troy said.

"Like I said, I've been through this before. We will get through it," Matt promised. "As long as Santelli and the others stay in the dining car, they are more trapped than we are. We are the ones who are going to be rescued, not them. When the rescue team comes, Santelli and the men with him will go to jail, and they will hang."

"Troy," Julius said, starting toward Morris's body. "Come help me take out the trash."

Chapter Twenty-six

Sugarloaf

"It's been two days. Do you think the train will get in before Christmas?" Sally asked as she took two dried-apple pies from the oven. "Because, if it doesn't I'm going to have a lot of extra food to get rid of."

"Oh, I'm sure the train will get here before Christmas. But even if it doesn't, you don't have to worry about getting rid of the extra food. Duff and I can take care of that for you. And we may as well start by having a piece of pie." Smoke picked up a knife and started toward one of the pies.

"Absolutely not!" Sally said authoritatively. "The pies haven't even cooled yet."

There was a knock on the door, and Smoke smiled. "I'll bet that's Eddie telling me the train got there and Matt is waiting at the station."

Smoke hurried to the door and opened it. "So, Matt's here, is he? What time did the train get in?"

"No, sir, he ain't here and the train ain't got in," Eddie said. "And it ain't goin' to get in."

"What do you mean, it isn't going to get in?"

"They've done sent a rescue train for it. They'll be takin' ever'one back down the mountain to Buena Vista."

"Oh," Sally whispered. "That means Matt for sure won't be here for Christmas."

"No, it doesn't seem likely that he will," Smoke said, disappointment in his voice. "But at least, if the rescue train takes them back to Buena Vista, he won't have to spend Christmas Day trapped in the snow on the top of the mountain."

"Eddie, it is nearly lunchtime. Won't you stay and eat with us before you start back?" Sally invited.

"Yes, ma'am!" Eddie replied enthusiastically. "And thank you, ma'am."

The table was laden with food; roast beef and gravy, mashed potatoes, stewed carrots, and green beans Sally had canned. She had also made a loaf of bread, which disappeared quickly. For dessert they had hot apple pie, over which had been put a piece of melted cheese. Sally had prepared a much larger meal than normal, partly in anticipation of Matt's presence. The meal did not go to waste, though, as the two men and Eddie showed their appreciation by eating second helpings of everything.

"Well, I'd better be getting back," Eddie said after he finally pushed away from the table.

"I appreciate you coming out here to tell us about the train," Smoke said.

"Yes, sir, well I thought you might want to know."

"You will come tell us if you get any more word about the train, won't you?"

"Yes, sir, you can count on that."

"Eddie, would you like to take a bear claw along with you to eat on your ride back?" Sally asked.

"Oh, I don't know. I ate so much, I hate to take anything else."

"Well, I can understand if you are too full."

A broad smile spread across Eddie's face. "Only, I've near 'bout always got room for another bear claw."

"I swear, Sally, I'd hate to see this boy and Cal in an eating contest," Smoke said. "I don't know who would win, but they'd likely run us out of food trying to determine a winner."

Duff and Sally laughed, then Smoke walked outside to see Eddie off.

"It is cold out there." Smoke came back in, clapping his hands together. "And it is getting colder. No telling how cold it is up at the top of the pass."

"Oh, those poor people," Sally moaned. "I wonder how much longer they'll have to stay up there."

On board the rescue train

Doodle Reynolds, the engineer of the rescue train, moved the Johnson Bar and the train came to a stop.

"What is it, Doodle? What'd you stop for?" the fireman asked.

"Look up ahead of us, Greg, and tell me what you think."

The fireman leaned out the window and looked ahead. His gaze carried along the side of the engine, the brass work, the green paint of the boiler, then past the snowplow attached to the front. Fifty yards ahead of the train was a pile of snow across the tracks as high as the engine itself.

"Jehoshaphat, Doodle! I don't think we could even make a dent in that. How far up the track do you think it goes?"

"I don't know." Doodle put the train in reverse. "But I don't plan to get a second train stuck up here."

"I hate we can't get them out."

"They aren't in any trouble yet," Doodle said. "They probably have enough food to last a couple weeks, anyway. For sure by that time, they'll either be able to leave, or the snow will be melted enough that we'll be able to get through to them."

"The folks back in town are goin' to be mighty disappointed."

"No more disappointed than I am." Doodle laughed. "I would love to come to the rescue, just so I could lord it over my brother-in-law for a while."

"That's right. Don is your brother-in-law, isn't he?"

"Yeah, he didn't have any more sense than to marry my sister."

"She's going to be upset and some worried, I reckon," Greg said.

"I reckon so."

The train beat its way back down the track toward Buena Vista, leaving behind an impenetrable wall of snow and the Red Cliff Special.

On board the train

Every passenger on the train, plus the crew, were now gathered in the last car, making it very crowded, but Matt was convinced they had enough fuel to last for a while. He'd already decided wood pieces from the car would have to be the next fuel supply. Of course, he would dismantle the car ahead.

Again, some of the men were playing cards. Bailey was napping, the three porters were talking together, the five active children—Becky remained on her mother's lap—had found a game to play, Ed Webb and his wife were sitting quietly, while Senator Daniels sat in the seat facing his wife and daughter. The scowl had not left his face. Luke and Jenny were cuddled together in the front seat, and looking at them, Matt smiled. He could almost believe they were enjoying the situation.

Matt was still smiling as he looked out the window, then the smile left his face, replaced by an expression of surprise and hope. Alongside the car, in the area right by the track, was a coyote, probably looking for food and to get out of the snow.

He pulled his pistol and started to raise the window, thinking to shoot the coyote, but changed his mind. A gunshot outside the car might bring down more snow. He quickly devised a plan and looked back into the car. He was going to need help, and had to figure out which of his fellow passengers would most likely be able to help him.

Looking over everyone, he decided and called, "Julius. Julius, come here."

"Yes, sir?"

"Look out the window, right down there," Matt said, pointing.

"It's a coyote."

"No it's not. It's a small deer."

"Mr. Jensen, you done gone crazy from not eatin'? That ain't no deer. That's a coyote."

"Shh," Matt hushed. "Once when I was very hungry, I barbecued a coyote, and it tasted like deer meat. As far as these folks are concerned, it's a small deer, and by the time they see it, they won't be able to tell the difference."

"You goin' to shoot it?"

Matt shook his head. "I'm afraid if I shoot, it might bring down a lot more snow. I've got another idea, but I'm going to need your help."

"Yes, sir," Julius said enthusiastically. "I'll do whatever I can to help."

"I'm going out on the back vestibule. You go out on the front. Then I want you to chase the coyote toward me."

"Yes, sir, but what if the coyote runs under the car?"

"Let's just pray that he doesn't," Matt said.

"Yes, sir. I'm a prayin' man, sir."

"Good. We better get started."

"Yes, sir," Julius said again.

Matt went out onto the back vestibule, then leaned around just far enough to see the coyote. It was still there, sniffing around. He pulled out his pocketknife and flipped it open

Julius climbed down from the vestibule at the front end of the car and slowly walked toward the coyote. Matt watched and, as he had hoped and planned, the coyote started in his direction.

Matt moved to the edge of the vestibule, then, timing his jump, leaped off, landing in a belly flop into the snow. That he was successful was evidenced by the fact that he could feel the coyote under him. The coyote was moving rapidly, squirming around trying to get free, and Matt knew he had to be very careful that it not get away.

Carefully, Matt lifted his body just far enough to reach his hand under, grab the coyote by the back of the neck, and cut its throat. He lay on the creature until it stopped moving.

"Praise the Lord, Mr. Jensen! You got 'im!" Julius shouted.

Still holding the coyote, Matt rolled under the car to prevent anyone inside from seeing what he was doing, then he cut off the head and legs, and skinned it. When he rolled back out from under the car, he was holding an unidentifiable carcass.

Julius carried the carcass into the car and held it up. "Mr. Jensen kilt him a small deer!" he shouted, to the joy of the others in the car.

"How big is the small deer?" Don asked.

"He's about this big," Julius said, demonstrating with his hands.

"Oh, my, that is rather small, isn't it?" Clara asked.

"Yes, ma'am, I reckon it is. But we're goin' to cook him up and ever'one is goin' to get some of it."

"I hate to deflate everyone's joy," Senator Daniels said. "But there are thirty of us. How is a deer that small going to feed all of us?"

"We're going to make a soup," Matt said, coming into the car just in time to hear the Senator's question. "And we aren't going to waste any of it."

"It's going to be an awfully thin soup," Senator Daniels complained.

Matt smiled. "Trust me, it'll be the best thing you've ever eaten."

"It won't be all that good," Bailey said. "We don't have any vegetables. We don't even have any salt."

"Oh, yes, we have salt." Matt smiled. "I learned from an old mountain man friend of mine to never be without salt." He pulled a little cloth bag from his pocket.

"And I've got some pepper I brought from the diner," Pete offered.

"All we have to do now is gather up some snow, melt some water, and start cooking.

"What are we going to cook it in?" Purvis asked.

Bailey smiled. "I have the perfect stew pot for it. There is a brand-new chamber pot in the toilet that hasn't even been put out yet, so it hasn't been used. It'll be just right to cook this in."

"A chamber pot? We are going to make soup in a spittoon?" Barbara Lewis made a face.

"Trust me, it hasn't been used, not one time," Bailey said. "It'll make a fine pot for cooking."

"It'll be all right, honey," Anita said to her daughter. "Why, if it's never been used, what is the difference between it and a stew pot?"

"I guess nothing." Barbara looked at her brother and Timmy. "But don't either of you dare ever tell anyone we cooked soup in a chamber pot and actually ate it," she demanded.

"Why not?" Steven replied. "I think it's funny."

"Oooh!" Barbara thumped her thigh in frustration.

"They aren't going to tell anyone, are you, boys?" Matt looked the boys straight in the eyes.

"All right," Timmy agreed. "We won't ever tell anyone."

"All right, so we can cook," Purvis said. "But how are we going to eat it? We don't have bowls or spoons."

"I have a knife, a spoon, and a collapsible cup," Matt said. "We'll pass the cup around, and eat one at a time. The children will go first."

Using his penknife, Matt began to cut up the carcass.

Troy also had a knife, so he went to the back to help. He started to make a cut, then looked up at Matt with a questioning expression on his face. "Mr. Jensen, I have to tell you, this don't look like no deer I done ever seen before."

"You don't say."

"It looks more like a dog."

"In some cultures, dog is a delicacy."

"But this ain't no dog, is it?"

"No."

"What is it? A wolf? A fox? A coyote?"

"You've heard of mule deer, haven't you, Troy?"

"Yes, sir, but I know this ain't no mule deer."

"It's a coyote deer."

Troy laughed. "We ain't goin' be tellin' the others this, are we?"

"No."

Troy laughed again. "I expect this will be the best coyote deer I done ever ate."

While Troy was cutting up the rest of the carcass, Matt went back up to the front of the car. "You men, go outside and start gathering snow. Use your hats. Oh, and stay behind the train as much as you can, there's less chance Santelli and the others will see you that way."

"I want to help, too," Timmy declared.

"Me, too," Steven added.

"If it's all right with your parents, it's all right with me," Matt said.

"Are you sure they won't get in the way?" Ed Webb asked.

Luke smiled at the two boys. "I think they would be a great help, Why, I wasn't much older than these two boys when I went to sea for the first time."

"All right, Timmy, you can go with them."

"Mama?" Steven asked.

"Go ahead," Mrs. Lewis said.

"Miss McCoy, if you would, please get the fire going a little hotter, at least hot enough to boil water," Matt asked.

"All right," Jenny agreed.

"I'll help you," Mrs. Lewis offered.

An hour later, the entire car was permeated with the enticing aroma of the soup.

"When will it be ready?" Timmy asked. "I'm really hungry."

"Soon, I think," Matt said.

"Matt, I have a suggestion," Luke said. "It's something we did a few times on board ship when our rations were running low."

"I'm open to any suggestion," Matt said.

"For the first time, we'll just have the broth. It will be nourishing enough to maybe take some of the edge off. Then we can put more water in, cook it a second time, maybe even three times before we eat up all the meat."

"That's a good idea."

"You know somethin'? What is happenin' to us now, has all come right out of the Bible," Troy pointed out.

"What do you mean, it's all come out of the Bible?" Daniels asked. "I don't remember reading anything about a trapped train in the Bible."

"Well, 'cause there weren't no trains then. But the rest of it." Troy quoted, "'*For I was hungry, and you gave me food.*' Well, ain't that what Mr. Jensen has just done? Provide us with food? *'I was thirsty, and you gave me drink.'* That's what all the snow is, givin' us water to drink. *'I was a stranger, and you took me in.'* That's me 'n Pete and Mr. Stevenson and Mr. Evans. We was strangers, out in the cold, but you good folks took us in. *'I was naked, and you clothed me'.*" Troy put his thumbs behind the serape and held it out. "That's what this here thing is. *'I was sick, and you visited me.'* That's the sweet little girl that's lyin' over there now. She is some awful sick, but we done ever' one of us took her into our hearts. *'I was in prison, and you came to me.'* Well, ain't we all sort of in prison now, I mean, what with bein' trapped in this car and all? So that last one, the part about bein' in prison, is for all of us. Yes, sir, ever'thing Jesus said in that parable just fits us."

"What parable is that, Troy?" Beans asked.

"That's from the twenty-fifth chapter of Matthew, Mr. Evans. It's the Parable of the Sheep and the Goats."

"Troy, how come you know that?" Julius asked.

"I thought I told you, Julius. My daddy is a preacher man."

"No, you ain't never done told me that. If you know all that stuff, how come you ain't never become a preacher man your own self?"

"My daddy is a godly man," Troy said. "I don't reckon I ever met a man who is finer 'n my daddy. But I ain't never been nowhere near as good a man as he is. I've done lots of things that ain't nowhere near godly. I just don't figure I'm fit to be a preacher man."

"Maybe being here like this is some kind of test for you," Don suggested.

"I don't mind Troy being tested," Pete said. "Only if he's the one bein' tested, how come the rest of us has to be with him?"

The others laughed, and it was the first good, deep laugh any of them had had since the ordeal began.

Chapter Twenty-seven

"If you ask me, Morris has done got hisself kilt, just as sure as a gun is iron." Kelly sat in the dining car with Santelli and Compton. "Otherwise, he'd be back here by now."

"More 'n likely," Santelli agreed.

"What if they come into this car after us?"

"They tried it once before, remember?" Santelli pointed out. "I don't think they're likely to try it again. The only way they can get into the car is through that door, and they can only come through the door one at a time.

"You know what?" Compton interjected. "We're goin' to run out of coal pretty soon. We won't have enough to cook our food or heat the car."

"No problem, just go into the next car and take whatever coal they have," Santelli suggested.

"Yeah, good idea." Compton stepped out onto the vestibule, pulled his pistol, then moved on into the car immediately behind the diner. Except for the bodies of the three men who had attempted to take back the diner, the car was completely empty.

Compton checked the stove and saw that the coal scuttle was empty. Walking through that car he looked into the next one, and it was empty as well, and was also missing a coal scuttle. As soon as he stepped onto the vestibule leading to the last car he heard laughter.

He frowned. Laughter? What did they have to laugh about?

Then he smelled the aroma of something being cooked. What could they be cooking?

Compton hurried back to the diner.

"Where's the coal?" Santelli growled out as soon as Compton entered.

"There ain't no coal in either of the next three cars," Compton answered. "There ain't no people there, either."

"What do you mean, there aren't any people? What happened to them?"

"They've all moved into the last car. And I figure they must've took their coal with them."

"Damn."

"And I'll tell you somethin' else. They're cookin' somethin'."

"What do you mean, they are cooking something? What have they got to cook?"

"I don't know, but I could smell it as soon as I got to the door. And the way they are laughing, you'd think they're having a party."

"Well, why don't we just go stop their party?" Kelly suggested.

"You really want to do that?" Santelli asked. "Morris ain't come back. Besides, Matt Jensen is with them."

"Are we not going to do anything?" Kelly asked in a huff.

"Why? Whatever food they have, it can't be much. And they have a lot of people to feed. We've got all the food we can eat for two weeks if necessary. As long as nobody does something foolish, things are fine just as they are."

Becky was the first person to be fed, and because it was a clear broth she was able to take it. She didn't take a full cup, but she took a little, and Matt was sure it would be good for her.

Timmy was offered the next cup. "I think my sisters and Barbara should get it before me and Steven. They're girls."

"Good for you, Timmy," Matt said with a smile. "And you are right, they should be next."

After the children took the cup, it went to the women, then to the men. When Troy started to drink it, Senator Daniels protested. "Are those colored men going to drink from the same cup as we?"

"Do you see any other cup?" Matt asked impatiently.

"That isn't right," Senator Daniels said adamantly. "I mean having a colored man drink from the same cup as whites." He shook his head. "No, sir, I won't share a cup with a colored person."

"All right, Senator Daniels, have it your way," Matt said.

Troy hadn't taken a swallow yet, and upon hearing Matt's comment, he looked up questioningly.

"What are you waiting on, Troy? Go ahead."

"Wait a minute!" Senator Daniels exclaimed. "I thought you said to have it my own way."

"I did say that," Matt replied calmly. "You said you won't share a cup with a colored person, so I'm not going to ask you take any of the soup. Which is fine, it'll just mean more for the rest of us."

"What? That's not what I meant."

"It's up to you, Daniels," Matt maintained, specifically omitting the title. "You can either share the cup with Troy, Julius, Pete, and the rest of us, or you can choose not to take the cup at all. Which will it be?"

"I'll, uh, I'll take the cup," Senator Daniels muttered.

"Yeah, I rather thought you might."

By the time they settled for the night, the coyote had been fully consumed. Nobody had a full stomach, but neither was hunger gnawing at them as much as it had the day before.

"Matt, I think we should post a watch tonight," Luke suggested as they sat in the darkened car. "Like we have onboard ship. There are enough of us that it won't require anyone to stay awake for too long."

Matt agreed. "Since we have all the coal now, I could see our friends in the dining car getting a little anxious, perhaps even anxious enough to try something. We'll post the watch."

Big Rock

Bob Ward had left Hannah's and started his evening in Longmont's, but he got loud and abusive and the owner had invited him to leave. Ward didn't want any trouble that might cause him to wind up in jail, so he'd moved on to the Brown Dirt Cowboy Saloon. He had to be in Big Rock when the train arrived, assuming it would arrive eventually.

He'd spent too much money at Hannah's. With barely enough to sustain himself over the next few days, he was trying to solve that problem by playing cards, but had not been successful in Longmont's, and was even less successful in the Brown Dirt Cowboy. "Well, you fellas have just about cleaned me out," he said jovially as he got up from the table.

"Don't feel like you are the only one, mister. This seems to have been Corey Calhoun's day." The player pointed to the winner, a cowboy who was temporarily out of work because of the season.

Smiling, Calhoun raked the pile of money toward him. "There must be near a hunnert dollars here. Why, this'll be enough to tide me over till spring roundup."

Ward tipped his hat. "Gentleman." He moved away from the table, but didn't go far.

"Some folks have it and some don't, Calhoun," one of the players griped.

"You got that right. I got the skill," Calhoun bragged.

"Ha! I was talking about luck," the player said. "I've never seen a worse player with better luck than you."

The others laughed.

"Oh yeah? Well, I'll tell you—" Calhoun paused in mid-sentence. "You're right. It was just dumb luck. But as my old pa used to say, it's better to be lucky than good. I probably should quit while I'm ahead. I'll put this money away, and when I come in here to play tomorrow, I'll bring no more 'n what I started with today."

"The way it's been snowing, what makes you think you'll even be able to make it to the saloon tomorrow?" one of the other players asked. "For that matter, we may all have a hard time gettin' home tonight."

"Yeah, well, at least we are down here," Calhoun said. "Think of all those poor folks trapped in a train up on top of the pass."

"Where are you sleeping tonight, Corey? You goin' to use some of your winnin's to get a hotel room?"

"No way am I goin' to waste this money on a hotel room. I'll sleep tonight the same place I sleep ever' night when I'm not out on the range," Calhoun replied.

"Yeah, that's sort of what I thought. You don't have a place, so you'll go over to the livery and bed down in an empty stall, won't you?"

"Mr. Vickery, he don't mind it. And there's plenty of clean straw to sort of burrow down into."

"How 'bout one more hand before you leave, Corey?" one of the other players asked.

"One more, but that's all," Calhoun agreed.

From his place near the wall, Ward heard every word and smiled. It was going to be just too easy.

He hurried through the cold, dark night, his feet making crunching sounds as he walked through the snow. Reaching the livery stable, he stood in the shadows outside for a long moment, making certain he hadn't been seen. Then he stepped into the barn.

It was almost as cold inside as it was outside. The only difference was the walls blocked the wind. The air reeked of horseflesh and horse apples. He moved into a dark corner and waited.

Calhoun was singing when he came into the stable.

"O bury me not on the lone prairie.
These words came low and mournfully
From the pallid lips of the youth who lay
On his dying bed at the close of day."

He moseyed over to one of the stalls. “Hey, Horse, what do you think?” I won a lot of money tonight and tomorrow, I’m goin’ to buy you some oats to go along with the hay you been eatin’. What do you think of that?”

The horse whickered and stuck his head over the gate. Calhoun rubbed the horse behind his ears. “Yeah, I thought you’d like that.”

Ward was sneaking up on Calhoun’s back, walking as quietly as he could, but he stepped on a twig and it snapped.

“What?” Calhoun said, turning toward the sound.

Hiding a knife in his hand, low and by his side, Ward made an underhand jab toward Calhoun, holding the blade sideways so it would slip in easily between his ribs. The knife penetrated Calhoun’s heart, and he went down without another sound.

Ward found the money in Calhoun’s coat pocket, then quickly crossed the street and entered the Ace High Saloon, where he stayed just long enough to establish an alibi. After a couple drinks and a little flirtatious banter with the bar girls, he walked down to the Rocky Mountain Hotel, where he took a room.

Chapter Twenty-eight

On board the Red Cliff Special—December 23

They had selected the time of their duty by lot, and had decided whoever was on duty would stand, not sit, at the door, looking out through the door window. That way nobody would fall asleep while on watch, and since they were only doing one hour at a time, it didn't seem too harsh a duty.

Luke had the watch from one until two in the morning, but couldn't help taking frequent glances toward Jenny. Often, he caught her looking at him. For the first few times he caught her, she would smile in embarrassment at being caught. But after a few times, the embarrassment was gone, and they looked at each other openly and unashamedly.

He recalled a conversation he'd had with his sea captain.

"You aren't married, are you, Mr. Shardeen?" Captain Cutter asked once, when the Pacific Clipper *was anchored off Hong Kong.*

"No, sir."

"You are a smart man not to be married. No sailor should be married, for 'tis no life for a woman to always be waiting for her man to come home to her."

"But you are married, aren't you, Captain?"

"Aye, and 'twas the dumbest thing I've ever done."

Because of that conversation, and because he believed the captain was right, the thought of marriage had never before crossed Luke's mind.

But he wasn't a seaman any longer. He was a rancher with land and a house. What better could he offer a wife, than her own home? Working the land, there would be no long separations. He could get married. They could have children . . . a boy would be nice. He could start him in ranching when he was . . .

Shaking his head, Luke abruptly turned his thoughts in a different direction. He was going to jail for four years. There were very few voyages where a seaman would be absent for four long years. If he couldn't subject a woman to being married to a seaman, what made him think he could subject her to being married to someone who was in jail?

He clenched his jaw and turned away from Jenny. Thinking was getting him nowhere.

Jenny watched Luke turn away from her. *What is he thinking?* she wondered. *Does he think that because I worked at the social club I am a loose woman? Am I but a temporary diversion for him?*

Life had been a good teacher to Jenny, and she had learned well. She had developed an intuition that she trusted, and it was telling her Luke's feelings for her were genuine. She concluded the answer to those questions was no.

But what about her feelings for him? She had made a mistake once, succumbing to foolish infatuation. Was she experiencing the same thing? They had known each other for only three days. Love couldn't develop in three days . . . could it?

She knew Luke was going to jail, the result of an unjust verdict. She was certain his impending jail time was weighing heavily on his mind . . . so heavily it would undoubtedly cause him to put aside any feelings he might have for her.

Giving thought to the comment he had made about the Samoans, and how there is no difference in the heart of a flower that lives but a single day and the heart of a tree that lives for a thousand years, she decided that was exactly how she would look at their current situation. If but a few days, or even a few hours remained for them she would fill what was left with love for Luke Shardeen.

The morning dawned bright and sunny, heating the car inside. But there was little chance another opportunity for food would present itself as the coyote had done.

Abner Purvis went back to talk to Matt. "Me, Jones, Turner, and Simpson have come up with a plan."

"What is your plan?"

"We're goin' to walk out of here."

"Which way are you going?" Matt asked. "The snow in front is three hundred feet high."

"That's why we are going to go back to Buena Vista. If we can get through, we'll get a rescue train back up here."

"Mr. Purvis, there is absolutely no doubt in my mind but that there has already been a rescue attempt. If they could have gotten through, they would be here by now. That tells me that the way behind us is as blocked as the way before us."

"That may be, but we been talkin' about it, and we don't plan to stay here 'n starve to death. Besides which we had a little somethin' to eat yesterday, so we ain't goin' to be any stronger than we are right now."

"You might have a point there," Matt agreed. "But you aren't going to get anywhere without snow shoes."

"We can try," Purvis said.

"When do you plan to leave?"

"The sooner the better. If we leave now we might be over the worst part of it while there is still light."

It took Purvis and the other three men about five minutes to get ready, then everyone in the car wished them luck. With hopeful hearts they watched through the back window as the men attempted to go over the wall of snow piled up behind the train.

Their attempts to climb the snow met with utter failure. They got a few feet up the side, only to slide back down again, or the very act of climbing itself pulled down large slides of snow. They kept at it for half an hour without the slightest bit of success. Finally, breathing hard and tired of bringing frigid air into their lungs, they had no recourse but to give up and return to the train.

"I'm sorry," Purvis said as he and the other three men huddled around the stove. They were so cold and exhausted Matt had thrown in a few extra lumps of coal for more heat. He feared they might contract pneumonia.

"We tried, but we couldn't get over the snow," Jones explained, then sipped from the cup Matt was passing between the men. He had heated snow in the same chamber pot used to make the soup the day before, and though it was nothing but warm water, it made them feel better to drink it.

"What do we do now?" Bailey asked.

"We'll just have to wait and see what develops." Matt looked over toward Millie and Becky. "How is she doing this morning?"

"Not well," Millie said, choking back a sob. "Not well at all. She's not even conscious anymore. I'm—I'm afraid she might be dying."

Matt took some warm water over to them, making certain the water wasn't too hot. "Bathe her face in this," he offered. "It won't help with the illness, but if she can feel it, it might make her feel a little better.

"Bless you." Millie tore some of the hem off her skirt and using it as a washcloth, bathed Becky's face gently with the warm water.

Becky made no response.

"Mrs. Daniels, you have been sitting in that same position for ever so long," Jenny said. "Why don't you let me sit there and hold your little girl's head in my lap while you get a little rest?"

"Oh, thank you, dear. That would be wonderful . . . if you are sure you don't mind."

"No ma'am. I don't mind at all." Jenny changed places with Millie, and put Becky's head in her lap.

"I'm going to hold you for a while now, Becky, while your mama gets a little rest. I hope you don't mind." Jenny looked down and smiled at the girl but got no reaction. Concerned, she put her hand on the child's forehead and found her burning with a very high fever.

Dear Lord, Jenny prayed silently. *I haven't always led the life I should, and I know I have no right to ask you for anything. But maybe since I'm not asking for anything for myself you will hear this prayer. Please, Lord, don't let this innocent child die. It's nearly Christmas. Please send her the Christmas gift of life. Amen.*

"How many more days until Christmas?" Jenny heard Timmy ask.

"Christmas is in two days," Timmy's mother answered.

"I'll be glad when it's Christmas," Timmy's younger sister Molly said. "Won't you be glad when it's Christmas, Mama?"

"Yes, dear," Clara replied quietly. "I'll be glad when it's Christmas."

"Will we still be on this train at Christmas?" Timmy asked.

"I don't know," Clara answered.

"Can Santa Claus find us if we are still on the train?" Molly asked.

"If he can't find us on the train, he will find us as soon as we get home."

"This isn't like Christmas," Timmy declared. "We don't have a Christmas tree. We don't have any cookies. It's nothing like Christmas."

"Oh, but we have snow," Jenny said. "And every Christmas should have snow. Think of all the boys and girls who live way down south and have no snow at all."

Luke laughed. "You are quite a woman, Jenny, to find a bright side to the snow."

"Well, without snow, how would Santa Claus land his sleigh?" Jenny asked. "His reindeer, Dasher and Dancer, Prancer and Vixen, Comet and Cupid, Donner and Blitzen need snow."

"How do you know the names of Santa Claus's reindeer?" Steven asked.

"Why, from the poem 'A Visit From St. Nicholas,'" Jenny said. "Have you never heard that poem?"

"No, ma'am, I ain't never heard it," Steven said.

"I've never heard it either," Molly said.

"Why, that is such a wonderful poem for children. Would you like to hear it?"

"Yes, ma'am." Steven nodded.

"Me, too," Timmy said. "Do you know the poem?"

"Oh, yes, I know it. It was written by a man named Clement Moore for his children. Why don't all of you gather round, and I'll tell you the poem. And maybe Becky can hear it, too."

"Becky is very sick," Molly said somberly.

"Yes, dear, I know she is. But sometimes you can hear things, even when you are too sick to talk. I think Becky will be able to hear it. And I think she will feel better on Christmas Day."

Timmy and his two sisters, as well as Barbara and Steven, gathered around Jenny and Becky. Seeing all the eager young faces made Jenny feel good, and she could almost believe she was teaching a class again.

Smiling, Jenny began to recite the poem.

"*'Twas the night before Christmas, when all through the house*
Not a creature was stirring, not even a mouse.
The stockings were hung by the chimney with care,
In hopes that St Nicholas soon would be there."

"St. Nicholas? Who is that?" Timmy asked.

"That's Santa Claus's real name," Barbara said. "Isn't it, Mrs. McCoy?"

"Indeed it is," Jenny said. Then she continued.

"*The children were nestled all snug in their beds,*
While visions of sugarplums danced in their heads.
And mamma in her 'kerchief, and I in my cap,

Had just settled our brains for a long winter's nap.
When out on the lawn there arose such a clatter,
I sprang from the bed to see what was the matter.
Away to the window I flew like a flash,
Tore open the shutters and threw up the sash.
The moon on the breast of the new-fallen snow
Gave the luster of mid-day to objects below.
When, what to my wondering eyes should appear,
But a miniature sleigh, and eight tiny reindeer.
With a little old driver, so lively and quick,
I knew in a moment it must be St Nick."

"St. Nick. That's Santa Claus!" Steven exclaimed.

"That's Santa Claus all right," Jenny said. She continued reciting the poem.

"More rapid than eagles his coursers they came,
And he whistled, and shouted, and called them by name!
'Now Dasher! now, Dancer! Now, Prancer and Vixen!
On, Comet! On, Cupid! On, Donner and Blitzen!
To the top of the porch! To the top of the wall!
Now dash away! Dash away! Dash away all!'
As dry leaves that before the wild hurricane fly,
When they meet with an obstacle, mount to the sky.
So up to the housetop the coursers they flew,
With the sleigh full of toys, and St Nicholas too.
And then, in a twinkling, I heard on the roof
The prancing and pawing of each little hoof.
As I drew in my head, and was turning around,
Down the chimney St Nicholas came with a bound."

Molly laughed. "That's funny—Santa Claus coming down through a chimney. Why, what keeps him from getting burned in the fire?"

"That's how Santa Claus gets into people's houses. And he doesn't get burned in the fire 'cause he's magic," Barbara said.

Jenny continued.

"He was dressed all in fur, from his head to his foot,
And his clothes were all tarnished with ashes and soot.
A bundle of toys he had flung on his back,
And he looked like a peddler, just opening his pack.
His eyes—how they twinkled! his dimples how merry!
His cheeks were like roses, his nose like a cherry!
His droll little mouth was drawn up like a bow,
And the beard of his chin was as white as the snow.
The stump of a pipe he held tight in his teeth,
And the smoke it encircled his head like a wreath.
He had a broad face and a little round belly,
That shook when he laughed, like a bowl full of jelly!
He was chubby and plump, a right jolly old elf,
And I laughed when I saw him, in spite of myself!
A wink of his eye and a twist of his head,
Soon gave me to know I had nothing to dread.
He spoke not a word, but went straight to his work,
And filled all the stockings, then turned with a jerk.
And laying his finger aside of his nose,
And giving a nod, up the chimney he rose!
He sprang to his sleigh, to his team gave a whistle,
And away they all flew like the down of a thistle.

But I heard him exclaim, ere he drove out of sight,
'Happy Christmas to all, and to all a good night!'"

"Oh, that was a wonderful poem, Jenny," Millie said. "And you spoke it so beautifully."

"Yes," Clara added. "And I think the children really enjoyed it, didn't you, children?"

"Yes, ma'am, I liked it a lot," Timmy said. "I just wish that Santa Claus could find us on the train."

"If he could find us, what would you have him bring?" Jenny asked.

"Something to eat for us." Timmy looked at Becky. "And some medicine for Becky, so she wouldn't be sick anymore."

"That is a wonderful gift to wish for," Jenny said.

"That won't happen, though," Steven said.

"Oh, I wouldn't be all that surprised if it happened." Jenny smiled. "Sometimes, wonderful things happen on Christmas. Christmas was the day Jesus was born, you know."

"I know," Timmy said. "He was borned in a barn."

"Why was the baby Jesus borned in a barn?" Molly asked.

"Because they didn't have hotels way back when Jesus was borned," Timmy said.

"Yes they did," Barbara said. "But they didn't call them hotels then. They called them inns. And Jesus was born in a stable and put in a manger, because there was no room at the inn."

"How do you know that?" Timmy asked.

"Because it's in the Bible," Barbara said.

"That's right. The whole Christmas story is in the Bible." Luke began to tell the story.

"'*And there were in the same country shepherds abiding in the field, keeping watch over their flock by night. And, lo, the angel of the Lord came upon them, and the glory of the Lord shone round about them: and they were sore afraid. And the angel said unto them, Fear not: for, behold, I bring you good tidings of great joy, which shall be to all people. For unto you is born this day in the city of David a Saviour, which is Christ the Lord. And this shall be a sign unto you; Ye shall find the babe wrapped in swaddling clothes, lying in a manger. And suddenly there was with the angel a multitude of the heavenly host praising God, and saying, Glory to God in the highest, and on earth peace, good will toward men.*'"

"Wow! I'm impressed!" Jenny said with a smile. "How were you able to do that?"

"I've spent many a Christmas at sea," Luke explained. "And I've often been called upon to read the Christmas story to the sailors. I've read it so many times that I finally memorized it."

"You know what?" Timmy said. "I think that, even if we are still on this train, it will be a good Christmas."

"Now why on earth would you say something like that?" Senator Daniels snarled. "We are stranded here, with no food."

"But we have friends," Timmy said with a broad smile. "And friends are about the best things you can have."

"Timmy, you are wise beyond your years," Luke said.

Chapter Twenty-nine

Big Rock

Again, Smoke and Duff took the sleigh into town. This time, though, Sally went with them. Smoke let Sally off in front of the Big Rock Mercantile, Duff got out in front of Longmont's, then Smoke drove on to the livery barn. Stopping just outside, he unhitched the team, then led them into the barn.

Liveryman Ike Shelby was just inside the barn talking to three other men—Sheriff Monte Carson, Dan Norton the prosecuting attorney, and Allen Blanton, editor and publisher of the *Big Rock Chronicle.*

"Gentleman," Smoke greeted. "Ike, I'd like to leave my team here for a while so they are somewhat out of the cold."

"Sure thing, Smoke. Billy, take Mr. Jensen's team," Ike called to one of his employees.

"What's going on?" Smoke asked.

"We had a murder here, last night," Sheriff Carson said.

"A murder? What happened?"

"When Billy came to open up this morning, he found Corey Calhoun's body lying over there." Ike pointed to a spot in front of a stall.

"Shot?" Smoke asked.

"He had been stabbed," Sheriff Carson answered.

"You knew him, didn't you, Smoke?" Blanton asked.

"Yes, I knew him."

"How well did you know him?" Norton asked.

"I knew him fairly well. He worked for me from time to time. He was a good man, and he, Pearlie, and Cal were friends. Stabbed, you say?"

"Through the heart," Ike said.

"Do you have any ideas on what happened?"

"According to some of the boys over at the Brown Dirt, Calhoun had a pretty good night at poker and won well over a hundred dollars."

"Let me guess. You didn't find any money on him," Smoke said.

"Not a cent," Sheriff Carson replied. "My guess is that someone saw him leave the table a winner, followed him over here, and killed him.

"What about footprints in the snow?" Smoke asked.

Sheriff Carson shook his head. "No help. There are hundreds of footprints everywhere, none that will do us any good."

"I hope you find him," Smoke said.

"We will."

Leaving his team with Ike, and his sleigh parked outside, Smoke walked down to the depot to see what he could find out.

"The rescue train tried to get through to them," Phil said, "but it failed because the tracks are blocked by snow."

"How do you know they failed?"

"These stories were wired to the *Big Rock Chronicle*." Phil showed Matt the newspaper.

Special to the CHRONICLE *by wire, from the* BUENA VISTA NUGGET

RELIEF EFFORT UNSUCCESSFUL

TRAIN FORCED TO TURN BACK

The train that was to relieve the trapped Red Cliff Special was forced to return to Buena Vista when a wall of snow presented an insurmountable impediment. Doodle Reynolds, the engineer, stated that, not even with the plow affixed to the front of his engine could the snow be removed.

Hodge Deckert has assured those who have loved ones on board the train that the passengers are in no danger or great distress as the diner carries extra food for just such a contingency. It is expected the snow will be sufficiently melted within a few days to allow another rescue attempt to be made.

Amon Briggs Removed From Bench

MAY FACE PRISON TERM

Word has reached the Nugget that Amon Briggs, formerly a district judge located in Pueblo, has been removed from the bench by order of Governor Davis Hanson Waite.

According to Sheriff McKenzie, Briggs, who is now a guest of the Pueblo County Jail, was involved in a nefarious scheme with Sheriff Ferrell of Bent County. Briggs would inform Ferrell when money was being transferred, and Ferrell and his partner in crime, usually one of this deputies, would rob the victim so identified.

The latest attempt at robbery failed when Ferrell and his deputy were both killed by the heroic action of Mr. Nugent, who was riding shotgun guard.

Though Sheriff McKenzie has not yet disclosed the incriminating evidence discovered as a result of the failed robbery attempt, it is sufficient to result in the incarceration of Briggs until such time as a judge can be made available to try the case.

"Ha!" Smoke thumped his fingers on the paper. "That doesn't surprise me about Briggs. I never have trusted him. But what about the train, have you heard anything? Do you know if they are going to try again?"

"I'm sure they will when the some of the snow melts."

"I hate it that Matt and the others are trapped up there. But I figure they haven't run out of food yet."

Phil laughed. "They're probably having a good old time. I mean, what else can you do under a situation like that?"

"I guess you're right," Smoke agreed. "Listen, Phil, I'm probably going to be in town for the rest of the day, so if you get any further word about the train, you'll let me know, won't you?"

"Yes, of course I will. Where will I find you?"

"I don't know, at Longmont's I suppose. Sally came into town with us, and she'll want to have lunch, probably at Kathy's Kitchen. But if you don't find me, I'll be checking in with you from time to time.

"That's a good place for lunch, I often eat there myself."

Smoke stepped into Longmont's a few minutes later. Duff sat at a table, drinking coffee and reading the newspaper. Smoke joined him.

"The rescue train was turned back," Duff said, thumping the paper with his fingers.

"Yes, Phil told me that."

"There is an interesting story here. The deputy sheriff from Pueblo County is escorting two prisoners. One of the prisoners has had all the charges against him dropped but he doesn't know that, and there will be no way for him to know until they are freed."

"Who are the prisoners?" Smoke asked.

Duff referred back to the paper. "Michael Santelli and Luke Shardeen."

"I hope Santelli isn't the one who has been pardoned," Smoke said.

"Na, 'tis Luke Shardeen. Do you know Mr. Santelli?"

"I've never had the displeasure of a personal encounter with him, but I certainly know who he is. And he is a bad one. I don't like to think of him being on the same train, trapped in a snowslide, with a bunch of innocent people."

"Aye, the longer one has to hold him in custody, the greater the mischief he can create."

Louis Longmont brought Smoke a cup of coffee without being summoned. "Did you hear about the murder we had here in town last night?" Longmont asked.

"Murder is it?" Duff said looking up from his paper. "I've nae heard a thing about it."

"It happened over at the livery stable," Smoke informed him. "I was talking to Monte and a few others about it. Corey Calhoun got killed."

"Och, 'tis sorry I am to hear of it. Did you know him?"

"Yes, he worked for me from time to time. He was a good man, and a friend of Pearlie and Cal. They'll be upset to hear about it."

"I haven't talked to Monte since I heard about

it," Longmont said. "Does he have any ideas as to who might have done it?"

"Only indirect ideas," Smoke said. "It seems that Corey won quite a bit of money in a card game over at the Brown Dirt. Sheriff Carson thinks someone may have seen him win, then followed him from the saloon. He killed him in the livery stable."

"That means nobody saw it." Duff leaned back and crossed his arms.

"Yes, I'm afraid that is exactly what it means. And if nobody saw it happen, I think the chances of finding out who actually did it are rather slim," Smoke sipped the hot coffee.

"I'll keep an eye open," Longmont promised. "Oftentimes, when someone comes into an unexpected sum of money, they'll come in here and be big spenders all of a sudden."

A couple of Smoke's friends came in then and invited Smoke and Duff to join them in a friendly game of poker. They were still playing three hours later when Sally came into the saloon.

"Sally, ma belle, bienvenue à ma place," Longmont greeted effusively.

Sally smiled. "Thank you, Louis." She turned to the poker players. "Smoke, Duff, are you two getting a little hungry?"

"Hungry?" Smoke glanced over at the wall. "Oh, oh. It's one-thirty. Uh, we were supposed to meet you at Kathy's at noon, weren't we?"

"That was my understanding," Sally said, though her response was ameliorated by her smile.

"Sally, you should leave this man who so mistreats you," Longmont said. "If you had chosen me over him, never would you be disappointed by such forgetfulness."

"Louis, I would be impressed, but I know you say that to every married woman in town."

"Only to the pretty ones," Longmont assured.

"And only to the married ones," Sally replied.

Smoke laughed. "Louis, she has you pegged. You only carry on so with women you know are safe. You wouldn't dare say such things to a single woman for fear she would take you up on your offer."

"Ah, how well my friends know me," Longmont replied. "Enjoy your lunch at Kathy's. And tell her that I long for her."

"You never give up, do you, Louis?" Sally said with a laugh.

On board the Red Cliff Special—December 24

Bailey was looking through the window of the car, and called Matt over.

"Yes?"

"I'm sure they've tried to reach us, but gave up when they couldn't get through. They probably aren't that worried, figuring we have enough food to last. But if they knew our situation, I think they would make more of an effort." Bailey pointed toward the telegraph wire. "If I could reach that wire, I could send a message back to Buena Vista telling them of our serious condition."

"You could send a message? You mean you know telegraphy?"

"Yes, before I was a conductor, I was a telegrapher for Western Union."

"But, how would you send a message? We aren't connected."

"I am pretty sure the wire going forward is down. But it looks like the wire going back toward Buena Vista is still up. I can see it over the top of the snowbank behind us, and if it didn't go down here, I'm sure it is up for the rest of the way. All I have to do is connect to it."

"Connect what to it?"

"I have a telegraph key," Bailey said with a smile. "But I don't know how to get up there."

Luke had overheard the conversation and he went over to join in. "Did I hear you right? You can send a telegram?"

"If I could connect to that wire I could. But in order to do that, I would have to climb that pole, and it is covered with snow and ice. Climbing it would be impossible."

Luke looked at the pole for a moment, then he shook his head. "It will be difficult," he agreed. "But it isn't impossible."

"Wait a minute," Matt said. "Are you saying you think you can climb it?"

"Why not?" Luke replied. "I've climbed ice-slickened mainmasts before, and that's with the ship rolling in the sea. Yes, I think I can get up there."

"Oh, Luke, no," Jenny put in. She'd followed Luke. "That's much too dangerous."

"Ha! I laugh at danger," Luke said, thrusting his hand out in an exaggerated fashion.

"I'm serious," Jenny argued.

"Don't worry, Jenny. I've done this kind of thing before."

Matt and Bailey went outside with Luke to see how he would attack the pole. Worried about Luke, Jenny trailed behind. They studied the pole for a moment or two, rising as it did from the midst of a huge drift of snow.

"How are you going to even get to the pole?" Bailey asked.

"I don't know. That does seem to be a problem." Luke looked at the pole, then looked back at the train and smiled. "I'll climb up onto the top of the car, then leap over to the pole."

"Luke, no, you can't be serious!" Jenny cried.

"I don't have to leap onto the pole, just into the snowbank close enough to it to be able to grab hold," Luke explained.

Matt smiled. "You know, I think that might work. I wouldn't want to be the one to do it, but I think it might work."

Luke climbed to the top of the car, then stepped to the edge to examine the pole for a moment. Satisfied with what he saw, he moved to the opposite side. With a running start, he leaped across the opening and disappeared into the snowbank at the foot of the pole.

"Luke!" Jenny called in fear.

After a moment of anxious silence, Luke appeared out of the snowbank, his arms and legs wrapped around the pole. They watched as he climbed to the top, threw a leg over the crossbeam, and pulled himself into a secure sitting position. He looked down and threw his arms open with a big smile.

"Oh, Luke, hold on!" Jenny called.

"I'm all right. Why, this pole isn't even moving. Mr. Bailey, what do I do now?"

"Cut the wire," Bailey instructed. "And toss it over here so I can get to it."

"Will I get shocked?"

"No," Bailey explained. "Telegraph works by direct current. There's no danger."

"If I cut the wire, won't it mean you can't send a signal?"

"It'll be fine, as long as there isn't another break in the wire between here and Buena Vista."

Luke cut the wire as Bailey instructed, then tossed it down. Matt caught it and handed it to Bailey, who attached the cut end to his instrument.

Luke came back down the pole about halfway, then leaped into the snowbank. Again, he disappeared, but reappeared a moment later, covered in snow.

"I'm going to have to quit doing that," Luke teased as Jenny helped brush the snow away.

Bailey got the wire attached, then sent a BV signal.

"Is it working?" Matt asked.

"I don't know. I haven't gotten a reply." Bailey sent a BV signal again.

There was no reply.

He tried it a third time, then, with a sigh, looked up at Luke. "I'm sorry, Mr. Shardeen. It looks like I sent you up the post for nothing. We may as well get out of the cold. It was—"

Clackclackclackclackclack.

"We're through!" Bailey shouted excitedly. "We're through!" He listened to the clicks for a moment, then chuckled. "Bernie is apologizing because he was away from the key. He wants to know who is calling him."

Bailey began sending a message, his fingers moving rapidly as the clicks went out over the line.

Chapter Thirty

Sugarloaf Ranch

Once breakfast was on the table, Sally joined Smoke and Duff. "I just hate to think of Matt being on that train. I was so looking forward to having him join us for Christmas."

"Matt's younger and resilient," Smoke said. "I imagine he can get through just about anything. But I would have enjoyed having him here for Christmas. Christmas should be with family, and we're the closest thing to family he has."

"We aren't just the closest thing to it," Sally said. "We *are* it. We are family."

"You're right. We are family."

Their breakfast was interrupted by a knock on the door. Sally started to get up, but Smoke held out his hand. "I'll get it."

He hurried to the front door and opened it to see Eddie standing on the porch.

"Eddie? Don't tell me the train is in?"

"No, sir, it ain't in. And it's worse 'n we thought."

"Worse how?"

"We got a telegram from the train. It's been sent out all over. Mr. Wilson thought you might want to read it."

SITUATION DIRE STOP PROXMIRE DEAD STOP
GUNMEN IN DINER STOP NO FOOD STOP
COME SOONEST STOP BAILEY CONDUCTOR

Smoke's expression was grim as he read it, then he looked up at the messenger. "Why don't you come on into the house, Eddie, have some breakfast?" Smoke invited.

"Thank you, sir!" Eddie said as a wide smile spread across his face.

Smoke led Eddie back into the dining room.

"Eddie," Sally said. "It's so nice to have your company. I'll get another plate. Smoke, you . . ." Sally stopped when she saw the expression on Smoke's face. "Smoke, what is it? What's wrong?"

Smoke showed the telegram to Sally, who read it quickly. "Oh, no."

Duff reached for the message and she gave it to him. He looked up after reading it. "What can we do?"

"I'm going up there," Smoke decided. "I'm going to load a sled with as much food as I can get on it and I'm going up there."

"Smoke, if a train can't get through, how are you going to get there?"

"I will get there because I must get there," Smoke said emphatically.

"I'll be going with you," Duff said.

"No need for you to go," Smoke protested. "This isn't going to be easy."

"Smoke, what kind of friend would I be if I didn't go with you? And what kind of friend would you be, if you didn't allow me to go?"

Smoke smiled, then nodded. "All right. Let's get ready. We need to get as much under our belt as we can while we've still got light. I've no doubt but that it'll be well dark before we get there."

"Aye," Duff said. "I'll find some warm clothes."

"Eddie?"

"Yes, sir?" Eddie replied, his mouth full of biscuit.

"I hate to interrupt your breakfast, so just grab yourself a couple bear claws. I want you to get back into town as quickly as you can and go by Ebersole's Bakery, and get as much bread as he has available. Then go to Dunnigan's store. Tell him to pack up as much jerky as he can get together. Tell him we're going to have to feed a lot of people. We'll be in to pick it up before we leave."

"Yes, sir," Eddie said, getting up quickly.

Sally handed him two bear claws and he left immediately.

Big Rock

Bob Ward was having lunch at Little Man Lambert's café and reading a special edition of the *Big*

Rock Chronicle. It had only two stories, and as it happened, both were of intense interest to him.

No Clues on Murder

Sheriff Monty Carson told the Chronicle he has no leads on the murder of Corey Calhoun. A well-known and well-liked young man, Calhoun worked as a cowboy during the season and was spoken highly of by all who knew him, employers and fellow workers alike.

Calhoun's body was found Friday morning by an employee of the livery stable.

Train Passengers in Peril

The conductor of the Red Cliff Special has sent a telegram in which he says Deputy Sheriff Proxmire is dead and gunmen occupy the dining car, denying food to the starving passengers.

That someone could be so evil in this Christmas season defies all understanding. We can but pray for the safe delivery of those unfortunate passengers, and the ultimate capture and execution of the evil men responsible for this reprehensible act.

With eight crates of bread loaded onto their sled, Smoke and Duff went to Dunnigan's for jerky.

"I don't have near enough jerky to do you any

good, Smoke," Ernest Dunnigan said. "But I tell what I do have. I have forty tins of sardines. And because they are in tins, it'll be pretty easy for you to carry them."

"All right," Smoke said. "Sardines it will be. Get them out here, and Duff and I will load them."

"Yes, sir," Dunnigan replied.

While Smoke and Duff were loading the sled, Ward left the restaurant and hurried to the livery where he was boarding six horses and tack to be used for the getaway.

"How much longer you plannin' on leavin' them horses here?" Ike asked. "Reason I ask is, they're takin' up a lot of room, and folks that's comin' into town are wantin' to board their horses to keep 'em out of the cold while they're here."

"I don't know how much longer," Ward said. "Until I need them."

"Here's the thing. You see them two horses there? They belong to Smoke Jensen and Duff MacAllister, and they're wantin' to leave them here while they go up to rescue them folks on the train. I reckon you heard about that, didn't you?"

"I heard about it," Ward said. "You mean they ain't goin' to go up on horseback?"

Ike shook his head. "There ain't no horse that can get up there now, and more 'n likely, no mountain goats either. The only way a body could get up there now is to climb the mountain. And that ain't goin' to be easy. Not with all this snow. But I reckon if anyone can do it, Smoke can."

"Yeah, that's what I heard someone say. They talk about Smoke Jensen like he is some kind of a hero or somethin'."

"Well, sir, you might say that he is," Ike said. "And that brings me back to them six horses you got boarded here. Would you mind if I sort of put some of 'em together? Like say, three stalls, with two horses in each stall. It would help me out, and you'd be savin' money."

"That'll be fine," Ward agreed. "But I need some of my tack, first."

"Sure, what do you want?"

"I want a poncho, blanket, and my rifle."

"Look here, mister, it sounds like you're goin' huntin'. If that's true, be awful careful 'bout where you shoot your rifle. You could cause an avalanche, and you for sure don't want to get caught in one of those."

"I'll be careful," Ward insisted.

"All right. You can come on back and get your tack." As they passed one of the stalls, Ike pointed. "I reckon you heard about the murder. Billy found 'im lyin' right there. He'd been stabbed."

"I read about it in the paper," Ward said.

"There's your tack, all there as you can see. Your stuff is safe here. Yes, sir, in all the years I been runnin' this livery, ain't never been nothin' stole from it."

"Just somebody murdered," Ward mumbled.

"What? Oh, yes, sir, I guess that's right. I sure ain't proud of it, but I guess it is right."

Ward pulled his rifle from the tack. Reaching down into his saddlebag, he opened a box of ammunition and scooped out a handful of extra rifle rounds, which he put in his pocket. The poncho and blanket were rolled together in a tight roll. He put the roll over one shoulder, let it fall diagonally across his body, and tied the two bottom ends together. This allowed him to carry the blanket and poncho while keeping his hands free.

"I appreciate you lettin' me put your horses together," Ike said. "That'll free up three more stalls."

Ward nodded, then stepped into the street in front of the livery. He looked toward the market, where, a few minutes earlier he had seen two men loading a sled. The men were gone, and he felt a moment of apprehension that he had lost them. Then, looking up the track, he saw them plodding along, pulling the sled behind them.

On board the train

The wire from the telegraph line had been run through the window of the car so Bailey could send and receive messages from the relative comfort of the car. Newspapers and pieces of carpet were stuffed into the open section of the window to keep as much cold air out as possible.

Some of the passengers had asked that he send messages back to let their family know that they were still alive. Senator Daniels asked if he could send a message to the Denver newspapers.

"All right," Bailey agreed.

Senator Daniels cleared his throat, then began to speak. "My fellow citizens. I am addressing you by the magic of harnessed lightning, to tell you that I am safe, though I, and the others with me, are being held hostage by a convicted criminal, Michael Santelli. He and other brigands with him have taken control of the dining car, wherein is stored all the food on this train. The result is four days of starvation and want.

"I want all my constituents to know that I, and the others herein exposed to such danger and privation, are doing all we can to fight against this evil, and it is my belief that we will prevail. But, I ask—no, I demand—the Denver and Pacific do whatever is necessary to come to our rescue.

"It is unthinkable that in this day of mighty steam engines and powerful, steam shovels, of telegraph and telephone, that a loud and resounding hue and cry has not gone out over all the land to cause a mighty mobilization of forces, sufficient to overcome any such barriers as may stand between us, and our eventual rescue.

"I further demand that—" Senator Daniels stopped in mid-sentence and looked down at Bailey. "You aren't sending this."

"Senator, I can't send all that. I can't send more than twenty-five words in each message."

"Why not?"

"Because this is not a regular Western Union station. We have what is called emergency access, which allows us but limited use of the line. If I attempted to send everything you just said, we would be cut off. And I feel that it is vital we keep this line open."

"Hrrumph," Senator Daniels grumped. "Very well, very well."

"If you have something you can send in twenty-five words or less, I would be happy to send it."

"All right, send this to the *Colorado Rocky News.*" Again, Senator Daniels cleared his throat as if about to deliver a speech. "Though we face starvation and privation, I have rallied the beleaguered passengers to show courage in the wake of hardship. We will prevail. Jarred Daniels, State Senator."

"That's twenty-seven words, Senator."

"Change 'we will prevail' to 'I will prevail' and sign it Senator Daniels."

Bailey sent the message, along with several other messages. Then, after a few minutes of quiet, the telegraph key began clacking. Bailey responded, then listened.

"Mr. Jensen," Bailey called. "There is a message coming in for you."

"For me?" Matt asked, surprised by the announcement.

"Yes, sir."

"What does he say?"

The machine clattered again, and Bailey recorded the message. Then he chuckled. "I'm sure this has some meaning for you."

"What?"

Bailey read aloud what he wrote. "Will pull your behind from snow again. Hang on. Rescue soon."

Matt smiled, broadly. "Yes, sir, it has a lot of meaning for me. It means Smoke is coming to get us. And it means that we will be out of here sometime within the next twenty-four hours."

"Smoke? Are you talking about Smoke Jensen?" Senator Daniels asked.

"Yes."

"I am well aware of the exploits of Smoke Jensen. However, he is but one man, and I don't see how one man can possibly come to our rescue. I mean, even if he gets here, what can he do? He can't free the train, and he is no more capable of taking the dining car back than we are."

"Never underestimate Smoke Jensen," Matt warned. "If he says he is going to rescue us, that is exactly what he is going to do."

"It must be refreshing to have such childish confidence in a person," Senator Daniels said sarcastically.

"Oh, there's nothing childish about it, Senator. As I am sure you will see soon enough."

The telegraph began clicking again, and once more, Bailey recorded the incoming message on a tablet. When finished, he reread the message. "Well, I'll be."

"What is it?" Matt asked.

Bailey showed him the message, and a big smile came across his face after he read it. "Luke, you might want to hear this message," Matt called.

Luke was sitting in the seat just across from Jenny, who was still holding Becky's head in her lap. He turned to Matt. "Yes?"

"This message pertains to you," Matt said.

Luke came over to Matt and Bailey, his face reflecting curiosity and a slight bit of anxiousness.

Matt read aloud from the paper. "Sheriff Ferrell killed robbing stagecoach. Judge Briggs indicted for collusion. Removed from the bench. Shardeen's charges dropped. Governor vacated sentence."

"Does that mean I'm free? Really free?" Luke asked.

"It does indeed," Matt congratulated. "When we are rescued from this train, you can go back to your ranch, a free man."

Chapter Thirty-one

On the mountain

Smoke and Duff had been climbing for the better part of four hours, encountering one obstacle after another. On three separate occasions, they had come to an absolute halt. Each time, they had to backtrack, sometimes for two or three miles, until they found another route.

With each subsequent try the trail became more difficult. Walking in snowshoes made the trek more manageable, but it was still exhausting. They stopped, then sat down under a juniper tree, drawing in huge, heaving breaths that filled their lungs with cold air and caused their chests to hurt.

"It's hard enough just to get your breath at this altitude," Smoke pointed out. "It's even more difficult when you are exerting yourself as hard as we are."

"This trail seems somewhat more difficult than any of the others we have tried, so far," Duff said.

"It is. The other trails were much easier going, but as you saw, each of those trails reached a point to where we could go no farther. I would rather have the trail difficult, but with no insurmountable obstacle, than to have an easy trail that comes to a dead end."

"Aye, you have a point there," Duff agreed.

Ward was exhausted. He had not thought about bringing snowshoes, and struggled mightily with each step he took. Twice he lost trail of the two men he was following, only to see them coming back down the trail toward him. In those cases he was glad to be far enough away they didn't come across his tracks.

Panting hard, he pulled his feet up from the snow, feeling agony from the cold and the heavy breathing.

Grumbling about snowshoes, he continued on through the snow, step by agonizing step, when he noticed the men had stopped. Resting. Immediately, the solution came to him. He would kill them, take their snowshoes, then go on to the train carrying the extra pair of snowshoes. Once he reached the train he would give the other pair to his brother, abandon the men he had recruited to help him, and he and his brother would split the five thousand dollars between them. He gauged the distance between him and the two men to be no more than about fifty yards, an easy shot with the rifle. Raising the Winchester .30-06 to his shoulder, he aimed at the one farthest away, then pulled the trigger.

Smoke leaned forward to adjust his foot in the snowshoe, which proved to be a fortuitous move. He heard the pop of the bullet as it passed close to his ear, and knew what it was, even before he heard the sound of the rifle shot.

"What is it?" Duff called, looking around.

"Get down!" Smoke called.

As both men began clawing at their heavy coats, trying to get to their pistols, they heard another sound. Not that of a second gunshot, but the heavy thunder of cascading snow.

"Avalanche!" Smoke shouted, and he and Duff crouched behind the tree, looking up at the snow as it came barreling down the side of the mountain.

Smoke was certain he was going to die. He felt no fear, just a sense of wonder that he had survived so many gunfights and close calls only to be killed by an avalanche. His biggest concern was that he had failed Matt and the others on the train.

About three hundred feet above, the avalanche changed direction, and Smoke and Duff watched in fascination as more than a hundred feet of snow snapped trees and gathered rocks as it roared down the side of the mountain and right past them. Miraculously, the avalanche left them in the clear.

Following the moving mountain of snow with their eyes, they saw the shooter swept up into the massive slide. His head and shoulders protruding from the great slide, the man's face contorted in pain and terror just before he went under. A moment later, the snow appeared red with blood in spots, then the avalanche continued down the hill, breaking trees off at the trunk, the loud pops sounding like explosions. As the avalanche rolled on down the side of the mountain, the sound, in Doppler effect, decreased in volume until, way down at the bottom of the mountain, the crashing trees sounded more like snapping twigs.

"That was close." Smoke stood up in amazement.

"Aye, indeed it was. Who was that fellow, Smoke, and why was he shooting at us?"

Smoke shook his head. "I don't have the slightest idea." He let out a long, frustrated sigh. "After this, though, I don't see how we are ever going to make it up the rest of the way. I wouldn't be surprised if this didn't close every path there was. I'm not ready to give up yet, but—" Smoke stopped in mid-sentence and looked up the side of the mountain. "God in heaven! It can't be!"

"What is it? What are you talking about?" Duff craned his neck to see what Smoke was looking at.

"You don't see him?"

"See who?"

"How can you not see him? He's no more than fifty feet away!" Smoke said, pointing.

"The shooter? How can that be?" Duff asked in confusion.

"No, not the shooter. The mountain man! But it can't be who I think it is. It can't be!"

"Lad, have ye gone daft? There is no one in the direction you are pointing, be it fifty or a hundred feet away."

The man Smoke saw was an old mountain man dressed in buckskins and a bear coat. He was carrying a Hawkens .50 caliber muzzle-loading rifle, and he was smiling at Smoke. "It's good to see you again, boy."

Smoke shook his head. "This isn't possible."

"Smoke, what are you talking about? Who are you talking to?" Duff asked, puzzled by Smoke's strange actions.

"Are you going to tell me that you don't see anyone there?" Smoke asked.

Duff looked again in the direction Smoke was pointing, then looked back at Smoke with an expression of confusion on his face. "I see nothing."

"Never mind the Scotsman," the old mountain man said. "Follow me. I'll show you the way."

"How did you—?" Smoke asked, but the mountain man interrupted him.

"We've no time for palaverin' now, boy. We have to get a move on it. Ain't that right, honey?"

A little girl, who appeared to be about nine years old, stepped out from behind the old mountain man.

"We need you, Mr. Smoke," the little girl said. "Please come help us."

"What? God in Heaven, who are you?"

"My name is Becky."

"What are you doing here?"

"I came from the train."

"Where are your mama and daddy? Do they know you are here?"

"They think I'm asleep," Becky said.

"Yes, and well you should be. You've got no business being out in this weather. You'll freeze to death!"

"Please hurry," the little girl said. "We need you. Everyone on the train needs you."

"What is she doing here?" Smoke asked the old mountain man. "Did you bring her?"

"No, she came on her own, just to show you how much those folks on the train need you."

"Smoke, would you be wanting me to drag the sled now?" Duff asked.

Smoke looked at Duff, then back at the mountain man and the angelic little girl who was standing beside him. Both seemed to be glowing in some sort of ethereal light.

"Old man, can I ask you something?"

The old mountain man chuckled. "Now, Smoke, would you tell me when, for as long as I have known you, you have ever needed permission to ask me a question?"

"I've never seen you . . . uh . . . quite like this, before," Smoke said.

"All right, ask the question."

"Why hasn't Duff said anything about you or the little girl? Does he see you?"

"Duff has his own reality," the mountain man said. "And you have yours."

"Reality? Is that what you call this?"

"What do you call it?" the old mountain man asked.

"I don't know what to call it." Smoke looked at the little girl again, and thought that he had never seen a more beautiful child.

Smoke turned to Duff. "Do you see this old man and this young girl standing here before us?"

Duff was down on one knee, adjusting the cord to the sled. He gave no indication he had even heard Smoke.

"Why doesn't he answer me?"

"He doesn't hear you."

"How can he not hear me? He's right here."

"I told you. He has his own reality."

"Are you saying I'm not a part of his reality?

"Sometimes you are and sometimes you aren't."

"That doesn't make sense."

"Do you think that when a caterpillar is born, he knows someday he will be a butterfly?" the old mountain man asked.

"I don't know."

"Then let's leave it at that. Just because you don't know, doesn't mean that it isn't real."

"All right, let's accept this as my reality. How are we going to get up to the train? There's no way up the side of this mountain. It's for sure the avalanche has closed every passage."

"Not every passage," the old mountain man explained. "Come along and follow me. I know a way. Have I ever steered you wrong?"

"Are you sure the avalanche has closed every passage?" Duff asked Smoke. "Or would you like to go on and see if we can find something? If you want to go on, I'm willing to go with you."

"You heard that? You heard me say that the avalanche had closed all the passages?"

"Of course I heard it. I'm standing right here."

"But you didn't hear me talking to the little girl."

"What little girl?"

"Never mind. Are you game to keep going?"

"Aye. 'Tis for sure 'n certain we can't turn back now," Duff said. "You know this mountain, I don't. But I've got confidence you can find a way up for us."

"He's got faith in me, and he doesn't even see me." The old mountain man snickered.

"Ha. He said he has faith in *me*," Smoke boasted.

"It's the same thing, my boy."

"Where is the little girl? What happened to her?"

"What little girl?"

"She said her name is Becky."

The old mountain man chuckled. "Like I said, boy. You've got your own reality. Now, are you ready or not?"

"I'm ready," Smoke said.

"Good. Then I'm with you," Duff answered. "I'll draw the sled for a while."

The old mountain man led the way, trudging up the hill. He wasn't wearing snowshoes, but that didn't matter because he wasn't sinking into the snow. The trail became much easier as they went through areas that looked as if a channel had been dug just to clear the way.

"Smoke, have you noticed something curious?" Duff asked as they made their way up the mountain.

"Everything about this is curious," Smoke replied. "I'm glad to see that you have finally noticed."

"How can you not notice this trail?" Duff asked. "It's just seems too easy to be real, and I've got a feeling we're going come upon a sheer rock cliff, or something else just as impassable. I can't actually believe we've found a path that leads to the top."

"It's all a matter of reality," Smoke said. "Yours and mine."

"What?"

"Nothing. Apparently we have found a good trail, at least so far. But you may be right. We might wind up somewhere that is totally impassable."

Chapter Thirty-two

Pueblo

Adele declared an open house on Christmas Eve. A huge, silver bowl was filled with eggnog, and cookies, fudge, pies, and cakes were laid out on the table beside it. Several of the town's leading businessmen were present, though she had put out the word earlier the night was to be social only. None of her girls would be available for anything more than friendly parlor conversation.

One of Adele's girls was playing the piano in the keeping room and a group of carolers, men and women, were gathered around it.

"God rest you merry gentlemen,
Let nothing you dismay,
Remember, Christ our Saviour
Was born on Christmas day,
To save as all from Satan's power
When we were gone astray.

O tidings of comfort and joy,
Comfort and joy,
O tidings of comfort and joy."

The Social Club was well decorated for Christmas, with staircase and fireplace mantel festooned with bunting and evergreen boughs. A large tree was decorated with ornaments and red and green rope, as well as candles. The candle flames were shielded by glass globes to prevent the flames from coming into contact with the pine needles.

"This is quite a party you are putting on, Adele." Charles Matthews was president of the largest bank in Pueblo.

"If you can't celebrate at Christmas, when can you celebrate?" Adele replied.

"You have certainly gone all out with the food. I don't believe I have ever eaten so well. So far I've had cookies and a piece of cake. I thought I might try a piece of cherry pie as well, if I can find room. But I'm stuffed."

"I feel a bit guilty," Adele said. "Here we are surrounded by food, while up at the pass, an entire trainload of people are starving. And that includes Jenny McCoy, bless her heart."

"Jenny McCoy? She's on that train? Well, no wonder I haven't seen her tonight. I figured she would be sitting on a sofa somewhere, holding court with her many admirers."

"No, she's been gone for the better part of a week now."

"Gone to visit someone for Christmas, has she?"

Adele shook her head. "No. Mr. Matthews, are you not aware that she was run out of town by Judge Briggs?"

"Ha! You mean former Judge Briggs, don't you? He's in jail now, which is exactly where he should be. And no, I wasn't aware. What do you mean she was run out of town? Why would that be? From what I know of Jenny McCoy, she has done nothing that would cause her to be run out of town. Why, she wasn't even one of your girls. Not in the traditional sense. Unless there were certain, uh, special people who could enjoy her favors, of whom I'm not aware. At least, I was never able to do more than have a conversation with her."

"There were no special people who could enjoy her favors," Adele said. "For all the time she was here, she remained chaste."

"Then what happened to cause Briggs to run her out of town?"

"She was hosting the Honorable Lorenzo Crounse, Governor of Nebraska, in the tearoom, when some armed brigands broke in on them. They forced poor Jenny to disrobe, then took a picture of her, sitting nude beside the governor."

"Uh-oh. That sounds like political chicanery," Matthews said.

"Yes, I'm sure it was," Adele said. "And I wouldn't be surprised if Briggs was behind it."

"I don't doubt that for a moment. Well, he won't be doing things like that anymore. I expect he is going to spend a long time in jail." Matthews chuckled. "And here is the interesting thing. A lot of his fellow inmates will be people that he put there."

"What poor timing. If Briggs had gone to jail a week or so ago, Jenny would be right here, enjoying the party along with the rest of us." Adele was quiet for a long moment. "Instead she is trapped on that train, starving to death."

"Well, it's too late to do anything about her being on that train, but we can certainly make it so she can come back to Pueblo," Matthews said. "That is, if she wants to. After the shabby way she was treated, she may not even want to come back."

"You are right about that. Jenny is a young woman with a lot of personal pride and self-confidence. Coming back to Pueblo might be about the last thing she has on her mind. But I think she ought to have to option to come back if she wants to."

"Yes, well, I don't know what made Briggs think he could run her off in the first place. But with him no longer on the bench, his order that she be run out of town is certainly without authority now. I tell you what, the mayor is over there. I'm sure he has the authority to vacate Briggs's order. Especially since Briggs has been removed from the bench."

"Oh, do you think so?" A smile of hope crossed Adele's face.

"I not only think so, I'm so sure of it I'll go ask him right now."

"I'll go with you."

His Honor Mayor C. E. "Daddy" Felker, a man of

rather imposing girth, was sitting on the sofa, squeezed between two of Adele's girls. It was obvious he didn't mind the closeness, as he had a big smile on his face when Matthews and Adele approached him.

"Merry Christmas, Mr. Mayor," Adele greeted.

"Yes, yes indeed, Merry Christmas," Felker replied. "What a wonderful party you are throwing tonight."

"It would be more wonderful if Jenny were here."

"Oh, that's right. She was forced to leave town, wasn't she? Such a shame. She would have been a wonderful addition to the party."

"She was run out of town by Amon Briggs," Matthews informed.

"Amon Briggs. What a disreputable character he turned out to be," Felker said. "I expect we will find that he was involved in a lot more chicanery than we even know about."

"Mr. Mayor, you could undo some of the evil Briggs did," Matthews suggested.

"Oh? And how is that?"

"You could vacate his order that Jenny McCoy be banished."

"Do I have the authority to do that?"

"Who is going to tell you that you don't? You are the mayor."

"Yes." Felker pounded his knee. "Yes, by golly, I am the mayor, aren't I? You know, I believe I do have the authority to do that."

"And will you do it?" Adele asked.

"Consider it done, my dear."

* * *

Fifteen minutes later, Adele was at the telegraph office in the Denver and Pacific Depot. "I understand that we have been getting telegrams from the trapped train."

"Yes, that is true. Mr. Bailey, the conductor, used to be a telegrapher and they have tapped into the wire."

"Is it possible to send a telegraph to someone on the train?"

"Yes, we have already sent a few. Do you wish to send one?"

"Yes."

"Who will be the recipient?"

"Jenny McCoy."

"Jenny McCoy? You mean the young woman who was run out of town?"

"Yes, that is the Jenny McCoy I'm talking about," Adele said pointedly.

"All right." The telegrapher picked up a pencil and a pad. "What is the message?"

"Judge Briggs is gone. Mayor Felker says you can come back. I hope that you are willing to do so. And sign it Adele."

"Very well. I'll send it," the telegrapher said.

As Adele left the telegrapher, she heard some carolers singing, and she stopped, just long enough to listen.

"Silent night, holy night
All is calm all is bright
'Round yon virgin Mother and Child
Holy infant so tender and mild
Sleep in heavenly peace
Sleep in heavenly peace."

Adele stepped into the narthex of St. Paul's Episcopal Church. Despite her profession, she was a very religious woman. Dipping her fingers into the baptismal font, she made the sign of the cross and thought back to when she had asked Father Pyron, the Episcopal priest, if he would accept her in his parish, and if she would be allowed to take the Eucharist.

"And why wouldn't I allow it?" Father Pyron replied.

"Because I am a prostitute," Adele said. "Well, I'm not really a prostitute, at least, not any longer. But I'm sure you know that I run a house of prostitution."

"Have you considered closing it?"

"I have considered closing it. But if I did, where would my girls go? What would they do? They would wind up in cribs somewhere, barely eking out a living. And without my protection, some might even be killed."

Father Pyron smiled. "You do have a powerful argument for your sin. But it has been suggested that Mary Magdalene was a prostitute. 'She whom Luke calls the sinful woman, whom John calls Mary, previously used the unguent to perfume her flesh in forbidden acts.' And of course, we know that Mary Magdalene was present at the crucifixion, the burial, and the resurrection. So if Jesus could accept Mary, then who am I to deny you the rite of communion?"

That conversation had taken place two years ago, and Adele had been a regular parishioner ever since.

She walked down to the chancel, genuflected before the cross, then knelt at the rail, crossed herself again, and prayed aloud. "Please, Lord, be with Jenny and all the other poor people trapped on that train. And let her find it in her heart to forgive the town, and return."

She crossed herself again, stood and genuflected one more time, then left the church. She walked back to the depot, on the chance that Jenny might answer the telegram.

On board the train

When the telegraph began to clatter again, Bailey hurried over to it to write down the message. "Mrs. McCoy. This message is for you."

"For me?"

"Yes, ma'am."

"Who would be sending me a message?"

"It's signed by the person who sent it," Bailey said.

Jenny read the message, then felt tears welling up in her eyes."

"Jenny!" Luke said. He hurried to her. "What is it? Is something wrong?"

"No. Something is right." She smiled through her tears and showed the message to Luke. "It's from Adele, and it looks like we might be able to have that dinner together after all."

Luke read the message, then embraced Jenny.

"Mr. Bailey, can I send a message back to Adele?"

"Yes, ma'am," Bailey said. "What do you want to send?"

"I want to say, Thank you, Adele, so much for this welcome news. I am sure you had a lot to do with it, and I'm very grateful. And sign it Jenny."

Bailey translated the message into telegraph speak and sent it on its way.

Chapter Thirty-three

On the mountain

Smoke and Duff took turns pulling the sled. Unlike the first part of the journey where pulling the sled had been laborious, it trailed behind Smoke as easily as if it weren't loaded. They followed the wide, flat path set out in front of them, amazed at how much easier it was to climb and how clearly it could be seen. The snow shimmered so brightly it looked as if it were being illuminated by lanterns.

Duff had never seen anything quite like it and he stared at it in curiosity. "'Tis a miracle of sorts, don't you think?"

"What do you mean?"

"I mean, here it is, so dark you can't see your hand in front of your face, and yet the path before us is glowing in the moonlight, almost as if it had lights of its own."

"Yes. You could say it is a miracle." Smoke looked

at the old mountain man who was leading them. He was about twenty feet ahead of them, moving as easily if he were walking across a parlor floor. As before, there was an aura around him, an enveloping silver glow that looked, not as if it were shining on him, but as if it were coming from him. That same light spread out along the path they were following.

Smoke knew, of course, it wasn't possible the light was coming from the old man. A full moon could be really bright, especially when reflected by the snow. No doubt what he was seeing was, as Duff had said, a reflection of the moonlight.

Smoke had climbed, hunted, and trapped on this mountain, many, many times in the past. He knew every inch of it as well as he knew his own backyard. But he had never seen a path like that, and had no idea how it had gotten there. He wasn't one to turn his back on opportunity, though, so he kept putting one foot in front of the other, following the path that was making their climb incredibly easy.

"How much farther do you think it is to top of the pass?" Duff asked.

"Do you smell that?" Smoke called back to Duff.

Duff took a deep sniff, then smiled. "Yes. I do smell it. It's smoke."

"And not just any smoke. It's coal smoke. That means we are very close now. I would say we are within a mile, maybe even closer."

"I don't know how you found this trail," Duff said. "But it has certainly made our effort much easier."

"I didn't find it. Preacher did."

"You have mentioned Preacher before. Tell me about him."

"Preacher is as fine a man as I've ever known. One of the original settlers of Colorado, he came out here to live in the mountains when there weren't more than two or three hundred white men within a thousand miles. He trapped beaver, lived off the game he took—bear, deer, elk, mountain goat."

"Why do call him Preacher? Was he an ordained minister? A man of God?"

"He wasn't an ordained minister, but he was, and I have to say is, definitely a man of God."

"Aye, 'tis a pleasure when one can find such a man, and a treasure when you can call him your friend. You are truly blessed, Smoke."

"Yes, I am." Smoke looked back to the path in front of him, but the old mountain man was gone. "Where did he go?"

"Who, Preacher? What do you mean where did he go? I thought you said he had died."

"Yes. Yes, that's true. Preacher is no longer with us."

They continued their trek up, following the path to the top of the mountain.

"What now? We're at the top of the mountain, and there's no train," Duff said.

Smoke realized then that the path had taken them all the way to the summit of the mountain, to the very top of the cut, above the pass. Approaching the edge very carefully, he looked down and saw the train, or rather, what could be seen of the train, well below them. It was sticking out from a high wall of snow, almost like an arrow protruding from a target. Lights could be seen in the windows of the last car and the coal smoke they had smelled earlier was drifting up from the chimney.

"Come over here, but be careful," Smoke said. "This is the top of the cut and there's a sheer drop here."

Duff approached, and Smoke pointed. "There's the train."

"Aye. 'Tis easy to see why they are trapped. There's a mountain of snow in front of them."

"And behind them as well. It looks to me like this train could be stuck here for a month."

"How are we ever going to get them out?" Duff asked.

"Let's feed them first, then we'll worry about getting them out," Smoke proposed.

"My word," Duff marveled.

"What is it?"

"Look at the moon. I thought it must be full, but it's only in its last quarter. Now, would you be for tellin' me, how a moon like that could produce enough light to make our path glow as it did?"

"I don't know," Smoke admitted. "Maybe it was the way the snow was spread out, just right to reflect what light there was."

"That can't be it. I mean it was almost like the snow itself was lighting our way for us. I know that sounds strange, but if you will look back at the path you'll see what I'm talking about. It—" Duff paused in mid-sentence. "Smoke? The path!"

"What about the path? Is it still glowing?"

"There is no path!" Duff's voice was laced with awe. "Look behind us, Smoke. There is nothing there but rocks and trees and snow. There is no path, lit or unlit. How did we get here? We could not possibly have come up that way."

"You aren't making sense, Duff. We're here, aren't we?"

"Yes, but—"

"But nothing. We are here, which means there had to be a path. We just aren't standing where we can see it clearly, that's all. Anyway, what is behind us doesn't matter. We still have to get down to the train."

"Aye. 'Twould be a shame to have come this far, and not be able to go the rest of the way. There's nothing now but the sheer wall of the cut. And even if we could climb down it, how would we get the sled down? If we show up without any food, we've just made the situation worse. We have to go on, or our trip has been nothing but a waste of time."

"I am determined that it not be a waste of time," Smoke declared. "We will get there, and we will deliver the food."

"Aye, 'tis my belief as well that we will succeed. I *dinnae* think the Good Lord would be for bringin' us this far if we *cannae* go on."

"Let's wait until sunup. I'm sure we'll find a way.

If nothing else, we'll just push the sled over, then find a way to climb down."

"I'm putting my trust in you, my friend. You haven't failed us yet," Duff avowed.

"I thank you for your vote of confidence, Duff," Smoke replied. "I just hope I can live up to it. What do you say we take a breather for a while?"

"Good idea," Duff replied.

The two men sat down in the snow and leaned back against the sled.

"Duff, do you believe in ghosts?"

Duff chuckled. "How can I not believe? I'm from Scotland. Do you not know the story of the Scottish King MacBeth and Banquo's ghost?"

"I've never heard of it."

"'Tis a story told by Shakespeare. I'll quote a bit for you." Duff extended his arm.

"What are you holding your hand out like that for?"

"Have you never been to a Shakespearian play? "Sure m'lad and 'tis necessary for me to establish the mood, tone, and tint."

Duff began reciting, as if on stage.

"Avaunt! and quit my sight!
let the earth hide thee!
Thy bones are marrowless, thy blood is cold;
Thou hast no speculation in those eyes
Which thou dost glare with!"

"Very good," Smoke said.

"So, why did you ask me about a ghost? Have you seen one?"

"I don't know exactly what I've seen," Smoke replied. "Let's nap until daylight."

"Yes, we seem to have lost our mysterious light, so it probably is smart to wait until daylight before we look for a way down," Duff agreed.

After a few more minutes, both men had drifted off to sleep.

On board the train

As they had on previous nights, Luke and Jenny were sitting side by side in the very front seat of the car. They were protected against the cold by her coat and the serape, and by their body heat.

She could hear Luke's deep, measured breathing, and knew he was asleep beside her. She knew also it was more than just the wraps and the shared body heat that warmed her. It was something else, some visceral reaction she was having to his closeness.

As she thought about it, she found the situation a little frightening. When she knew that he was going to be gone for four years, and that she was being forced to leave Pueblo, there was a certain degree of detachment between them. They were like that passage from one of Longfellow's poems:

Ships that pass in the night, and speak each other
in passing,

Only a signal shown and a distant voice in the darkness.

That very detachment protected her. She could enjoy his company and lose herself in fantasy. As long as she realized that it was but fantasy, she wouldn't be hurt when it didn't come to pass.

But everything had changed. Luke wasn't going to jail, and she wasn't being banished from Pueblo. What did that mean? Would Luke return to Two Crowns, and she to the Social Club? If they met on the street, would they acknowledge each other's presence? Or would they look away, and pass each other with no outward sign that they had ever even met?

It wasn't fair. It just wasn't fair to have met someone she could truly love, only to have that love denied her. And she was certain that once they returned, that love would be denied.

Jenny wept quietly.

On the other side of the car, Herbert Bailey drummed his fingers on the cold window and looked out into the night. It was his fault everyone was stuck on the mountain pass. He was the one who'd insisted the train move on ahead—because he knew the railroad would lose money if the trip wasn't completed—even though Don had been hesitant about it. And by that foolish insistence, he had put every soul on the train in danger.

He had believed the railroad would recognize his

boldness, and as a result, his position and authority, to say nothing of his salary, would be increased, even though he had only been a conductor for a couple months.

Bailey had been a telegrapher, but though the job was interesting and provided a much-needed service to others, he'd wanted the money and prestige that came with being a railroad conductor. Looking into the dark night he remembered his father's attempt to change his mind.

"You are being foolish, Herbert," his father said when Bailey told him of his intention. "You are the only telegrapher in this town. If you leave it may be a long time before we can get another to take your place. What if there is an emergency, a need for a message to go forth, and there is no one to send it? It could be a matter of life and death, with no one to turn to, because you are gone."

"But, Father, don't I have to think of myself, first?" Bailey had replied. "I will make much more money as a railroad conductor, and people will respect my position."

"You put money and importance ahead of all else. The mark of a good man is his service to others. Don't you know that when you die, the only thing you can take with you are the good deeds you have done? When you answer to the Almighty, will He be more pleased that you made money and had prestige by your position? Or would it please Him more if you could bring Him a lifetime of service to others?"

"I must do what I must do," Bailey said.

Bailey's father handed him a Bible. "I know you have made your decision, so I will not try to change it. But I ask, only that you read Luke twelve, verses sixteen to twenty-one."

To satisfy his father, Bailey read the recommended text.

> *"And he spake a parable unto them, saying, The ground of a certain rich man brought forth plentifully:*
>
> *"And he thought within himself, saying, What shall I do, because I have no room where to bestow my fruits?*
>
> *"And he said, This will I do: I will pull down my barns, and build greater; and there will I bestow all my fruits and my goods.*
>
> *"And I will say to my soul, Soul, thou hast much goods laid up for many years; take thine ease, eat, drink, and be merry.*
>
> *"But God said unto him, Thou fool, this night thy soul shall be required of thee: then whose shall those things be, which thou hast provided?*
>
> *"So is he that layeth up treasure for himself, and is not rich toward God."*

His father's attempt to change his mind had had no effect, and Bailey had eventually become a conductor. Ironically, it wasn't his position as conductor making a difference during the Red Cliff Special ordeal. It was through his ability as a telegrapher. His father had been right. If he died during this ordeal, what good would the increased salary and position be?

He knew the small town of Higbee had been

unable to locate a replacement telegrapher. Making a fist, he tapped the window once as if confirming his decision. When he got out of this situation, if he got out, he intended to go back to his old job as telegrapher for the town of Higbee.

Chapter Thirty-four

On the mountain—Christmas morning, December 25

Wrapped tightly in several blankets, Smoke was the first to awaken, and when he opened his eyes, he saw the old mountain man standing in front of him. The butt of his Hawkens was on the ground before him, and his hands were crossed and resting on the muzzle. His head, covered with a coonskin cap, was tilted to one side, and he was smiling down at Smoke. "I wondered when you were going to wake up."

"I thought you were gone," Smoke mumbled as he stretched.

"You didn't think I would bring you this far, then not let you finish the job, did you?"

"You've brought us to the train, now what? There's no way down to it."

"I'll show you the way."

"There *is* no way," Smoke said emphatically. "I've

been here dozens of times. I know this pass like I know my own ranch."

"Wake up Duff, and follow me," the old mountain man said.

"Duff, wake up." Smoke gave his friend a poke, then threw off his blankets to start the morning.

Duff opened his eyes, but didn't move a muscle, staying snug in his blankets.

"Come on, we're going down to the train."

"How?"

"Just trust me."

"I'm with you." Duff stretched, then climbed out of the blankets and stomped his feet. "Whew. Didn't get any warmer overnight, did it?" He made a few quick jumps to get the blood flowing and picked up the leader to the sled. "Where are we going?"

"That's a good question," Smoke said. "Where are we going?"

"Don't worry about where we are going. In all the years you have known me, have I ever steered you wrong?" the mountain man replied.

"What do you mean, where are we going?" Duff asked. "Don't you know? You're in front of me. Sure, lad, and I'll be going where you go."

"I wasn't asking you," Smoke muttered.

"Well, who were you asking? There's nobody else here, but the two of us."

"I . . . I guess was just talking to myself."

Duff chuckled. "Don't talk to yourself like that. It makes me nervous to think I'm wandering around out here in the mountains with a man who has suddenly gone mad."

Smoke laughed as well. "What makes you think I suddenly went mad? If you ask Sally, she'll tell you I've been crazy from the moment she first met me."

"Ha!" the old mountain man put in. "You were crazy long before you ever met Sally."

"You haven't changed, have you?" Smoke said. "You are as cantankerous now as you ever were."

"Cantankerous am I?" Duff questioned.

"No, not you. I'm not talking about you."

"Oh, I see. You're talking to your invisible friend, are you?"

Smoke chuckled. "I guess I am."

On board the train

"Oh, Jarred," Millie said, her voice choked by sobs. "I can't wake Becky up."

"Becky! Becky! Wake up, child! Wake up!" Senator Daniels called.

"Oh! Jarred! Is she . . . Is she . . . ?" Millie couldn't finish the question.

"I . . . I don't know." Senator Daniels pinched his nose. "Oh, Millie, it's my fault, it's all my fault. I'm sorry. You were right. We should have stayed in Pueblo and taken her to a doctor. It's all my fault, I got us into this mess."

"It's not your fault," Millie said. "You had no way of knowing anything like this was going to happen. If it had been a normal train trip, we would have been to Red Cliff long before now, and a doctor would have seen her."

Senator Daniels knelt on the floor beside Becky, then leaned over to kiss her on her forehead. "I'm sorry, I'm so sorry."

Senator Daniels stood up. It was morning, and the sun was streaming into the car. Those who had slept fitfully through the night were awakening. Some had overheard Daniels and his wife and were looking toward them with concern.

"Could I have your attention, please?" Jarred called. "I want to make a public confession and a public apology. I have been, well, there is no other way to say it, but to just come out and say it. I have been a jerk on this trip. No, not just on this trip. I have been a self-centered, arrogant jerk for some time." He looked down at his daughter for a moment, trying to compose himself. "And now my daughter is dying . . . if she hasn't already . . ." He couldn't force himself to say the word *died.* "If we had stayed in Pueblo, a doctor might have been able to help her. Or maybe not. The point is, against my wife's instincts, I insisted we make this trip because I had a very important speech to make tonight.

"But as it turns out, it wasn't really all that important after all. It was important only as far as my political career is concerned. The fact that I missed the speech is of no consequence to anyone.

"I want to apologize to everyone in this car." Senator Daniels looked over toward the porters. "And I especially want to apologize to you three gentlemen.

My actions and comments toward you have been bigoted and small-minded, and I am heartily sorry. I ask your forgiveness, and from all of you, I ask your prayers for my daughter."

"Senator, I been prayin' for your little girl from the first I learned she was sick," Troy said.

"Thank you, Troy." Senator Daniels lowered his head and pinched the bridge of his nose. "And I thank the rest of you for giving me a moment of your time to let me make this public apology."

"Senator, I would say the speech you just made is a hundred times more important than any speech you would have given at that dinner in Red Cliff," Matt said.

"Hear, hear," Luke said, and when he began to applaud, the others joined in.

After Senator Daniels's apology, the passengers settled back into the routine they had established during the long ordeal. Luke and Jenny sat together, warmed by her coat, his serape, and the closeness of their bodies.

"Luke, when you asked if I would have dinner with you when you came back in four years, I said yes, because I didn't know what else to say. The truth is, I had no idea where I would be four years from now, and I still don't. But I do know where I will be if we ever get off this train. I'll be back in Pueblo, and if you were serious, if you really want to see me again, I would be happy to have dinner with you."

"Why wouldn't I want to see you again?"

"You know who I am. You know where I work."

"I'd rather you not go back to work at the social club, though," Luke said.

"I . . . I don't really want to go back there, either. But Adele has been a wonderful friend. And I don't know where else I would be able to work."

"What about raising our children?" Luke asked. "Wouldn't that be work enough for you?"

"Raising our children?"

"Yes, I would like to have children, wouldn't you?"

"Luke, let me get this straight. Are you asking me to marry you?"

"Well, yes. I mean, we really should get married before we start having children, don't you think?"

Jenny laughed. "But . . . that's insane! We've only known each other for four days!"

"Remember the Samoans."

"There is no difference in the heart of a flower that lives but a single day, and the heart of a tree that lives for a thousand years," Jenny repeated what Luke had told her earlier.

"We've known each other for a thousand years, Jenny. Will you marry me?"

"Yes! Yes, Luke, I will marry you!"

They sealed the decision with a kiss.

Suddenly, Timmy shouted, "It's Christmas morning! Hey, everybody, Merry Christmas!"

Bailey chuckled. "Oh for the spirit of a youngster. At a time like this, he can still be excited by the fact that it is Christmas."

"He's right, though. It is Christmas," Luke said, getting to his feet. "And it is the most wonderful Christmas of my life. I've an announcement to make, folks. Jenny McCoy has agreed to be my wife. Merry Christmas "

"Merry Christmas to you as well, young man, and congratulations," Purvis said.

For a few moments after the announcement, and despite the fact that they were stranded and without food, a bit of good nature prevailed among the passengers. Anita and Clara came to talk excitedly to Jenny about her upcoming marriage.

Matt went over to Becky, who was lying on the seat, either asleep, or unconscious, or perhaps even dead. It was difficult to tell. "When was the last time she was awake? Do you know?"

"I don't know," Millie said. "I think she may have been awake for a bit, yesterday. But I don't think she was awake at all during the night. I . . . I don't even know if she is still alive. She is so . . . so unresponsive."

Matt opened his knife, then took one of her fingers and pricked it with the point of the knife, studying the little girl's face as he did so. She gave no reaction to the stimulus.

"Do you have small mirror in your handbag?"

"No, I'm afraid I don't."

"I do," Jenny said, having overheard the conversation. She opened her handbag and took out a small compact, opening it to expose the mirror.

Matt held the mirror under Becky's nose. A small cloud of condensation appeared on the mirror, and he smiled, then showed it to Millie. "She's still breathing, Mrs. Daniels, so she's alive. Don't lose hope. She may be in what they call a coma. I've known people to be in them before and come out of them. All the people in this car are praying for her. And like Timmy said, this is Christmas. I've seen things happen on Christmas, wonderful things that defy understanding. One Christmas I saw a baby born in a barn when all the odds were against it.* That birth reminded us all of that first Christmas."

"If you folks don't mind, I'd like to say a Christmas prayer," Troy offered.

"I don't think we would mind at all, Troy," Senator Daniels said. "In fact, I think we would appreciate it. I know that I would."

Troy nodded and bowed his head. "*Lord, we thank you for the sweet baby Jesus that was born so many years ago. Thank you that He paid for our sins by dying on the cross. We are in a dark time now, and we pray that you guide us through it, and Lord, we pray for this sweet child, Becky, who is so sick. Put your healin' hand on her Lord. In Christ's name we pray. Amen.*"

"Thank you, Troy. That was a wonderful prayer." Senator Daniels turned to the conductor. "Oh, and Mr. Bailey?"

"Yes?"

**A Lonestar Christmas.*

"Forget about what I said about holding the Denver and Pacific responsible. I am going to make a report to the Denver and Pacific, but it will be to praise you and all the rest of the train crew for your exemplary service under extraordinary conditions."

"I deserve no praise, Senator. It was my insistence that we continue on that put you, your family, and everyone else on this train in danger."

Chapter Thirty-five

On the mountain

"I dinnae believe my eyes," Duff said. "There is a path down the sheer side of this cut, and 'tis no ordinary path, but one that is wide and flat and hard packed with snow for the sled."

"I told you we should wait until sunrise." Smoke grinned.

"You mean you knew about this path? Of course you did. You live here. How could you not know?"

Smoke was silent for a long moment. Taking a deep breath, he said honestly, "I've never seen this path before in my life."

"How could you nae see it? 'Tis almost like a ramp."

"It wasn't here before."

"Then how did it get here?"

"I don't know," Smoke admitted. "Maybe it was created by the storm. Weather does such things, you know."

It took less than ten minutes to reach the bottom of the cut, where they found themselves at the back of the train. A black man lay on the ground just off the track, a dark shadow against the brilliant white of the snow.

Duff knelt on one knee and put his hand to the man's neck, though the fact that he was lying there, unmoving, and with both eyes open, made any further investigation unnecessary. "Och, the poor man is dead."

Smoke and Duff climbed up onto the rear platform and tapped on the door to the car.

Nobody inside the car had seen the approach of the two men and the sled, so the tapping on the door was unexpected.

"It must be Santelli!" Purvis shouted.

"Everyone down, behind the seats!" Matt called, pulling his pistol and pointing it toward the back.

The passengers scurried to follow his directions.

The door opened and two men bundled in winter coats came in.

"Hello?" Smoke called out tentatively.

"Smoke!" Matt shouted happily. Holstering his pistol, he rushed to him. "You made it!" Matt grabbed Smoke's hand and pumped it vigorously."

"Why is it I always find you bottom-lip deep in snow?" Smoke teased.

Matt grinned and turned to Smoke's friend. "Duff!"

"Aye. Happy to be able to help."

Matt called the others from their hiding places and introduced Smoke and Duff. "I told you he would come." Matt couldn't stop grinning.

The passengers expressed their happy gratitude.

"Oh, by the way, is anyone hungry? I've got food on the sled outside," Smoke said.

Several people made a mad rush for the door.

"Wait, wait!" Smoke held up his hand. "We'll bring it in to you. It's only bread and sardines, but that should hold you until we get you out of here."

"Praise the Lord, he's done delivered us loaves and fishes!" Troy called out.

"By golly, Troy, you are right!" Bailey acknowledged. "But I hope it's more than five loaves and two fishes."

Smoke stood on the rear platform as Duff took the food from the sled and passed it up to him. Smoke passed it to Matt, who handed it to Luke. Luke and Bailey opened the tins of sardines and passed them out, one each to everyone in the car. There was no crowding or feeling of fear that they wouldn't get their share. On the contrary, everyone was solicitous for others.

"Mama, this is the best Christmas dinner I've ever et," Timmy said.

Clara laughed. "You mean the best that you have ever eaten, and I agree with you. It is delicious."

"I wish Becky could enjoy it," Barbara said.

"So do I, Sweetheart," Anita said. "So do I."

"Becky?" Smoke asked, the name piquing his interest. "You have someone here named Becky?"

"Yes. She is Senator Daniels's daughter, and she has been ill from the time we left Pueblo. Over the last twenty-four hours she has been unconscious." Matt looked around to make certain he wasn't overheard, then he added, "I've been trying to keep their spirits up, but to tell you the truth, I'm not sure she is going to make it."

"And her name is Becky? You are sure that it's Becky?"

"Yes. Why are you so curious about that particular name?"

"Because I—" Smoke stopped in mid-sentence. Duff already thought he had gone mad. If he told Matt he'd seen Becky out on the trail, that she had come to him, Matt would also think he was crazy. "Nothing. I would like to see her."

"She's over here." Matt led Smoke over to the seat where Becky lay, still covered by Matt's coat. Senator Daniels and his wife were sitting together in the seat across from Becky, eating their sardines and bread.

"This is my friend, Smoke Jensen," Matt said.

Senator Daniels started to get up, but Smoke held out his hand. "No, don't get up."

"Mr. Jensen, I know I speak for all of us when I tell you how thankful we are for your courage in tackling this mountain to bring us food and hope. I didn't think you could do it, but here you are."

"I heard about your daughter," Smoke said. "I just thought I'd like to take a look at her."

"Of course you can," Millie agreed.

Smoke pulled the coat down slightly, so he could get a better look at her. He wasn't at all surprised she was the same little girl he had seen on the mountain. He didn't understand it, but he wasn't surprised. He reached down to place the back of his hand against her cheek. "I have come, Becky," he said quietly. "Can you hear me? I have come."

"We are so worried about her." Millie's voice shook a little.

"She will be all right," Smoke declared.

"I pray that you are right."

"I know that she will be all right," Smoke said emphatically. "I can't tell you how I know, but I know."

Tears welled in Millie's eyes, and she took Smoke's hand in hers, the same hand that had touched Becky's cheek, and she raised it to her lips to kiss. "I believe you."

Smoke nodded a confirmation to the Danielses and he and Matt walked back to the rear of the car. Matt tore off a piece of bread and picked up an open tin of sardines. "How in the world did you two get up here? I know this mountain, if you don't come up through the pass, it is practically impossible to climb."

"It was easier than you think. We just followed a path up to the top, then down here. Look, you can see the path coming down the—" Duff stopped in mid-sentence. There was no path. There was nothing but mountains of snow all around them. There weren't even any tracks in the snow left by Smoke, Duff, and the sled.

"What happened to the path? It's just like when we were coming up the mountain. That path was gone, too. I don't understand."

"The path left when Preacher left," Smoke said quietly. "He is the one who led us here."

"Preacher?" Matt exclaimed. "Who are you talking about?"

"You know who I mean by Preacher. You met him," Smoke pointed out.

Matt shook his head. "Excuse me, but you aren't making any sense. Preacher is dead. At least the one I know. But you're saying Preacher led you here. Unless you are talking about someone else."

"No, I'm talking about the same one. He's the one that guided us here."

"Smoke, sure 'n did the cold freeze your brain?" Duff asked. "There was no one that guided us here. You led and I followed, every step of the way. I heard you mumbling and talking to yourself, but you were in the lead. There wasn't anyone else."

"Then how do you explain there is no path, and that we left no tracks?" Smoke asked.

"I don't know. I can't explain it."

"I can. The path was there when Preacher was there. And when Preacher left, the path left. And I'll tell you something else. Becky?"

"What about Becky?" Matt asked.

"She was there, too. I saw her on the mountain. The same little girl that's lying over there on that seat." Smoke pointed toward the Daniels.

"That's impossible," Matt argued. "She hasn't left

this train. She's barely been conscious. So how do you explain that you saw her?"

"I can't explain it. Just like I can't explain how I saw Preacher. But I saw Preacher, and I saw Becky." Smoke was absolutely positive what he saw.

"Smoke, Matt, sure 'n let's not be for tellin' this tale to anyone else," Duff suggested. "They'll think we've all gone daft. And I don't know but that they would be right."

"Look!" Bailey suddenly shouted, pointing to the track behind them. "The track behind us is clear! We can get out now."

"I'm not walking back down this track," Senator Daniels fussed. "I'm not leaving Becky."

"There's no need to leave anyone," Don the engineer advised. "And there's no need for anyone to walk. I've made this run so many times I know every inch of this track. All we have to do is disconnect this car . . . and we can roll all the way back to Buena Vista."

"I believe he is right," Bailey said.

"Let's try it," Smoke suggested.

Matt, Smoke, Duff, Bailey, Don the engineer, and Beans the fireman worked on the coupler until they got it free. Then they strained against the car, pushing to get it started.

Suddenly, a bullet careened off the side of the car, raising sparks where it hit the metal frame, then ricocheting off with a loud, echoing whine.

They turned to see Santelli, Kelly, and Compton

coming toward them, all three with pistols in their hands. Santelli fired again, and again he missed.

Smoke and Matt drew their pistols, but Don called out. "No! Don't shoot! You might start an avalanche!"

Even as he shouted the warning, they heard a roaring thunder high up in the mountains. And, though they could hear it, as yet, they saw nothing.

"Get the car moving! We have to get out of here!" Matt shouted, and the men turned to the task at hand, starting the car to roll, slowly at first, then more rapidly, then faster still, until gravity took over and the car started rolling on its own.

Don and Beans jumped on first, then Smoke and Duff. Bailey and Matt were the last two aboard, barely catching up to the car, so fast was it rolling.

"Don't you leave us!" Santelli shouted. "Don't you dare leave us! *Don't . . . you . . . leave . . .*"

Beyond that, Matt couldn't hear him. Santelli's words faded as the distance increased, and were quickly silenced by the growing roar coming from the mountaintop.

"Look!" Bailey shouted in awe, pointing to the top of the mountain.

A fifty-foot-high wall of snow, half a mile wide, came sliding down the side of the mountain, its churning white wave filled with rocks and broken tree trunks.

Santelli, Compton, and Kelly stood looking up at it, their mouths and eyes wide open in horror. Matt was sure they were crying out a death scream of terror, though from his position on the car, he couldn't hear anything but the roar of the avalanche.

The gunmen disappeared under the huge wave of snow, rocks, and broken tree trunks as the avalanche smashed against the train cars, crushing them as if they were naught but children's toys.

As the men watched from the free-rolling car, the avalanche was increasing in width as more and more of the mountain began coming down. It moved fast, racing down the track behind them, easily matching the car in speed.

Fortunately, it wasn't going *faster* than the car, and therefore, not overtaking it, though Matt feared it might, so close was it behind them. He literally willed the car to go faster until, finally, the distance between the cascading snow and the rapidly moving car was increasing. After a full minute, he was satisfied the car was no longer in danger and went back into the car.

The engineer had gone to the other end of the car and was standing out on the platform, looking ahead as the car swept rapidly down the track. Matt joined him, and felt the cold air knifing through him as the car rushed ahead.

"We are really going fast," Don said. "I'm pretty sure I've never gone this fast."

"I don't know how fast we are going, but we

needed every bit of it. The avalanche was coming down the track toward us, and we barely escaped."

"Count off twenty seconds. I'll count the number of rail joint clicks. The number of clicks we hear in twenty seconds will tell us how fast we are going in miles per hour."

Matt counted off the seconds, but when he got to twenty, Don shook his head. "We're going too fast for me to get an accurate count, but my guess would be that we are doing at least sixty miles per hour."

"Wow! Sixty miles per hour? Is there any danger of us running off the track?"

"I don't think so. Most of the turns are long and gentle. Though, certainly none of them have ever been taken at this speed."

"What do you say we go back inside the car and get out of this cold wind?" Matt suggested.

"Yes," Don replied. "That's a good idea."

Duff was standing just inside the car, and he had a question. It was a question Matt had already considered, but hadn't yet asked.

"How do we stop this thing when we get there?" Duff asked.

"That won't be a problem," Don said. "The track flattens out for the last half mile before we get into the station. By the time we get to the depot, we won't be going any faster than a walk."

Senator Daniels came over to join them. "Well, all I can say is this. Gentlemen, this has certainly been an adventure."

"You can say that again," Don replied.

"We sure are going fast," Becky said. The little girl's words stunned everyone into shocked silence. She was standing just behind her father.

"Becky!" Senator Daniels shouted.

"Oh, Becky, Sweetheart! You are up!" Millie said, hurrying over to her, and sweeping her up into a big hug.

"Jarred! The fever! I don't feel it! It's gone!" Millie said excitedly.

Everyone else in the car reacted in amazement at seeing the little girl who, but a short time ago, had been in an unresponsive state of unconsciousness. Now she was up and talking. All called out in excitement, and Barbara ran over to her, spontaneously giving her a hug.

"Daddy, I'm hungry," Becky said.

Half a dozen passengers offered her food, and she accepted a piece of bread from Anita.

"How do you feel, honey?" Millie asked.

"I feel good, Mama. I feel real good. Just like Mr. Preacher said I would."

"*Who* said that?" Smoke asked curiously.

"An old man. He was dressed in funny clothes, with a furry coat and a little furry cap that looked sort of like a squirrel." Becky laughed. "You know who he is. You were with him out there in the cold. I saw you. You were with him, weren't you?"

Smoke glanced over at Duff and smiled at the

expression of shock on his face. "Yes, honey. I was with him."

When the car finally rolled in to the depot at Buena Vista the news was spread far and wide. A Christmas celebration was held at the depot, and the entire town participated. People brought roast turkey, duck, chicken, beef, and ham, as well as vegetables of every hue and description, along with pies, cakes, and candy.

"Hey!" one of the railroad employees shouted, coming into the depot. He was holding up a Hawkens .50 caliber buffalo rifle. "Somebody left this back in the car. Anybody know who it belongs to?"

CHAPTER THIRTY-SIX

Pueblo—January 15, 1894

An article appeared in the *Pueblo Chieftain*:

> ***Track Cleared, Ten Bodies Recovered***
>
> The Denver and Pacific Railroad has cleared the track through Trout Creek Pass of the terrible wreckage left by the avalanche, which has, for these last three weeks, rendered traffic through the pass impossible.
>
> Our readers are well aware of the ordeal the passengers who took the Red Cliff Special five days before Christmas, with the intention and full expectation of spending Christmas with their loved ones have endured.
>
> The nefarious scheme of Michael Santelli and the four brigands he had

enlisted to aid him ruined Christmas for the innocent passengers. They suffered great hardships during the time they were trapped in the train, with no food and little fuel for warmth.

The train was subsequently reached by Smoke Jensen and Duff MacAllister, their bravery supplying a happy ending to the unhappy adventure. It may also be said that poetic justice was served, as the perpetrators of the crime: Michael Santelli, Felix Parker, Roy Compton, Gerald Kelly, and Melvin Morris, were all killed by avalanche. Their mangled bodies were found in the wreckage.

Also found were the bodies of five innocent men: Deputy Braxton Proxmire, Dennis Dace, and Andrew Patterson of this city, Paul Clark, Deputy City Marshal of Red Cliff, and Fred Jones, a colored porter.

Red Cliff—January 16

Abner Purvis was a passenger on the first train to make the trip to Red Cliff after the pass was reopened. He walked the seven miles from the Red Cliff train station to his father's farm.

His brother was out feeding the pigs, and was the first to see him. He reacted in great surprise at seeing his older brother coming down the road toward him. "Abner? Is that you?"

Abner held his hand out toward Aaron. "Don't

disturb yourself. I know that I walked away from my inheritance. I know the farm is yours. I want only to be treated as a hired hand."

Aaron smiled. "Come with me to see Pop."

Abner followed his brother into the machine shed, where their father was working on a plow shear.

"Pop, look who is here," Aaron said.

Arnold Purvis looked up to see who Aaron had brought to him. There was only a second's hesitation before his face was wreathed by a huge smile.

"Abner? Abner, my boy! You have come home!" Arnold cried excitedly, getting up from the workbench and hurrying over to embrace his son.

"Aaron, run quickly to tell your mother. Tell her I will kill a hen, so she can make chicken and dumplings." The elder Purvis looked back at Abner. "I know that is your favorite meal."

"Pop, I've already told Aaron. I've no wish to deprive him of the inheritance. The farm shall rightly be his."

The elder Purvis looked at Aaron with a confused expression on his face. "You haven't told him?"

"No, Pop. I haven't told him."

"Told me what?" Purvis asked.

"Abner, I have an appointment to West Point. I'll be leaving soon. I don't want the farm. It's all yours."

"Welcome back, son," Arnold said with a wide grin.

Pueblo—January 18

Luke had suggested they get married in the Colorado Social Club. Jenny was hesitant at first, but then she thought, *why not?* Adele Summers had been a very good friend to her, as had all the other girls who worked there. It was a bit unconventional, but Jenny didn't care. For those who declared themselves her friends, no explanation was necessary. For those who were openly hostile toward her, no explanation would be understood.

Adele had gone all out to decorate the club, and insisted the girls dress demurely as if they were going to church.

Father Pyron of St. Paul's Episcopal Church had never been in Adele's establishment before. While he was drinking a cup of coffee before the ceremony, he admitted he was looking forward to it. "I always wanted to know what this place looked like inside. This way I can come here without compromising myself."

Father Pyron wasn't the only one whose appearance in the club had caused no small degree of curiosity. Troy, Julius, and Pete were also there, the first time anyone of their color had ever set foot through the doors.

Senator Daniels and Millie were there. Becky was very proud to serve as Jenny's flower girl. Also in attendance was Herbert Bailey, who was no longer a railroad conductor, having been rehired as a telegrapher for the town of Higbee.

Smoke, Matt, and Duff were present for the wedding, and Duff had volunteered to play Pachelbel's "Canon in D" on his pipes. It was the first time anyone had heard the traditional wedding song played on the pipes, and so beautifully was it played there wasn't a single dry eye among the girls of the Colorado Social Club.

After the wedding, everyone went down to the train depot to wish the happy couple well as they left by train on the first leg of their wedding trip.

"Where in the world is Samoa?" Adele asked. "And why do they want to go there?"

Nobody had an answer.

As Smoke turned to leave the depot, he thought he saw an old man dressed in buckskin, carrying a long-barreled, Hawkens .50 caliber buffalo rifle and wearing a coonskin cap.

When he blinked, the man was gone.

Epilogue

Lambert Field, St. Louis—December 20, 1961

"Attention, passengers, the runways have been cleared, and the airport is now open. Please check with the schedule board to learn the status of your flight." The announcement came over the speaker.

"I fully recovered from my illness, whatever it was, and never had another recurrence," Rebecca said, completing the story of that Christmas, sixty-eight years ago.

"And your father went on to become governor," Margaret pointed out.

"That's right, he served two terms as governor, then in 1912, he was very nearly selected as the Vice Presidential candidate for Mr. Roosevelt. After that, he gave up politics and became a successful businessman in Denver."

"Speaking of successful, your life has been a steady string of successes. You have been a schoolteacher, a college professor, an accomplished author, and finally the United States Ambassador to Greece."

"Yes, my life has been blessed," Rebecca agreed.

"Mrs. Robison, in the story you just told, you met Mr. Jensen and Mr. MacAllister out on the mountain as they were coming to rescue the passengers."

"Yes."

"But that's not possible, is it? I mean, particularly when Matt Jensen said that you were in a coma, and that you never left the train."

"You would think so, wouldn't you?" Rebecca replied. "But I clearly remembered seeing Mr. Jensen and Mr. MacAllister out on the trail. It was probably a dream, but if it was, Mr. Jensen had the same dream, because he remembered seeing me out on the trail, as well."

"You also said someone named Preacher came to see you while you were in a coma and told you that you would be all right. Was that just a dream?"

An enigmatic smile spread across Rebecca's face. "I don't know. Was it? I'm still here, nearly seventy years later."

A uniformed airport attendant walked over to where Rebecca and Margaret were having their discussion. "Mrs. Robison, we are now loading first-class passengers for your flight to Denver."

"Thank you, young man."

"Will you need help in boarding?"

"No, thank you, I'm still quite mobile." Rebecca got up then, but before she left the lounge, she looked back. "Margaret, your young man is going to propose to you over dinner tonight. Say yes. You will have a wonderful marriage."

"What?" Margaret gasped.

"Merry Christmas, dear," the old lady said as she turned and walked toward the boarding gate.

Turn the page for an exciting preview

With his epic novels of the Jensen family, William W. Johnstone has captured the pioneer spirit of America. Now he reveals the untold story of Luke Jensen, a haunted gunman who survived the fiercest war in our nation's history to become the greatest bounty hunter who ever lived . . .

THE JENSEN FAMILY SAGA CONTINUES

During the last days of the Civil War, with Richmond under siege, Confederate soldier Luke Jensen is assigned the task of smuggling gold out of the city before the Yankees get their hands on it—when he is ambushed and robbed by four deserters, shot in the back, and left for dead. Taken in by a Georgia farmer and his beautiful daughter, Luke is nursed back to health. Though crippled, he hopes to reunite with his father and brother, but a growing romance keeps him on the farm until then fate takes a tragic turn. Ruthless carpetbaggers arrive and—in a storm of bullets and bloodshed—Luke is forced to strike out on his own. Searching for a new life. Hunting down his enemies. Gunning for revenge.

This is the making of a bounty hunter: the sprawling saga of one fearless man who would stop at nothing to bring outlaws to justice—and freedom to America.

LUKE JENSEN, BOUNTY HUNTER

Prologue

A rifle bullet smacked off the top of the log and sprayed splinters toward Luke Smith's face. He dropped his head quickly so the brim of his battered black hat protected his eyes. A splinter stung his cheek close to his neatly trimmed black mustache.

Luke looked into the sightless, staring eyes of the dead man who lay next to him. "Those amigos of yours are getting closer with their shots, José. Too bad for you that you're not alive to watch them kill me. Reckon you probably would've enjoyed that."

José Cardona didn't say anything. A bullet hole from one of Luke's Remingtons lay in the middle of his forehead, surrounded by powder burns. Most of the back of his head was gone where the slug had exploded out.

More shots rang out from the cabin about a hundred yards away, next to the little creek at the bottom of the slope. The sturdy log structure had been built for defense, with thick walls and numerous loopholes where rifle barrels could be stuck out and fired.

Luke had no idea who had built the cabin. Probably some old fur trapper or prospector. Those mountains in New Mexico Territory had seen their fair share of both.

Currently, it was being used as a hideout for the Solomon Burke gang. Luke had been on the trail of Burke and his bunch for several weeks. There was a $1,500 bounty on Burke's head and lesser amounts posted on the half-dozen owlhoots who rode with him. If Luke was able to bring in all of them, it would be a mighty nice payoff for him.

Unfortunately, it didn't look like things were going to work out that way. Luke had tracked the gang to the cabin and had been crouched in the timber up on the hill overlooking the creek, trying to figure out his next move, when someone tackled him from behind, knocking him out into the open. They rolled down the hill together, locked in a desperate struggle, even as the man screeched a warning to the others at the top of his lungs.

The big log, which had also rolled about twenty feet down the hill when it toppled sometime in the past, brought the two men to an abrupt halt as they slammed into it. Luke barely had time to recognize the *bandido* as Cardona from drawings he had seen on wanted posters when he realized the man was about to bring a knife almost as big as a machete down on his head and split his skull wide open.

Without having to think about what he was doing, Luke palmed out one of his Remingtons, eared back the hammer as he jammed the muzzle against Cardona's forehead, and pulled the trigger.

The point-blank shot blew Cardona away from him, and the dead outlaw flopped onto the ground behind the log. Luke had rolled over and started to get up when a bullet had whipped past his ear. Instinct made him drop belly down behind the log. A second later, more rifles opened up from the cabin and a volley of high-powered slugs smashed into the fallen tree. If it hadn't been there to give him cover, Luke would have been shot to pieces.

As it was, he was pinned down on the slope. The trees above him were too far away. If he stood up and made a dash for them, Burke and the others in the cabin would riddle him with rifle fire. Trying to crawl up there would make him an even easier target. The grass was too short to conceal him.

He was stuck with a dead man for company, and it was only a matter of time until some of those varmints slipped out of the cabin and circled around to catch him in a crossfire. Luke's craggy face was grim, in spite of the ghost of a smile lurking around his mouth.

In plenty of tight spots during the years he'd spent as a bounty hunter, he had always pulled through somehow. But he had known his luck was bound to run out someday.

After all, he had already cheated certain death once. A man didn't get too many breaks like that.

From time to time, he rose up long enough to throw a couple shots at the cabin, but not really expecting to do any damage—too long range for a handgun. His nature wouldn't let him die without a fight, though. He could put up a better one, if his Winchester wasn't still in the saddle boot strapped to his horse, a good hundred feet upslope. Might as well have been a hundred miles.

"Blast it, José, I must be getting old, to let a clumsy galoot like you sneak up on me," Luke said, keeping his eyes on the cabin.

Cardona had been a big, burly man, built along the lines of a black bear. Like all the other men in Solomon Burke's gang, he'd had a reputation for ruthlessness and cruelty. He had killed seven men that Luke knew of during various bank and train robberies, and was probably responsible for more deaths in addition to those. But he wouldn't be killing anybody else.

Luke took some small comfort from that. He tracked down outlaws mostly for the bounties posted on them, and he wasn't going to lie about it to himself or anybody else. It pleased him to know, because of him, men such as Cardona were no longer around to spread suffering and death across the frontier.

More bullets pounded into the log. One tore all the way through it and struck a rock lying on the slope, causing the bullet to whine off in a ricochet and bringing a thoughtful frown to Luke's face. He realized the log had been lying there long enough to be half-rotten in places. He holstered the Remington he was still holding and drew a heavy-bladed knife from its sheath on his left hip. Attacking the log with the blade, he hacked and dug at the soft wood.

It didn't take him long to break through and see what he'd been hoping to see. The log was partially hollow. Luke began enlarging the opening he had made and soon realized the hollow part ran all the way to one end of the log. He could see sunlight shining through it.

It took fifteen minutes of hard work to carve out a big enough hole for him to fit his head and shoulders through. By the time he was finished, sweat was dripping down his face.

He sheathed his knife and looked over at Cardona. "*Adiós, José.* If I see you again, I reckon it'll probably be in hell."

Luke wormed his way through the opening into the hollow log. Down below in the cabin, the outlaws hadn't been able to see what he was doing. He could only hope none of them had snuck around to where they could observe him. If they had, he was as good as dead.

He began shifting his weight back and forth as much as he could in those close confines. He felt insects crawling on him. His nerves twanged, taut as bowstrings. The log began to rock back and forth slightly. Bunching his muscles, he threw himself hard against the wood surrounding him. Over the pounding of his heart, he heard a faint grating sound as the log shifted.

Suddenly, it was rolling.

He let out a startled yell, even though rolling the log down the hill was exactly what he'd been trying to do. Up and down switched places rapidly.

With nothing between the log and the cabin to stop it, the crazy, bouncing, spinning, dizzying ride lasted only a few seconds.

The log crashed into the side of the cabin with a loud cracking sound just as he had counted on. Luke bulled his way out of the broken trunk, pulling both Remingtons from their cross-draw holsters as he did so.

He was on his feet when one of the outlaws appeared in the doorway, unwisely rushing out to see what had happened.

Luke shot him in the chest with the left-hand Remington. The slug drove the owlhoot back, making him fall. His body tangled with the feet of the man behind him. Luke blasted that hombre with the right-hand gun, then pressed himself against the cabin wall and waited. The men inside couldn't bring their guns to bear on him from those loopholes, and the log walls were too thick to shoot through. If anybody tried to rush out through the door, he was in position to gun them down. And, if the door was the only way out, he had them bottled up.

Of course, he couldn't go anywhere, either. But a stalemate was better than being stuck behind that log and his enemies having all the advantage.

As the echoes of the shots rolled away through the mountain valleys, a charged silence settled over the area. Luke thought he heard harsh breathing coming from inside the cabin.

After a few tense minutes, a man called out. "Who are you, mister?"

"Name's Luke Smith." He wasn't giving anything away by replying. They already knew where he was.

"I've heard of you. You're a bounty hunter!"

"Am I talking to Solomon Burke?"

"That's right."

"Who are the two boys I killed in there?"

Burke didn't answer for a moment. "How do you know they're dead?" he finally asked.

"Wasn't time for anything fancy. They're dead, all right."

Again Burke hesitated before saying, "Phil Gaylord and Oscar Montrose."

"José Cardona's dead up on the hillside. I blew his brains out. That's nearly half your bunch gone over the divide, Burke. Why don't you throw your guns out and surrender before I have to kill the rest of you?"

That brought a hoot of derisive laughter from inside.

"Mighty big talk, Smith. You step away from that wall and you'll be full of lead in a hurry. How in blazes are you gonna kill anybody else?"

"I've got my ways." Luke looked along the wall next to him. One of the loopholes, empty now, was within reach.

"We've got food, water, and plenty of ammunition. What do you have?"

"Got a cigar."

"Well, go ahead and smoke it, then," Burke told him. "It'll be the last one you ever do."

Luke kept his left-hand gun trained on the doorway. He pouched the right-hand iron and reached under his coat, bringing out a thin, black cigar. He bit off the end, spit it out, and clamped the cylinder of tobacco between his teeth. Fishing a lucifer from his pocket, he snapped it to life with his thumbnail. He held the flame to the end of the cigar and puffed until it was burning good. "Smell that?"

"Whoo-eee!" Burke mocked. "Smells like you set a wet dog on fire."

"It tastes good, though," Luke said. "I've got something else."

"What might that be?" Burke asked.

Luke took another cylinder from under his coat. Longer and thicker than the cigar, it was wrapped tightly in dark red paper. A short length of fuse dangled from one end. Luke puffed on the cigar until the end was glowing bright red, then held the fuse to it.

"This," he said around the cigar as the fuse began to sputter and spit sparks. He leaned over and shoved the cylinder through the empty loophole. It clattered on the puncheon floor inside the cabin.

One of the other men howled a curse and yelled, "Look out! That's dynamite!"

Luke drew his second gun and swung away from the wall as he extended the revolvers and squared himself up. As the outlaws tumbled through the door, trying to get away before the dynamite exploded, he started firing.

They shot back, of course, even as Luke's lead tore through them and knocked them off their feet. He felt the impact as a bullet struck him, then another. But he stayed upright and the Remingtons in his hands continued to roar.

Solomon Burke, a fox-faced, red-haired man, went down with his guts shot to pieces. Dour, sallow Lane Hutton stumbled and fell as blood from his bullet-torn throat cascaded down the front of his shirt. Young Billy Wells died with half his jaw shot away. Paco Hernandez stayed on his feet the longest and got a final shot off even as he collapsed with blood welling from two holes in his chest.

That last bullet rocked Luke. He swayed and spit out the cigar, but didn't fall. His vision was foggy, because he'd been shot three times or because clouds of powder smoke were swirling around him, he couldn't tell. The Remingtons seemed to weigh a thousand pounds apiece, but he didn't let them droop until he was certain all the outlaws were dead.

Then he couldn't hold the guns up anymore. They slipped from his blood-slick fingers and thudded to the ground at his feet.

I might not live to collect the bounty on these men, but at least they won't hurt anybody else, he thought as he stumbled through the cabin door. The single room inside was dim and shadowy.

The cylinder he had shoved through the loophole lay on the floor near a table. The fuse had burned out harmlessly. The blasting cap on the end was just clay and the "dynamite" was nothing more than a piece of wood with red paper wrapped around it. Luke had used it a number of times before. Outlaws tended to panic when they thought they were about to be blown to kingdom come.

Ignoring the fake dynamite, he stumbled across the room. Sitting on the table was the thing he had hoped to find inside.

It took him a couple tries before he was able to snag the neck of the whiskey bottle and lift it to his mouth. Some of the liquor spilled over his chin and throat, but he got enough of the fiery stuff down his throat to brace himself.

He leaned on the rough-hewn table and tried to take stock of his injuries. He'd been hit low on his left side. There was a lot of blood. A bullet had torn a furrow along his left forearm, too, and blood ran down and dripped from his fingers. The bullet hole high on his chest was starting to make his right arm and shoulder go numb.

He needed to stop the bleeding before he did anything else. With little time before his hands quit working, he pulled the bandanna from around his neck and used his teeth to start a rip in it. He tore it in half and managed to pour some whiskey on the pieces. He pulled up his shirt, felt around until he found the hole in his side, and shoved one wadded-up piece of the whiskey-soaked bandanna into the hole.

But that was just where the bullet had gone in. Wincing in pain, he located the exit wound and pushed the other piece of bandanna into it.

That left the hole in his chest. All the gun thunder had deafened him for a few moments, but his hearing was starting to come back. He listened intently as he breathed, but didn't hear any whistling or sucking sounds. The slug hadn't pierced his lung, he decided. That was good.

The bullet hadn't come out, either. It was still in there somewhere. Not good, he thought. Fumbling, he pulled his knife from its sheath and used the blade to cut a piece from his shirttail. Lucky he didn't slice off a finger or two in the process. He upended the bottle and poured whiskey right over the wound, then bit back a scream as he crammed the piece of cloth into the hole.

That was all he could do. His muscles refused to work the way he wanted them to. He had to lie down. He took an unsteady step toward one of the bunks built against the side walls. The world suddenly spun crazily around him. The floor seemed to tilt under his feet. His balance deserted him, and he crashed down on the puncheons, sending fresh jolts of pain stabbing through him.

He felt consciousness slipping away from him and knew if he passed out, he probably wouldn't wake up again. He tried to hold on, but a black tide swept over him.

That black surge didn't just wash him away from his primitive surroundings. To his already fevered mind, it seemed to lift him and carry him back, back, a bit of human flotsam swept along by a raging torrent, to an earlier time and a different place. The darkness surrounding him was shot through with red flashes, like artillery shells bursting in the night.

Chapter One

The bombardment sounded like the worst thunderstorm in the history of the world, but unlike a thunderstorm, it went on and on and on. For long days, that devil Ulysses S. Grant and his Yankee army had squatted outside Richmond, pounding away at the capital city of the Confederacy with their big guns. Half the buildings in town had been reduced to rubble, and untold numbers of Richmond's citizens were dead, killed in the endless barrages.

And still the guns continued to roar.

Rangy, rawboned Luke Jensen felt the floor shake under his feet as shells fell not far from the building where he stood. It had been one of Richmond's genteel mansions, not far from the capital itself, but recently it had been taken over by the government. One particular part of the government, in fact: the Confederate treasury.

Luke was one of eight men summoned tonight

for reasons unknown to them. They were waiting in what had been the parlor before the comfortable, overstuffed furniture was shoved aside and replaced by desks and tables.

In the light of a couple smoky lamps, he glanced around at the other men. Some of them he knew, and some he didn't. The faces of all bore the same weary, haggard look, the expression of men who had been at war for too long and suffered too many defeats despite their best efforts.

Luke knew that look all too well. He saw it in the mirror every time he got a chance to shave, which wasn't very often these days.

For nearly four long years, he had worn Confederate gray—ever since the day he had walked away from the hardscrabble farm tucked into the Ozark Mountains of southwestern Missouri and enlisted. Behind him he'd left his father Emmett and his little brother Kirby, along with his mother and sister.

It had been hard for Luke to leave his family, but he felt it was the right thing to do. Fighting for the Confederacy didn't mean a man held with slavery, although he figured that was what all those ignorant Yankees believed. Luke didn't believe at all in the notion of one man owning another.

At the same time he didn't think it was right for a bunch of Northern politicians in By-God Washington City to be telling Southern folks what they could and couldn't do, especially when it came to secession. The states had joined together voluntarily, back when they'd won their freedom from England. If some of them wanted to say "thanks, but so long" and go their own way, it seemed to Luke they had every right to do so.

Even so, if they'd just kept on wrangling about it in the halls of Congress, Luke, like a lot of other Southerners, would have pretty much ignored it and gone on about his business. But Abraham Lincoln had to go and send the army marching into Virginia, and the battle along the creek called Bull Run was the last straw as far as Luke was concerned. He'd been raised to avoid trouble if he could, but when a Jensen saw something wrong going on, he couldn't just sit back and do nothing.

So he'd been a soldier for four years, fighting against the Northern aggressors, slogging along as an infantryman for a while before his natural talents for tracking, shooting, and fighting got noticed and he was made a scout and a sharpshooter.

He knew three of the men waiting in the parlor with him were the same sort. Remy Duquesne, Dale Cardwell, and Edgar Millgard were good men, and if he was being sent on some sort of mission with them, Luke was fine with that.

The other four had introduced themselves as Keith Stratton, Wiley Potter, Josh Richards, and Ted Casey. Luke hadn't formed an opinion about them based only on their names. He didn't blame them for being close-mouthed, though. He was the same way himself.

Remy fired up a cigar and said in his soft Cajun

accent, "Anybody got an idea why they brought us here tonight?"

"Not a clue," Wiley Potter said.

"The treasury department has its office here now," Dale Cardwell pointed out. He smiled. "Maybe they're finally going to pay us all those back wages we haven't seen in months."

That comment drew grim chuckles from several of the men.

Remy said, "I wouldn't count on that, my frien'."

Luke didn't think it was very likely, either. The Confederacy was in bad shape. Financially, militarily, morale-wise . . . everything was cratering, and there didn't seem to be anything anybody could do to stop it. They would fight to the end, of course—there was no question about that—but that end seemed to be getting more and more inevitable.

The front door opened, and footsteps sounded in the foyer. Several gray-clad troopers appeared in the arched entrance to the former parlor. They carried rifles with bayonets fixed to the barrels.

A pair of officers followed the soldiers into the room. Luke and the other men snapped to attention. He recognized one of the officers as a high-ranking general. The other man was the colonel who commanded the regiment in which Luke, Remy, Dale, and Edgar served.

The two men in civilian clothes who came into the room behind the general and the colonel were the real surprise. Luke caught his breath as he recognized the President of the Confederacy, Jefferson

Davis, and the Secretary of the Treasury, George Trenholm.

"At ease," the general said.

Luke and the others relaxed, but not much. It was hard to be at ease with the president in the room.

Jefferson Davis gave them a sad, tired smile and said, "Thank you for coming here tonight, gentlemen," as if they'd had a choice in the matter. "I know you'd probably rather be with your comrades in arms, facing the enemy."

Stratton and Potter grimaced slightly and exchanged a quick glance, as if that was the last thing they wanted to be doing.

"I've summoned you because I have a special job for you," Davis went on. "Secretary Trenholm will tell you about it."

Luke had wondered if they were going to be given a special assignment, but he hadn't expected it would come from the president himself. It had to be something of extreme importance. He waited eagerly to hear what the treasury secretary was going to say.

"As you know, Richmond is under siege by the Yankees," the man began rather pompously as he clasped his hands behind his back.

Luke preferred Confederate politicians to Yankees, but they all had a tendency to be windbags, as far as he was concerned.

"Although I hate to say it, it appears that our

efforts to defend the city ultimately will prove to be unsuccessful," the secretary continued.

"Are you saying that Richmond's going to fall, sir?" Potter asked.

Trenholm nodded. "I'm afraid so."

"But that doesn't necessarily mean the Confederacy is about to fall as well," Davis put in. "Our glorious nation will persevere. The Yankees may overrun Richmond, but we will establish a new capital elsewhere." He smiled at the treasury secretary. "I'm sorry, I didn't mean to interrupt."

"That's quite all right, Mr. President. No one in this room has more right to speak than you." Trenholm cleared his throat and went on. "Of course, no government can continue to function without funds, so to that end, acting on the orders of President Davis, I have assembled a shipment of gold bullion that is to be spirited out of the city and taken to Georgia to await the arrival of our government. This is most of what we have left in our coffers, gentlemen. I'm not exaggerating when I say the very survival of the Confederacy itself depends on the secure transport of this gold."

Luke wasn't surprised by what he had just heard. For the past few days, rumors had been going around the city that the treasury was going to be cleaned out and the money taken elsewhere so the Yankees wouldn't get their grubby paws on it.

The secretary nodded toward Luke's commanding officer. "Colonel Lancaster will be in charge of the gold's safety."

"You're taking the whole regiment to Georgia, sir?" Dale asked.

The colonel shook his head. "Not at all, Corporal. That would only draw the Yankees' attention to what we're doing." Lancaster paused. "We're entrusting the safety of the bullion—and the future of the Confederacy—to a smaller detail. Eight men, to be exact." He looked around the room. "The eight of you who are gathered here."

Chapter Two

Luke had figured that out even before Lancaster said it. The idea seemed obvious. Getting the gold out of Richmond would require speed and stealth, and no one was better at moving fast and quiet than he and his fellow scouts.

It seemed like a mighty big risk, though, turning over a fortune in gold to only eight men. Of course, as long as they were loyal to the Confederacy, it didn't really matter.

"I'll be going along as well," Colonel Lancaster pointed out. "I've been relieved of my command of the regiment and given this task."

"I know you'd rather be with the men you've led in such sterling fashion, Colonel," Jefferson Davis said. "However, we all must make sacrifices for our noble cause."

"Of course, Mr. President," Lancaster said stiffly.

Davis turned back to Luke and the other scouts. "No one is going to order you enlisted men to accept this assignment. If there are any of you who don't want to go along, speak up now, and it won't be held against you. You'll be allowed to return to your units. All we ask is that you say nothing about this. Secrecy is the watchword until the bullion is safely on its way to Georgia."

Luke looked at his friends. Remy shrugged and told Davis, "Mr. President, I don't think any of us are gonna say no to this job."

"That's right," Edgar said. "If this is something that will help the Confederacy, you can count on us, sir."

"I knew that." Davis smiled. "I knew you valiant lads wouldn't let me down, but I felt it was only right to ask. Thank you for justifying my faith in you."

"You can thank us when we get that gold where it's goin', Mr. President," Stratton said.

Luke had been quiet so far, but he asked, "When are we leaving?"

"Tonight," Colonel Lancaster said.

"That soon?" Potter was surprised.

"Do you have a problem with that, Sergeant? Something you need to do here in Richmond before you leave?"

Potter grunted and shook his head. "Permission to speak freely, sir?"

"Go ahead," Lancaster told him.

"Richmond's turned into a hellhole ever since the Yankees showed up on our doorstep, and as far as I'm concerned, the sooner we get out of here, the better."

As if to punctuate his comment, another shell

fell somewhere nearby, and the blast shook the house enough that little bits of plaster sifted down from the ceiling.

The general said to Davis, "You should get back to somewhere safer, sir. The colonel and I can handle this."

"Very well, General." Davis turned to the treasury secretary. "Come on, George."

The troopers escorted the two politicians from the room. Once they were gone, Colonel Lancaster said, "The gold is being stored in a warehouse not far from here. It's packed in crates in a couple wagons and covered with canvas so they'll look like supplies."

"No offense, Colonel," Luke said, "but are you sure that's a good idea? With the city cut off like it is, people are starting to get pretty hungry. They're liable to come after food quicker than they would gold."

"How else would you suggest we transport it, Jensen?" the colonel snapped.

Luke shrugged. "I don't know, sir," he admitted. "As scarce as everything is these days, folks are going to be interested no matter what it looks like."

"That's why it's up to us to get the wagons out of the city quickly, and with as little fuss as possible. We have civilian clothes at the warehouse for all of you, as well. Hopefully that'll keep you from drawing too much attention."

Luke didn't know about that, but the idea of getting some fresh duds appealed to him. His gray uniform was worn and ragged and covered with stains from too many nights spent sleeping in the mud. The black bill of his forage cap was crooked and broken. His shoes were more hole than shoe leather.

His only possessions still in good shape were his Fayetteville rifle and his Griswold and Gunnison revolver, both of which he kept in excellent condition. His life often depended on them.

The general shook hands with all eight of the scouts and wished them luck, then Colonel Lancaster said gruffly, "Let's go. We'll dispense with military formality since we're supposed to be civilians, but don't forget who's in charge here."

Luke didn't think Lancaster was likely to let that happen.

"I don't know about you boys," Ted Casey said with a wide grin, "but I feel like a whole new man in this getup!"

The civilian clothes they had donned when they reached the warehouse weren't new—some of them even had patches here and there—but they were clean and in much better shape than the uniforms the eight men had been wearing.

Colonel Lancaster, as befitted his rank, was dressed in the only real suit, including a flat-crowned planter's hat. Other than his ramrod-stiff backbone, in those clothes and with his florid face and thick side-whiskers, he might have been mistaken for a plantation owner.

The other men were dressed more like overseers on that hypothetical plantation, in boots, whipcord trousers, linsey-woolsey shirts, and leather vests. They wore an assortment of headgear ranging from broad-brimmed hats to tweed caps.

Luke had snagged one of the hats he thought made him look like a plainsman. Such men rode through the Ozarks from time to time, on their way to or from the vast western frontier, and Luke had always admired them.

His revolver was tucked in the waistband of the trousers. Most enlisted men didn't carry handguns, but since scouts often had to do some close-quarters fighting, they had been issued revolvers along with their rifles. Luke considered himself pretty handy with either weapon, and with a knife, too, for that matter.

He didn't think about it very often, but he had killed quite a few men during his time in the army. It was war, of course. That was what soldiers did. He had killed more than his share up close, though, sneaking up on Yankee pickets and slitting their throats or driving his knife into their backs so the blade penetrated the heart. He had felt the hot gush of enemy blood on his hand, heard the death rattle, and borne the weight of a suddenly limp body that had to be lowered to the ground quietly. He had seen the terrible damage gunshots did to human flesh, especially at close range.

Those memories didn't haunt his sleep, but they were part of him and always would be.

Wiley Potter, Keith Stratton, Ted Casey, and Josh Richards clustered together near one of the wagons. Luke saw them casting furtive glances at the canvas-covered cargo in the back of the vehicle.

"Like dogs lickin' their chops over a big ol' soup bone, eh?" Remy said quietly as he came up beside Luke.

"You can't blame them. I sent some mighty hard looks at those wagons myself. I've never been this close to so much gold." Luke snorted. "Hell, back home I might go as long as a year without seeing as much as a double eagle."

"I suppose I'm more accustomed to it, seeing as I spent a lot of time in the gambling halls in New Orleans. The money always flowed freely there."

"Maybe so," Luke said. "Where I come from, money flows more like quicksand."

Dale asked Lancaster, "Are we going to be riding on the wagons, Colonel?"

"We'll have a driver and a guard on each wagon," Lancaster explained. "The other four of you, plus myself, will be on horseback and serve as outriders."

"Horses sound good," Casey said. "I always hankered to ride something better than an old mule. They turned me down for the cavalry because that was all I had."

"You'll take turns at the jobs, at least starting out. I don't care who does what, though. You can settle that among yourselves."

Dale commented, "I wouldn't mind handling one of the teams. I used to drive a freight wagon before the war."

"So did I," Edgar offered. "I reckon I'll take the other driver's job starting out."

None of the other men volunteered to ride on the wagons as guards. Luke and Remy looked at each other. Luke shrugged, and Remy said, "We'll take the wagons, too, Colonel."

Lancaster nodded. "Fine." He looked to Potter, Stratton, Casey, and Richards. "You men will find your horses in the alley behind the warehouse. Bring them around front and mount up. You can fetch my mount as well." He motioned to the uniformed soldiers who had been waiting in the warehouse, guarding the gold shipment. "Open the doors."

The troopers swung the big double doors back while Luke and his friends climbed onto the wagons. Luke settled down on the seat of the first wagon beside Dale. "Sure you can handle this?"

"Oh, yeah. To tell you the truth, I've never been that comfortable in a saddle."

"I was riding almost before I could walk, at least according to my pa," Luke told him.

The mention of Emmett Jensen put a pensive look on Luke's face. Luke had joined up first, back in '61, but he had suspected his pa wouldn't be able to stay out of the fight for long. Sure enough, Emmett had enlisted, too.

Proving that the world really was a small place, the two of them had run into each other at Chancellorsville, even though they were in different regiments. Hundreds of thousands of troops rampaging around those Virginia woods, and yet father and son had practically bumped heads.

That wasn't the last time, either. Anytime their units were anywhere near each other, one of them would seek out the other so they could visit in the lull between battles. Neither of them got much news from home, but Emmett was confident his youngest son Kirby was keeping things going on the farm.

"Kirby may be just a boy," Emmett had said during one visit, "but he's got something special inside him. I don't think I've ever seen a boy willing to work harder or more determined to do the right thing."

"He'll have the farm waiting for us when we come back," Luke had said.

"Shoot, he may not even need our help!" Emmett had replied with a grin.

It had been a while since Luke had seen his pa. He hoped Emmett was all right. Both were soldiers, so who knew what might happen. It was a dangerous line of work.

When the wagons rolled out of the warehouse into the darkness, Colonel Lancaster and the other four outriders were waiting on horseback.

"I'll lead the way," Lancaster declared. "I want a rider on each side of the wagons. Keep an eye out behind you as well. We don't want anybody sneaking up on us."

"Did the colonel tell any of us exactly where

we're going?" Luke asked Dale as the party set out over the rough, cobblestoned streets.

"Not that I know of," Dale replied.

"I might say something to him about that the first time we stop. He's bound to have a map or something, but if anything happened to him, we wouldn't know where we were supposed to take this"—Luke stopped himself before he said the word "gold"—"cargo."

"Yeah, that's true," Dale agreed. "All we know is that we're headed for Georgia, but Georgia's a pretty big place."

It was pretty far away, too, Luke thought, and almost anything could happen between here and there. He felt the unaccustomed burden of responsibility weighing on his shoulders. He wasn't used to taking care of anybody but himself or maybe two or three of his comrades. He'd never had anything like the fate of the Confederacy riding on his back before.

The city was dark except for the few fires started by exploding artillery shells. The Yankee bombardment continued. It went on almost around the clock. Luke didn't see how the city could hold out much longer.

A shell screamed overhead and landed maybe half a mile behind them, blowing up with a huge explosion. Dale looked back over his shoulder at the pillar of flame rising into the black sky. "What do you think it'd be like if one of those things landed right on top of us?"

"We'll never know," Luke said.

"Because it won't happen?"

"Because if it does, we'll be blown to smithereens before we know what happened."

"You really know how to make a fella feel encouraged, Luke—" Dale stopped short and hauled back on the reins. Colonel Lancaster had come to an abrupt halt in front of the wagon team. Garish, flickering light spilled over the cobblestones as a large number of men, many of them carrying torches, surged around a corner up ahead.

"That looks like trouble," Dale muttered.

Luke was thinking the same thing. He knew mobs made of desperate civilians and deserters had taken to roaming the streets of Richmond. The army was trying to keep things under control, but it was getting more difficult with every passing day as the Yankee siege continued. Already there had been several riots.

And it looked like the two wagons were in the path of another one, as one of the men in the forefront of the mob yelled, "There are some wagons! There might be food in them!"

It was an easy conclusion to jump to. A starving man saw food everywhere.

The man waved his torch forward, and with a full-throated cry sounding like the howl of a wounded animal, the mob surged toward the wagons and riders.